AN OUTSIDE PLAN

■ ■

Chris had to admit that things weren't so bad. At least now they had a plan, which the so-called experts inside had always told him was important. A man couldn't just drift through life and expect to end up anywhere at all—except maybe back in the joint.

But that wouldn't happen to them. They were getting on just fine, under the circumstances. They had a plan.

It had actually been Dwight's idea, and, to be perfectly honest, Chris had been more than a little skeptical about it in the beginning. After all, what the hell did they know about looking for treasure in Mexico? And getting a bankroll together was, unfortunately, a lot easier said than done. Especially when you were trying to do the job with Dwight St. John. Chris couldn't quite figure out if Dwight was crazier on the outside than he'd been in prison or if it just showed up more.

■ ■

FAULT LINES

ALSO BY TERI WHITE

Max Trueblood and the Jersey Desperado*
Tightrope*
Bleeding Hearts*
Triangle

***Published by
THE MYSTERIOUS PRESS**

ATTENTION: SCHOOLS AND CORPORATIONS

MYSTERIOUS PRESS books, distributed by Warner Books, are available at quantity discounts with bulk purchase for educational, business, or sales promotional use. For information, please write to: SPECIAL SALES DEPARTMENT, MYSTERIOUS PRESS, 666 FIFTH AVENUE, NEW YORK, N.Y. 10103.

**ARE THERE MYSTERIOUS PRESS BOOKS
YOU WANT BUT CANNOT FIND IN YOUR LOCAL STORES?**

You can get any MYSTERIOUS PRESS title in print. Simply send title and retail price, plus $3.00 for the first book on any order and 50¢ for each additional book on that order, to cover mailing and handling costs. New York State and California residents add applicable sales tax. Enclose check or money order to: MYSTERIOUS PRESS, 129 WEST 56th St., NEW YORK, N.Y. 10019.

FAULT LINES

TERI WHITE

THE MYSTERIOUS PRESS

New York • London • Tokyo • Sweden

MYSTERIOUS PRESS EDITION

Copyright © 1988 by Teri White
All rights reserved.

Cover design by Irving Freeman

Mysterious Press books are published in association with
Warner Books, Inc.
666 Fifth Avenue
New York, N.Y. 10103
A Warner Communications Company

Printed in the United States of America

Originally published in hardcover by The Mysterious Press.
First Mysterious Press Paperback Printing: August, 1989

10 9 8 7 6 5 4 3 2 1

For My Mother

FAULT: A fracture in the Earth's crust, on either side of which there has been relative movement. Faults seldom occur in a single plane; usually a vast number of roughly parallel faults take place in a belt (fault zone) a few hundred metres across. Faults may be large enough to be responsible for such features as rift valleys, or, in contrast, microscopically small.

Encyclopedia of the Planet Earth
Anthony Hallam, Ph.D.
Consultant Editor

1

Whitson frowned.

That was a bad sign. The very last thing a man in his position wanted was to have Emory Whitson showing any kind of displeasure. Please-the-Parole-Officer was the name of this particular game; if you lost, it was head straight back to jail, do not pass go, and, for sure, don't collect any goddamned two hundred dollars.

Chris shifted a little in the Leatherette chair. The burnt-orange plastic crackled beneath his thighs.

Whitson, still frowning, walked right past him and stopped in front of the only window in the room. Some kind of fern sprawled out of its pot and dangled over the edge of the sill. With one quick tug, Whitson pulled off a hapless leaf. He held it up so that Chris could see the yellowing tip. "You see that, Moore?" he demanded.

Chris blinked and nodded. What the hell was this? Had the parole system added one more piece of garbage to the twice-monthly rigamarole he had to go through? Were they going to be testing his eyesight now? "Yes, sir," he said, relieved to realize that the frown apparently hadn't been intended for him at all, but for the errant leaf.

There was a moment of silence as they both stared at the object of Whitson's disdain.

"This small thing could have spelled the beginning of the end for the whole plant," Whitson said finally. "If I hadn't spotted the problem and dealt with it. Immediately and firmly."

Now Chris knew damned well what was coming. He swallowed a sigh.

Whitson dropped the potentially deadly leaf into the wastebasket and watched its delicate descent with gloating satisfaction. One problem disposed of. Then he walked back to the chair on the other side of the desk—the power side—and sat, fixing Chris with the same stare he had used on the troublesome greenery. Now it was time, the look seemed to say, to deal with this other irritant. "That's a little like what I do on this job, Moore," he said. "Spot the little problems and then work to remedy them before they turn into major ones. Do you see my point?"

"I see your point," Chris said.

And a fucking stupid point it is, he wanted to add.

But he didn't, of course. Nobody ever accused Christopher Moore of being dumb enough to shoot himself in the foot. So, on the first and the last Tuesday of each and every month, he sat in this humid little office and listened to a first-class asshole make the same stupid points over and over.

Whitson thumbed through the file folder on his desk. "You still living at the same address?"

"Yeah, same place."

"Any change in the job situation?"

"No, sir."

This time, unfortunately, the frown was most definitely aimed at him and not at any of the green and growing things that crowded the small room. "I told you before that working through the temp-job agency is not really a satisfactory arrangement. Stability is important for someone like you."

That was a laugh. What the hell did this guy know about somebody like him? Chris reached for his crumpled pack of Camels, then remembered the THANK YOU FOR NOT SMOKING sign posted on the office door and dropped his hand. Whitson was such a fucked-up wimp. Afraid of a little cigarette smoke. Probably he was one of those guys who fastened his seat belt all the time and took a big dose of vitamin C whenever he sniffled.

Chris hated men who were afraid of life. Too goddamned chicken to take a chance now and then. What was the point of being alive otherwise? Of course, being such a candy-ass made Whitson the perfect civil servant.

After a moment, he realized that Whitson was looking at him expectantly; apparently, some kind of response was called for. He tried to remember what the hell Whitson had last said. The job thing, right? Something about not liking the temp service. "A steady job is hard to find," he said belatedly. "Especially when they hear I'm an ex-con."

"Life is hard," Whitson replied. "Some of us make it even harder on ourselves by screwing up and getting caught, right?"

"Right," Chris agreed. Of course he agreed. What the hell else?

"Let me ask you one very simple question. Do you want to make it on the outside?"

Chris gripped the wooden arms of the chair. "I sure as hell don't want to go back there," he said in a low voice. Did Whitson think anybody would, for chrissake?

Whitson nodded. "Then I suggest you get your act together. People who mess up the parade for the rest of us usually end up in trouble."

"I'll keep trying."

"Very good. That's all I ask of my men." He surveyed the file again. "Staying away from your old friends?"

"I don't have any friends left from before. Seven years is a long time to be away."

"Just as well, I'd say. Considering the trouble you were in back then."

"Hey, man, I'm doing just what I'm supposed to do." Chris's tone was sharper than it should have been, but the patience he could summon up for these meetings had a limit. That limit was reached at about the same time during every visit.

But Whitson, as usual, didn't seem to notice.

He only stood, signaling an end to the conversation. "See you next time," he said. "And work on getting a full-time job by then." There was an unspoken threat dangling at the end of the sentence.

"Yes, sir."

And fuck you, sir.

* * *

Chris didn't say that, either, naturally. He just left the office and took the elevator back to the first floor, pausing long enough in the lobby to light a cigarette. Blessed smoke filled his lungs. Then he exhaled deeply, feeling the built-up tension leave his body as well. Maybe the doctors were right about the dangers of smoking, but sometimes, when he couldn't inject a quick shot of nicotine into his system, he thought he'd lose his goddamned mind, and how healthy could *that* be?

Midday heat rose up from the concrete in brutal, almost visible waves that hit him like a blow as he stepped outside. And then there was the smog. Weren't they supposed to have cleaned all this shit up? He blinked a couple of times. Hadda be close to ninety, and a man could hardly even see the sun behind the gray-blue haze that lay over the city. It was Chris's opinion that the bastards who made the air so dirty ought to be sent up. Crime was crime. But what could you expect?

The sidewalk was jammed with lunchtime strollers, mostly just more civil-servant lackeys like that asshole Whitson, and others who might as well have been, by the beaten-down look of them. Chris glumly viewed the motley stream of humanity for a moment, then plunged into its midst. Most of these creeps weren't even speaking English. Whose country was this, anyway?

Despite the heat and the thick, almost choking air, Chris moved as quickly as the crowd would allow. His impatient jostling earned him a few cautiously dirty looks, which he blithely ignored.

Sweat was rolling down his face profusely by the time he had covered just two blocks. He checked the traffic, jaywalked across the street, and climbed into the passenger seat of a battered yellow Volkswagen bug that was parked just far enough from the fire hydrant to be legal.

Chris leaned back against the seat with a sigh. "Shit," he said after a moment.

"You know what I was sitting here thinking about?" Dwight asked lazily.

Chris took a Kleenex from the glove compartment and ran it

over his face. The tissue dissolved into a damp mess. "How the hell would I know that?" He tossed the soggy lump out the window.

"I was sitting here thinking that before we leave this city for good, we should do Whitson. I mean, the man deserves to die, right?"

Chris took one last, massive drag on the end of the cigarette, burning his fingertips in the process, then flicked the butt out into the gutter. It landed next to the discarded tissue. "Don't tempt me," he said. "Just don't fucking tempt me."

Dwight laughed softly and reached for the ignition.

Maybe he had only been kidding about offing Whitson. But maybe not. It was hard to tell with Dwight. Simple, everyday kinds of things made him nervous as hell, but he could talk about killing as if he were talking about running out for smokes.

Frankly, it made Chris more than just a little nervous. Throughout his career, he had prided himself on not getting real physical with people. A smart man didn't have to do that. But lately they seemed to be living on some kind of dangerous edge. Like at any moment, something violent might happen. It wasn't the way life should be.

He didn't like it. He didn't like it a whole lot.

The ancient car was hacking and groaning its way to life. Chris listened to the reluctant engine and shook his head. Damned thing was going to crap out in the middle of the Santa Monica Freeway one of these days and then what the hell would they do?

However much the car irritated him, though, Chris accepted the fact that Dwight wouldn't give it up until its last breath of life was gone. And he, himself, even felt a certain sentimental attachment to the damned thing. He could still remember the pleased shock he'd felt stepping down from the bus on his first day out and finding the lemon-colored bug waiting for him.

Dwight St. John, barely recognizable beneath the shaggy auburn crop of postprison curls and behind the mirrored sunglasses, was perched on the hood, grinning broadly.

Chris waited until the bus had gone and the lot was empty. Then he shifted the duffel to his other hand and strolled over to the car. He kicked one of the tires like a prospective buyer, then looked at Dwight. He was wearing a pair of faded jeans with one knee torn and a tie-dyed T-shirt. Chris hadn't seen a shirt like that in years. "What're you supposed to be? Some kind of damned hippie reception committee?"

Dwight lowered the glasses briefly and glanced around the deserted lot. He covered his eyes again. "Looks like I'm the best you've got," he said.

Chris couldn't really argue with that, so he just shoved the duffel in the back, and they both got into the car. It was a tight fit for him. When he was finally comfortable—or, at least, as comfortable as he was ever going to be in the passenger seat of a toy car—he turned to look at Dwight again.

Three months on the outside seemed to have loosened him up a lot, easing most of the familiar tension lines from his face. He looked younger than the thirty-three Chris knew he was.

Dwight glanced at him. "You grew a mustache," he said.

"Yeah."

"Looks good."

"Thanks." Chris fingered the thick, dark blond hair above his lip. "This isn't exactly kosher, is it?" he asked. "I mean, it seems to me that the rules don't allow us to get together. Something about avoiding bad companions. I have a feeling a former cellmate just might qualify."

"That's true," Dwight agreed cheerfully. "The rules do say that. You want to get out here and stay pure?"

Chris didn't bother to answer that.

Dwight snickered. "That's what I figured."

Something else occurred to Chris. "Thanks for the birthday card, by the way."

"You figured out it was from me? I didn't want to sign it."

"I figured it out." Actually, it hadn't been so hard. It was the first time he'd ever gotten one from the outside and there wasn't anybody else it could have come from.

Neither man spoke again until they were hurtling down the freeway, which seemed like even more of a madhouse than it had the last time Chris had seen it. Dwight was hunched over the steering wheel, watching the traffic. At least Chris hoped he was watching the traffic; with those damned mirrored glasses, it was impossible to be sure.

"Where are we going, anyway?" Chris finally asked.

"Home," Dwight replied.

He didn't know what the hell that was supposed to mean, but he didn't bother asking. After so many years inside, he didn't have anyplace else to go, and sure as hell nobody else was waiting for him.

So maybe another parolee in a broken-down VW wasn't the greatest welcome wagon a man could have, but, as Dwight had pointed out with deadly accuracy, this was as good as it was liable to get for one Christopher Moore.

He reached over and punched Dwight lightly on the shoulder. "Good to see you, you bastard," he said.

Dwight grinned at him. "Yeah."

Chris sat back, feeling fine all of a sudden. Maybe he didn't know where the hell he was heading or what was going to happen next, but that was okay. After he had some time to catch his breath, they could figure things out, he and Dwight.

And now, six months later, Chris had to admit that things weren't so bad. At least now they had a plan, which the so-called experts inside had always told him was important. A man couldn't just drift through life and expect to end up anywhere at all—except maybe back in the joint.

But that wouldn't happen to them. They were getting on just fine, under the circumstances. They had a plan.

It had actually been Dwight's idea, and, to be perfectly honest, Chris had been more than a little skeptical about it in the beginning. After all, what the hell did they know about looking for treasure in Mexico? But Dwight had a pile of books on the subject and he had pressed his case with enthusiasm. Sunken pirate ships. Buried hoards of Aztec gold. There was a fortune to be made for those smart enough to go after it. Chris had gotten the impression that Dwight had been thinking about this for a very long time. And it hadn't taken so much for him to be convinced, too. Even if they never found a damned thing, which he figured was likely, a change of scene would be good for both of them. Change your scene and change your luck.

The bad part was that making such a move would cost money. A lot of money, because they had no intention of starting this new life as a couple of paupers. They wanted a nice fat stake.

And getting a bankroll like that together was, unfortunately, a lot easier said than done. Espécially when you were trying to do the job with Dwight St. John. Chris couldn't quite figure out if Dwight was crazier on the outside than he'd been in prison or if it just showed up more.

Chris stared across the street at the small liquor store. He wiped sweat from his forehead. Although it was nearly midnight, the city was still almost as hot as it had been at noon when he'd left Whitson's office. To make matters even worse, the inside of the car they were using—a pale green Ford stolen two hours previously—smelled of sour milk.

Dwight, sitting behind the wheel, yawned hugely. "Pretty soon, huh?"

"Yeah, yeah," Chris replied irritably. "If you think you can stay awake that long."

"I'm awake."

The unrelenting heat and the stinking car were giving Chris one massive headache. He leaned back and closed his eyes.

"Hope this goes down right," Dwight said suddenly.

"Any reason why it shouldn't?"

"No, I guess not. That's an old man in there. He won't give us any trouble."

"Probably not," Chris replied. "Of course, he might have a double-barrel under the counter. He might pull it out and blow both of us away. That could happen," he added perversely.

"You think?"

Chris massaged his temples. "Dwight?"

"Yeah?"

"Shut the fuck up. You always do this."

"I always do what?" Dwight asked, sounding offended.

"You're worse than some old lady on a job. Worrying and fretting about the dumbest shit every damned time."

Dwight tapped the steering wheel. "Yeah, well."

"Yeah, well, nothing. I'm getting damned tired of it. If you don't want to do this, let's just go home. Tomorrow morning we can go into the temp service and maybe pick up some work. See how long it takes us to get to Mexico that way."

"We're going to do this," Dwight said. "Of course we are. Sometimes I think of things, that's all."

"Do me a favor, willya? Don't think."

It wasn't easy trying to pull jobs with a novice. The big problem was that no matter how willing he might be, a killer was just not a heistman. Sometimes he thought that Dwight's first transgression of the law, the one that got him incarcerated, really *had* been just a fluke, an accident, as Dwight always claimed, and that maybe he just didn't have the right kind of mind for this line of work.

Chris opened his eyes long enough to see a couple more customers go into the store, then shut them again. Another problem, he knew, was that Dwight had this overactive imagination. That might be a good thing in a guy you were locked up with for five years because it helped fight the boredom, but it was not an advantage on a job. It allowed him to see all kinds of possibilities—most of them bad—in what should be just easy little jobs. They'd been pulling one or two of these a week for almost six months now, and nothing ever went wrong.

Oh, a couple of times they'd had to use a little rough stuff—Dwight had, actually—just to convince people that they meant business (although it seemed to Chris that just the sight of a .357 should have done that), but nobody was dead. In his opinion, that made them successful. That and the fact that they hadn't gotten caught.

Successful and lucky.

Dwight lit a cigarette. "One for the road," he said. "How much longer do you think?"

Chris knew that he wasn't talking about this particular job but about their plans for the future. "Depends, man. If we could just get one big score, instead of fooling around with all this nickel and dime shit, we'd be on our way south in a hurry."

"Can't be too soon for me." Dwight exhaled with a sigh.

Chris glanced at him, frowning. They really had to get out of this city soon or Dwight was liable to do something too stupid for him to fix. One fuck-up with too much booze and a broad was all it would take to get him sent right back inside. If the bastard could just learn to control himself a little, life would sure as hell be less complicated.

They just had to get to Mexico. That was the only way Chris could see things settling down.

Dwight threw the unfinished cigarette away. "Well, here's hoping the bastard doesn't have a gun."

The last customer was leaving the store and the neon sign went off.

Chris sighed. "Can we just get this over with, please?"

Dwight followed him across the street and into the store.

The old man behind the counter looked up from the cash register as they entered. "We're closing," he said.

"This won't take long," Dwight assured him in a friendly voice, taking the Magnum out of his waistband.

Chris reached under his shirt and brought out the bag. "Let's see just how fast you can get all of that money out of the register and into this sack."

The senile fool just stood there, staring at the gun as if he'd never seen one before.

After fifteen or so seconds, Chris made an impatient sound. He went behind the counter himself and shoved the man out of the way. Opening the register, he reached in and started pulling money from the drawer and stuffing it into the bag.

Dwight glanced out the plate-glass window. "Hurry up," he said.

"Yeah, yeah," Chris muttered without looking at him.

Just as the last of the bills went into the sack, the old man moved. With a roar that didn't even seem to come from the small body, he lunged toward Chris.

Chris, startled, glanced at him, more from surprise than out of any real fear, and then Dwight fired once. The man fell out of sight behind the counter. "Damnit," Chris said.

"He dead?"

Chris glanced down quickly. "No, he's breathing. Looks like a shoulder hit, is all."

"Stupid bastard. He shouldn't of done that, huh?"

Instead of answering that question, Chris just said, "Come on, let's move."

Dwight tucked the gun safely out of sight once more, and they left quickly.

It wasn't until they were nearly three blocks away that they heard the first sirens in the distance. Neither man really relaxed until they had gone seven more blocks, to the spot where they abandoned the stolen car and got back into the VW.

Finally, Dwight let his breath out slowly. "Why would somebody want to die for just a little money? Can you answer me that?"

Chris had no answer; he only shrugged. Philosophy was not his thing. Anyway, as far as he was concerned, the real question was: Why the hell had Dwight fired? That old man was nothing. He could have knocked him down with one hand, for chrissake, and kept pulling out money with the other. But not Dwight. He sighed and opened the bag. "There isn't much in here. Not enough to help us a lot."

"I watched you fill the damned thing," Dwight said grouchily. "I know what's in there."

Chris closed the bag again and sat back. They absolutely had to find a big score. Sooner or later, something was going to go very wrong on one of these shitty little jobs. Or else Dwight would do something extra stupid and the whole plan would blow up in their faces.

One break, that was all they needed, for chrissake. It wasn't so much to ask for, was it? Just one big fucking break, and life would be white-sand beaches and cold tequila from then on.

2

He was on the beach again.

Bryan stopped at the ramshackle refreshment stand to buy a carton of orange juice. As he waited to get his change from the harried teenage boy working the counter, Bryan kept his eyes on the solitary figure sitting on a nearby bench. The usual Santa Monica beach crowd was already swarming over the sand—it was still early, but even so, the day promised to be a scorcher—but despite the mob, this guy stuck out.

It was the third straight day that Bryan had noticed him, always sitting on that same bench and intently watching the water. That, in fact, was all he seemed to do. No swimming or taking off his shirt to soak up the sun. No volleyball. He didn't even show much interest in trying to pick up any of the girls parading by, although it was clear that more than a few of the females wouldn't have minded catching his eye despite his somewhat scruffy appearance. Or maybe because of that; Bryan had no idea what young girls found attractive these days. If he ever had known.

At any rate, this guy just seemed real interested in the waves.

Bryan finally got his seven cents back. He pushed his way through the crush of waiting customers, then, when he was in the clear, stopped to open the carton. As his glaze flickered back toward the young man on the bench, he was feeling the same nagging sense of recognition that he'd experienced the previous two days. But, at the same time, he was convinced that he'd never seen the face before.

As he sipped the slightly waxy-tasting juice, Bryan studied the almost too-thin slouched figure and sharply planed features. A few days on the beach had given the guy some color, but the pink tinge barely covered a pasty pallor.

And, finally, it came to him. What he'd been recognizing was not a specific person but a type. A type he knew very well.

When the dark-haired wave watcher straightened and took yet another gulp of the salty ocean air, Bryan knew that he was right.

He smiled a little to himself, glad to know that he hadn't lost his touch.

Of course, it was none of his business. What once upon a time might have been excused as professional curiosity was now just plain nosiness. But so what? Frankly, he was bored. Although he tried not to think about it and fought using that word to describe his feelings, he faced the truth now: Bryan Murphy was bored.

So after another moment of hesitation, he decided what the hell and made his way across the sand to the bench. He sat. "Maybe it sank," he said.

Two brown eyes slid his way fleetingly, then returned to their perusal of the Pacific. "What?" The voice was almost too quiet to be heard above the mingled sounds of the surf and the nearby volleyball match.

Bryan swallowed some juice before answering. "The way you've been watching that horizon for the past couple of days, I thought maybe you were waiting for your ship to come in."

A derisive snort came from the other end of the bench. "Yeah, sure. Well, if I ever *had* a ship, it fucking well did sink. Yeah." He needed a shave and the T-shirt he was wearing hadn't been washed in a while.

"How long have you been out?" Bryan asked casually.

It was a moment before the other man spoke. "What have I got? A sign on my goddamned back?"

Bryan grinned. "No. I used to be a cop, is all."

"Oh, wonderful. Well, I've done my time, sir, all of it, so you can just go hassle somebody else. If you don't mind, sir."

Bryan held up a hand. "Hey, no hassle from me. I've done *my* time, too. What I said was, I *used* to be a cop. Not anymore." Now he extended the hand. "Former detective Bryan Murphy, N.Y.P.D."

After the slightest hesitation, the hand was accepted. "Detaglio. Tray Detaglio."

They shook, then each settled back on the bench. Two bikini-clad girls strolled by. Both men watched the deliberately slow journey the girls were making. When the two reached the water and then vanished in the crowded surf, Bryan finished his juice. "So, how long have you been out?" he tried again.

"Why the hell do you care?"

Bryan took off his Yankees cap and ran a hand through his sweat-damp graying hair. "Calm down," he said mildly. "This isn't a frigging interrogation, you know. This is what's called a conversation."

Detaglio seemed to think fleetingly about smiling, but the idea never quite reached his mouth. "Sorry. Guess my social skills are a litle rusty." He fumbled in the pocket of his jeans and took out an almost empty pack of Winstons, searched some more and came up with a book of matches. Then he took out one cigarette and extended the pack.

Bryan, who was still mulling over the incongruity of a con talking about his "social skills," just shook his head.

When Detaglio had his cigarette lit, he spoke again. "Besides, the last so-called conversation I had earned me a nickel inside. So maybe I'm a little gun-shy."

"That's understandable." Bryan crushed the empty juice carton between his palms. "You know, when I saw you sitting here, I had a funny thought."

"Well, gee, sir, I've been hoping for a good laugh all week. What was the thought?"

"It was just about people. See, I've been walking up and down this damned beach for over three months now. Talked to a lot of these sun worshipers"—he surveyed the crowded beach with some disdain—"and I could never really connect with any of them. It was like we were from different planets. And not because I'm from back East, because so are a lot of them. No, it was because I was a cop. Cops and civilians just don't relate."

"Don't they?" Detaglio exhaled through his nose. "What a shame."

"But when I saw you sitting here, I said to myself, That guy's a con—"

"Ex-con," Detaglio corrected. "That subtle distinction might not seem important to you, but it is to me. Ex-con."

"Right," Bryan agreed. "Sorry. Anyway, I figured that you and I could understand each other. Two different sides of the same coin. You get what I'm saying?"

Detaglio eyed him. "I get it, all right. But it's fairly weird."

Bryan shrugged and replaced his baseball cap. "Well, maybe. But you just think about it."

"I sure will. First chance I get."

Bryan got to his feet. "I better take off." Not that he really had any place important to go to, but he tried to stick to a daily schedule. It gave his life a certain sense of order. He looked down at Detaglio. "Take care of yourself, Detaglio."

"I intend to. *Sir*. I intend to."

Bryan aimed the flattened juice carton toward the wire trash basket, threw it, and hit the target. He sidestepped a wild Frisbee and trudged toward the parking lot.

Tray Detaglio watched as the cop—once a creep, always a creep, as far as he was concerned, no matter all that bullshit about not being one anymore—walked away.

So, just what the hell had *that* been all about, anyway? Casual beach conversation? He shook his head. Since when did cops have ordinary conversations with guys like him? "No way," he said.

Damn. Had to stop talking to himself. Didn't they lock people up for things like that? Maybe not in Los Angeles, though.

Detaglio smoothed his hair nervously. Was that cop tailing him for some reason? Shit. That was all he needed.

At last, he just settled back on the bench again, resuming his wave watching. Now, however, he frowned at the Pacific and played absently with the wide gold ring on his finger.

Everybody had told him that he would hate living in California. His partner, Grabowski, laughed right out loud at the very idea. "You're a New fucking Yorker," he warned at the going-away party. "Whattaya gonna do out there, anyway? Take up surfing and dating boys, like all them Hollywood types?"

Bryan just shrugged because the truth was, he didn't *know* what the hell he was going to do. But he knew that the move west, making a clean break with the past, was a start.

He didn't try to explain his reasons to Grab because the other man never would have understood. Maybe you had to come right to the brink of death before knowing what you wanted to do with your life.

He still got nervous thinking about it.

It had been three days before Christmas when his life changed forever. He'd already decided to stop eating lunch at Fat Patty's Diner. Never mind the fact that it was convenient as hell and cheap to boot, plus having the added charm of Patty herself, a foul-mouthed, three-hundred-pound former meter maid.

But all of those advantages aside, this time he meant it: no more meals at Fat Patty's.

He rubbed his chest irritably. Heartburn again. Jesus, every day for the past week, he'd had indigestion. Had to be Patty's cooking. Probably somebody—like the frigging health inspector, for example—should tell her to check the grease on the grill. It must be way past time for a hundred-thousand-mile oil change by now.

Bryan quit rubbing the nagging ache and tried to stop thinking about the pain. Instead, he forced himself to concentrate on the action across the street.

Karl Steinmetz was still perched on a stool in the Chock Full o' Nuts. He was clearly visible through the front window, sitting at the end of the counter where he'd been for over an hour, drinking coffee and talking to the little waitress. She was pretty, judging by what they could see, especially when she turned her smile on Steinmetz.

"You know," Grab said from the driver's seat of their unmarked sedan, "these dumb broads almost ask for it. It's been all over the fucking papers and TV about the Coffee-shop Rapist. You'd think that every waitress in the city would run double-time from a creep trying to put the make on her. Instead, she's doing everything but dropping her pants for him right there."

"Doesn't make much sense," Bryan agreed. "But people are funny."

Grab snorted.

His bad mood, they both knew, had nothing whatever to do with the innate stupidity of either the human race in general or waitresses in particular. He was just tired of looking at Steinmetz. Their just barely official surveillance of the man was going into its second week, while Bryan, whose particular obsession Steinmetz had become, tried to convince the captain and the D.A.'s office that they had enough to make a case against the wealthy commodities trader.

Whoever claimed that there was no class system in the good old U.S. of A. obviously never worked as a cop, Bryan figured. Had Steinmetz been some indigent third-worlder, he'da been rousted a month ago.

But this guy Steinmetz had even eaten dinner once at Gracie Mansion, for chrissake.

Today, however, was the day. "Pick him up," the captain had said with a pained grimace. "But keep it very low key, understand?"

Low key.

Bryan massaged his left arm absently, watching the scene through the window. He could see why Steinmetz, despite all the publicity about the case, kept getting away with it. A rapist, after all, was supposed to look like a bad guy. He should be big and dirty and probably black. That was what people like to think, anyway, no matter how far it was from the truth. Somebody who looked like that was undoubtedly what all the waitresses were on guard against. Somebody like that they'd run from.

But no way did Steinmetz fit that image. He was dressed in what looked like an expensive Italian suit, his hair was styled, and Bryan would have bet that he smelled real good, too, although he couldn't tell that from across the street. In short, the man they were watching was the answer to a midtown maiden's dream. A maiden who still believed in fairy tales, at least, and who kept expecting Prince Charming to walk into the Chock Full o' Nuts or the Steak N' Brew.

Bryan opened the glove compartment and took out the ever-present roll of Tums. He popped two of them into his mouth and chewed vigorously.

"We could just go in there and take him," Grab suggested. His partner had occasional flashes of TV-copitis, although he was certainly old enough to know better.

Bryan took two more Tums before shoving the rest of the roll back into the glove compartment. "We know that it's a pretty good chance he's carrying. I'd rather avoid a preholiday shoot-out in the damned Chock Full o' Nuts, if you don't mind."

Grab sighed but didn't argue. Instead, he turned his head to watch yet another Santa Claus pass the car. "That's seven for the day," he said. From Thanksgiving until Christmas every year, Grab kept a running tally on the number of St. Nicks they saw on every shift. On Christmas Eve, he would announce the grand total. He had never explained the reasons for his behavior, but by now Bryan sort of looked forward to it as just another ritual of the season.

"Don't you think it's hot in here?" Bryan said suddenly. He rolled the window down about six inches and let the icy December wind come rushing into the car. Leaning forward a little, he began to gulp the air into his lungs.

"What're you— Having them hot flashes again?" Grab said, huddling down in the seat. "Maybe you're going through the fucking change. Ever think about that?"

"It's that damned chili-and-cheese dog I ate," Bryan answered through gritted teeth. "Not one more lunch in that frigging grease pit, understand? You eat there again, you can just eat alone."

"I ate the very same thing you did, and I feel just fine."

He didn't bother to respond to that, partly because he didn't give a damn and partly because he was still trying to ease the tightness in his chest.

"Maybe you got the flu," Grab suggested cheerfully.

"Maybe."

Abruptly, Grab straightened. "He's leaving."

They both got out of the car and dodged through a sudden flurry of traffic to get across the street. Steinmetz was already moving briskly away from the coffee shop.

Bryan hurried to keep up with Grabowski, although each step was an effort. The cold, or something, was making his whole left side tingle.

Suddenly, Steinmetz looked around, saw them, and immediately knew his pursuers were cops. He started to run, and they moved quickly after him. Bryan nearly tripped over the curb but managed to regain his balance and keep going. As he moved, he clutched at his chest with one hand, trying desperately to ease the crushing, constricting sensation.

Steinmetz disappeared around the corner, with Grab closing in fast. To Bryan, they both seemed a hundred miles away. He tried to shove his way through the crowd to catch up with his partner, but his body seemed only able to move in slow motion. Damn that lunch, anyway. Now the food and the chocolate milkshake seemed to be battling their way back up from his gut.

Without warning, he wasn't running anymore. Instead, he was flat on the sidewalk, staring into the gutter and throwing up. Pain pressed down on him.

When Bryan finally stopped heaving, he rolled over onto his back and gazed up into a circle of New York faces—faces that managed, all at the same time, to convey curiosity, streetwise distance, and a visible desire to somehow be helpful. He tried to ask someone to call 911, but the words wouldn't come. The faces pressed closer as voices argued the best course of action.

Out of nowhere, he thought of his father. The way the old man used to holler about heaven. When it was your time to go, you went. Nobody could ignore a summons from the Lord. Of course, Bryan doubted that when his summons came he'd be going to sit at either hand of God.

Probably, he was on his way straight to hell.

Well, he owed Patty an apology. This sure as hell wasn't indigestion. What this was, he decided through a descending fog, was real bad.

Maybe this was what dying felt like.

But he didn't die after all.

No matter what his father had preached, this time Bryan

Murphy had cheated the Angel of Death. He had managed to avoid those damned pearly gates.

Instead, he had taken early retirement and moved to California. Some people, like Grab, had seemed to think that death would have been the lesser of the two evils.

Frankly, after some four months out here, Bryan still wasn't sure.

He headed home on the Pacific Coast Highway, almost absently maneuvering the small brown jeep through the traffic.

When he reached Topanga Canyon Boulevard, he veered off and entered a quiet corner of the world. What was the phrase the real estate agent had used? Rustic, that was it. Rustic and bucolic. He still wasn't quite sure what *that* meant, but it sounded good. And as a man who had spent much of the first four decades of his life on the concrete of New York City, he enjoyed living in a place where there were more trees than houses.

He turned the jeep into the graveled drive that led to his place. Finding this house and actually being able to buy it had been a stroke of luck, although he supposed there was a certain amount of gratitude due to the platinum-blond real estate agent with the phony smile and the big diamond (real) on her finger. She had found the house before it actually hit the market and talked the desperate owner—an on-the-skids rock star facing drug charges—into a great deal. If any house that cost almost five hundred grand could be called a great deal, that was.

But he knew how damned lucky he'd been to have the money.

Even if it was dirty.

The cash to buy this place had come from his mother. For all of the years since he'd inherited it, Bryan had left the full amount untouched in the bank. He hated the fact that it had come from several generations of crooked cops and even more crooked politicians in his old lady's family.

But, in the end, he'd been forced to use the blood money. Now he loved the house enough so that he could almost forget the source of the cash he'd used to buy it.

Bryan parked the jeep next to the little blue Italian job already there. He sighed and climbed down.

Ann Hamilton was sitting on the steps. She smiled and stood as he approached. "I was about to give up."

"Just walking on the beach," he said.

They were silent for a moment.

He liked Ann, a friend of a friend. What was there not to like? She was in her late thirties, divorced, an artist who lived on the beach and, it seemed, made a lot of money. She was also pretty, in a healthy California way, with long chestnut hair and an even tan.

And she was obviously interested in him. Which was the problem, as Bryan saw it. For chrissake, he was a man who'd had a heart attack. A man who had nearly died. What did he need with some hot-blooded woman trying to jump into his bed? Hell, he liked sex as much as the next man, but the best lay in the world wasn't worth croaking for.

She turned to look at the house. "You've made some progress since last week."

"Some." He surveyed the newly painted trim. "But there's still a helluva lot to do."

Apparently, drugged-out rock stars didn't care about the shape of their houses.

"Why not take a break later and come to dinner?"

Actually, he wouldn't have minded. She was a good cook, and once in a while he liked being around someone instead of always being alone. But being around *Ann* made him nervous. No matter what the doctor said. He kept remembering the pain and not being able to catch his breath and all the rest of it.

And, anyway, even if he could push aside that fear, there was another. What if his body wouldn't cooperate? Bryan felt like a jackass, thinking about things like that, but he couldn't change how he felt.

So he kept shuffling away from Ann Hamilton.

She never seemed to get discouraged, though, and this time was no exception. When he declined the dinner invitation, she just grinned and promised to ask again.

He knew she would.

* * *

It got very quiet at night. Sometimes he liked the peace, and sometimes he would have killed for the racket of midtown traffic. Tonight was one of the latter times.

Bryan ate his plateful of spaghetti on the porch, watching the distant flicker of lights from the Pacific Coast Highway. Maybe he'd get a dog.

Once, twenty years ago, he'd been married, but it hadn't lasted long. The match between a hotshot young patrolman and a beautiful girl who wanted to be an actress had probably been doomed from the start. It used to make him sad, but now it was such a distant memory that the whole marriage seemed more like something he'd seen in a movie than an actual part of his life.

Finally, he went back into the house, rinsed the plate and silverware, and stuck them into the dishwasher. As he did that, he caught sight of his reflection in the window. Twenty pounds lighter than before the attack. Hair still thick, although it was mostly gray now. And a goddamned California tan on his unmistakably New York Irish face.

Except for the eyes.

The stony gray gaze he saw looking back at him came not from the charming, larcenous Murphys. The eyes were the legacy, the only real legacy, of his father. Matthew Dawkins.

Bryan could see something cold and unyielding in the gaze, a hardness that probably sprang from the coal mines of West Virginia. That was where the Dawkins clan had its roots. The eyes warred with the rest of his Irish face, just the way the Catholic Murphys had battled the evangelical Dawkinses when their offspring married.

In the end, the gray Baptist eyes were all he had left of his old man. The divorce had happened when he was only five. Mary Margaret returned gratefully to Brooklyn, where she belonged, and took back her own name. His name changed at the same time. He never saw his father again.

In him, the eyes burned not with religious fervor but with the weary cynicism of a detective. They were cop eyes, even now. The frigging cop eyes. He sighed and punched on the dishwasher. Maybe there was something good on television.

3

The thin cotton curtains at the bedroom window did nothing at all to keep out the first light of the morning. Chris, as usual, awoke as soon as the sunshine hit the room. He didn't sleep well anymore, hadn't really since his first time inside. When he was in prison, he had the feeling that part of his mind should be kept alert all the time. Just in case. A deep sleeper just might wake up dead.

Maybe someday he would get over all those years and then he could start to feel like a normal person again. Maybe. In Mexico, probably.

He rolled out of the bed and walked barefoot into the kitchen. Although the tiny light in the refrigerator was still burned out, he could see that they were out of OJ—again, damnit—and so he dropped several ice cubes into a plastic tumbler and then filled it with water. Taking that and his cigarettes, he went out back to the porch and sat on the top step.

The narrow alley behind the house was empty at this hour except for a solitary tomcat prowling the garbage cans. After one glance, he ignored Chris. The weirdos who populated this neighborhood were not early risers.

Chris lit a cigarette, hoping that a good shot of nicotine would help to clear his head. Way too much tequila the night before had left him definitely fuzzy around the edges.

He gulped ice water.

The hangover wasn't really what was bothering him, though, and he knew it. He just couldn't stop thinking about the scene with the hooker the night before. Dwight, unfortunately, had gone a little crazy and hit her. Luckily, there had been no real damage done, just a bloody nose, and the woman had taken the two hundred dollars Chris had offered to go away and forget it. But the situation could have turned into a real major problem.

Damn that Dwight, anyway.

What the hell was his problem? You don't fuck everything up over some smart remark by a two-bit piece of ass. Although, as it turned out, she had cost them a whole lot more than two bits.

Chris flicked ash aside and shook his head.

Glancing around to be sure that the coast was clear, he reached down to the next step and pried up a board. He pulled out the metal box beneath. Although he knew damned well how much money was inside, he counted it, anyway: just short of ten grand. A lot of money, yeah, but not enough. Not enough to get them to Mexico and set up the way they wanted to be.

Twenty-five grand was the goal they had targeted for themselves six months ago, and it would have been an admission of failure to settle for less than that. It didn't make sense to start a new life already feeling like a loser.

But the money seemed to come in such pissing little amounts. And just living ate up a lot of their profits. Especially when he had to hand out hundred-dollar bills to whores.

He sighed and dropped the money back into the box before replacing it in the cubbyhole. What he had to do was quit screwing around with liquor stores and get something big together. He couldn't have lost his touch completely. Could he? He dismissed the thought impatiently.

One thing was certain: If anything was going to happen, it would be up to him to get it moving. Dwight sure as hell wasn't going to. Why couldn't he have been locked up with somebody who knew what the fuck was going on?

Chris sucked one ice cube into his mouth and crunched it noisily. Yeah, it was time to get off his ass and *move*.

The screen door banged open and Dwight appeared. "We don't have any juice left," he said in a voice still thick with sleep. It took him a long time to wake up because he slept like the dead. Even inside he'd never had a problem. Probably because he knew that I was awake and keeping watch, Chris thought with some bitterness.

He shrugged. "Your week to shop, Dwight, and you haven't."

"Hell, I forgot."

"Why don't you tie a fucking string around your finger?"

Dwight gave a weak smile of apology and dropped onto the step next to him. He held out his hand and Chris gave him the remains of the cigarette. After two quick puffs, he arced the butt out into the shadows. The cat gave him a dirty look. "Hey, Chris, I'm sorry about last night."

"Yeah, sure."

"I really am."

Chris ate another ice cube. "You're always sorry and still you keep fucking around with our future like that. Someday you're gonna blow it completely. And when that happens, Dwight, you're on your fucking own. I won't take the fall with you."

"I know that."

Chris could feel himself getting angry and tried to hold it in. Count to ten, like his old lady used to say. Because he was so big, he couldn't just let go of his emotions like most people. He counted slowly. Then he said, "You know? Do you, really? You act like you *want* to end up back on good old cellblock D. By yourself this time."

Dwight shook his head.

"You'd last a week."

"If that long." Dwight seemed to shiver suddenly in the muggy morning air. "Damn, I don't want that."

"So?" Chris said.

"So I better shape up."

"Fucking A," Chris said.

"I will. Swear to God."

"Okay."

They'd had the same conversation before. Many times. And Chris knew in his gut that despite Dwight's promises, they'd have it again.

Sometimes he wished that he'd followed his instincts and just stayed on the damned bus the day he'd gotten out and gone someplace else. Then all he'd have to worry about was the parole board tracking him down.

"You know," Dwight said suddenly, "I never mentioned it before, but the first time I saw you, it about scared the shit out of me."

Chris looked at him, surprised. "It did? Why the hell? I didn't do anything."

"*Do* anything? Hell, Chris, what'd you have to do? I was in jail, for chrissake, which was scary enough. And then they put me in the cell and there you were. What're you, anyway, six-three or -four?"

"About that, I guess," Chris muttered.

"And built like a damned Mack truck. So what the hell did you have to do? Just standing there looking at me was enough. I nearly dropped dead on the spot."

"Yeah, well, I didn't do anything," Chris repeated.

"I know."

He pushed himself up from the step. The sun was up far enough now so that the day could begin. "I'm going to put my pants on and walk over to the store for some juice."

Dwight nodded. "Get some doughnuts, too."

Chris let the door bang as he went back into the house. Doughnuts and orange juice. Jesus. He used to be a major-class second-story man; he had a rep, for chrissake.

Now he was a goddamned housewife.

Monday wasn't a good night to work.

Chris had never liked pulling a job on Monday even before he was busted the last time, which, in fact, had happened on a Monday. That job hadn't been his idea in the first place. Beware of Greeks bearing gifts, he should have told himself. Although Greco, who came to him with the scam, was not actually Greek at all but Cuban. The moral still held true, however.

So he avoided Monday jobs when he could. He and Dwight just stayed around the house, watching the ballgame for a while, but the Dodgers were colder than . . . well, colder than the Reds, who they happened to be playing. And also the house—which consisted of only living room, small kitchen, john, and small bedroom—tended to feel a little crowded if the two of them spent too many hours there. In addition to all that, those damned freaks next door were playing their stereo at full volume again. They did that all the time and it made Chris crazy. The music they liked was all crap. He could get a heavy metal headache after about ten minutes. One of these days he was going to turn Dwight loose on them. With his gun. After the fourth inning, with the score already ten to nothing, Dwight turned the set off and they went out for a drink.

After cruising Sunset for a time and seeing nothing that excited them, they ended up in a bar on Santa Monica. Chris got a pitcher of beer from the bar and brought it to the table in back. A halfhearted game of pool was going on in the corner and they watched it as they drank.

Dwight cracked a peanut. "I was thinking about what you were saying this morning," he said.

"What was I saying?"

"About me doing something stupid and getting busted again."

Chris waved a hand. "Ah," he said.

"No, you were right to come down on me like that. But I decided something."

"What?"

Dwight stayed quiet while one of the pool players tried a tricky shot. He missed, anyway. "I decided that I'd rather be dead than get sent back."

Chris frowned. "That's a stupid thing to say."

"No, I mean it. Before I let them send me back, I'd kill myself."

"Fine," Chris said shortly. "It's your life. Do whatever you fucking well want to."

Dwight threw a peanut at him. "Well, you don't have to sound so pissed about it."

"I'm not pissed." But he was and he knew it. People who talked about killing themselves made him mad. That was the coward's way out.

Before they could pursue the subject any further, although Chris wasn't sure they should, a shadow fell across the table. He glanced up.

"Hi," she said. "You have an empty chair. Mind if I join you?"

Chris looked around the room; Monday was a slow night for bars, too. "Lot of empty chairs," he said.

She smiled, looking like a woman who was used to getting what she wanted. And no wonder. She was about five-four, thin in all the right places, with long brown hair that fell in straight bangs above lively dark eyes. Nice set of tits inside a snug pink T-shirt. Anybody who looked like that could probably write her own ticket. Broads were lucky that way. She fingered a thin gold chain that hung around a perfectly tanned neck. The smile never wavered. "But I'd like some company, too," she said.

Chris ran a hand through his fading blond hair. "So sit, if you want."

She did.

Chris carefully picked up his beer mug and took a swallow. He wiped his lips. Pretty women always made him feel clumsy and even bigger than he was. She watched him for a moment, a small smile still on her face, then turned her attention to Dwight.

Well, that was typical. Women always took to him, drawn probably to the curls and the deep blue eyes. Dwight was the kind of guy broads felt like they could mother and cuddle. Who the hell wanted to cuddle somebody six-three and built like a goddamned truck?

Chris didn't care, of course. Broads were easy to find. And Dwight never minded sharing, anyway.

"My name is Kathryn," she said after taking a sip from a glass of white wine.

"Chris. And he's Dwight."

That seemed to take care of the introductions.

Dwight went into the men's room.

He took a leak, then stood in front of the mirror to splash some water on his face. Chris was playing pool with the girl and they probably hadn't even noticed that he was gone.

It was starting to make him nervous, this Kathryn hanging around. But Chris seemed to be having a good time, so there wasn't anything to be done but make the best of it. He stared at his dripping face in the mirror and sighed.

The cheap paper towels practically dissolved in his hands as he tried to dry off. He took another moment to comb his hair and to smooth the front of his Jams T-shirt.

Suddenly, the door was pushed open and a guy in a shiny green suit came in. Dwight started to leave.

"Hey, pal," the guy said.

He turned reluctantly, his body primed to move fast, if necessary. "What?"

"You be interested in acquiring some primo smoke?"

"Maybe." He took two steps back toward the creep. "What's it like?"

After the man showed him three joints in a Baggie, Dwight paid him and put them into his pocket. Maybe they would cheer Chris up a little.

Dwight left the bathroom and went back to the bar. He sat, propped his feet on the table, and watched the pool game.

Chris was never quite sure how or why Kathryn ended up coming back to Venice with them. Usually they didn't take the broads home. It was a tight fit in the VW, but since they were all sort of drunk nobody minded much.

When they got to the house, Dwight took a Coke from the fridge and went out to the back porch. Chris stood by the screen door. "Guess Kathryn and I will hit the sack," he said.

Dwight raised the can of soda in a mock toast.

"Unless you'd rather?"

He shook his head. "Maybe later."

Chris lingered. "Well, if you're sure."

"I'm sure." He grinned. "After all, it's not like you're getting the chance to deflower a virgin, right?"

"Do what to a virgin?"

"Deflower. I read that somewhere. Sounds a little classier than to say popping her cherry, right?"

"Lot classier. However, I don't think either phrase applies here."

"Uh, not hardly. But have fun, anyway."

"Right."

After another moment, Chris turned around and walked into the bedroom. Kathryn was sitting on the bed, smoking a cigarette. "What'd you do, toss a coin?"

"Yep. I lost."

"Very funny."

He smiled and went into the bathroom. Maybe he ought to do something about the beginnings of a beer gut he could see in the mirror. Then he shrugged and undressed. When he came back out, she was under the sheet. Her clothes were piled on the chair. "Hey," she said.

"What?"

"He isn't going to watch or anything, is he?"

"What?"

"Dwight. I don't want him watching us."

Chris stared at her. "Whattaya think? You think we're a couple of weirdos or something? Course he isn't going to watch. He knows how it's done, for chrissake."

"Well, you never know about people, that's all."

He shook his head and pulled back the sheet to slide in next to her. The beers he'd had at the bar were already losing their hold on him and he was tired. What he wanted to do was just roll over and go to sleep, but that really wasn't possible now, was it?

So, instead, he rolled toward her. She stubbed out the cigarette as he began to massage her breasts. Chris felt himself begin to respond. The body was a funny thing.

Sex with Kathryn turned out to be simple, uncomplicated fucking, which was the way he liked it. When they were finished, he lit a couple of cigarettes and they smoked, staring at the ceiling instead of at each other.

"You mind if I crash here tonight?" she said. "I'm sort of without a place to stay right now. Bastard I was living with threw me out a couple days ago."

"Why'd he do that?"

She shrugged. "A man like him doesn't explain things. He just gives orders. And the rest of us obey. Or else."

"Or else what?"

"Or else he sends one of his gorillas to make sure you do it."

"Sounds like a real fun guy."

"Oh, yeah."

Chris got out of the bed. He pulled his jeans on, then walked to the doorway and stopped. "Dwight might come in now. You mind?"

"I guess not."

"Don't worry. I won't watch, either."

She flipped him a finger and he left.

Dwight was still sitting on the step, looking at one of his *National Geographic* magazines in the glow from the porch light. Chris sat down next to him and picked up the soda can. There was only a swallow left and it was warm, but he drank it, anyway.

"So how was it?" Dwight asked.

He shrugged. "It was screwing. Screwing is screwing."

"What a fucking romantic you are."

"Right. Well, you can go on in, if you want to."

"I guess." He started to get up, then sat again. "Oh, I almost forgot."

"What?"

"I got a present for you."

"A present?"

He reached into his pocket and took out the Baggie. "If the salesman can be trusted, this should be good."

"Thanks."

"Yeah, sure." He stood and went to the door.

"Hey, Dwight?"

He paused, the door open. "What?"

"Take it easy, huh?"

"I will." He held up a hand, Boy Scout style. "Promise."

Chris nodded.

When he was alone, he took out one of the joints and lit it. Well, it wasn't great dope, but it was better than a kick in the balls. He leaned back against the porch and picked up the magazine. Dwight had been reading an article about a cache of Spanish gold found recently in Mexico.

Yeah.

He studied the pictures eagerly. Someday they'd find stuff like this. Not for any dumb museum, though. Unless the museum wanted to pay them big, big bucks.

Looking at the pictures, it was easy to forget his problems, like Whitson and piss-poor jobs and Dwight, and just let himself drift pleasantly along on the dope and the golden images of a better future.

4

Bryan inhaled deeply.

It smelled like a cop shop, just like every precinct house he'd ever been in. The familiar odor was comforting, as was the steady buzz of conversation and the seemingly constant activity. He knew enough to know that much if not most of the talk was insignificant garbage, and a lot of the activity pointless. But that didn't make it all any less enticing.

He lifted the Styrofoam cup to his mouth, sipped, and then grimaced. Even the coffee tasted the same.

Lieutenant Roger Blank closed his office door, cutting off most of the noise from the squad room just beyond. "So, how're you doing, anyway?" he asked, going to the chair behind his desk.

Bryan was sitting in the visitor's chair. That's all he was now: a tourist in the real world. The thought rankled, and he took another drink of the bad coffee—feeling dangerously defiant because it was the real stuff, not the decaffeinated brown water he'd been drinking since the heart attack. "You want me to feed you some bullshit line? Or do you want the truth?"

Blank shrugged. "Whatever." Then he leaned back. "Of course, hearing the truth from anybody would be a refreshing change in my life."

Bryan considered, then said, "I'm bored outta my freaking skull, that's how I'm doing."

Blank barked an unsympathetic laugh. He hadn't changed much since they'd both been rookies on the N.Y.P.D. He still favored a military crewcut, and the ancient baggy brown suit

33

hung on his body with the easy familiarity of an old uniform. On his cluttered desk were the usual photos: plump, smiling wife and fresh-faced Catholic schoolkids. He was drinking a bottle of diet orange soda.

Blank's foot was propped on the edge of the desk and he used the toe of his sturdy black shoe to poke at a pile of reports. "I wouldn't mind a little boredom like that."

Bryan frowned. "Be careful what you wish for, buddy, or you just might get it." He eyed the files almost hungrily. "Anything good in there?"

"Not especially." Blank put the bottle to his mouth and gurgled down soda. "Hey, there isn't any good crime anymore," he said, lowering the bottle. "Just punks and druggers. Two-bit perpetrators."

"You're getting cynical."

"Sure. That's the cop disease. Don't tell me you aren't?"

Bryan fought a smile. "I don't have to be. I'm not a cop anymore, remember?"

"Yeah, well." Blank leaned forward and picked up a couple of the reports. "Man killed his wife. Now that's a real exciting case. Two kids knocking over gas stations and killing the attendants. Probably they just think it's all fun and games. And just this morning Robbery shuffled a case to me, couple of guys holding up liquor stores. Once or twice a week, three people shot so far, though nobody has actually died. They figure it's just a matter of time, so they invited me in early. One of the victims is in a coma and probably won't make it." He threw the papers down in disgust. "Those're the kinds of things I deal with. Shit."

"What're you hoping for? Some nice mass murderer like Son of Sam or Zodiac or maybe an international jewel thief? An exciting case like you see on TV, right?"

Blank grinned a little sheepishly.

Bryan nodded. "Uh-huh."

"The question is, old pal, what the hell are *you* going to do with the rest of your life?"

"Hey, I'm keeping busy," he protested, ignoring his earlier complaint about boredom. "Lot to do around my place."

"Right. A full life just playing Mr. Handyman."

"Fuck you." Bryan finished the coffee and set the cup on the edge of the messy desk. It could go unnoticed for months. "Yeah, I know," he said then. "But what the hell can I do about it?"

"Get a job."

"All I know is being a cop. You want to hire me?"

"Would if I could."

"Yeah. Or maybe I should hire on someplace as a security guard. Me and all the other washed-up little old men. Except that I'm not old. Just washed up." He shut up then and shrugged, dismissing the subject.

The phone rang and Blank picked it up. He listened for a moment, then covered the mouthpiece. "This is liable to take some time, Bryan."

"S'okay. I better take off, anyway."

"Keep in touch."

"Oh, sure."

He left Blank's office and walked slowly through the squad room. Nobody seemed to notice him.

Leaving Parker Center, he walked through the steamy city toward the lot where he'd parked the jeep. This place still didn't feel like home. The rhythm was different from what he was used to. There was something almost hypnotic about Los Angeles; he just couldn't quite give in to the seduction yet. Bryan wanted to be a part of it all—the excitement, the almost palpable sense of lazy sin—but still he held himself back. Maybe it was fear.

But on days like this, when the restlessness was like an itch that couldn't quite be reached, he was determined to *do* something about the half life he seemed to be living. If only he knew what the hell to do.

After inserting the key into the ignition he sat there a moment longer, remembering the smell and the feel of the police squad room.

"Hell," he said aloud. "Cut the crap, Murphy."

Oh, great. Now he was sitting in public talking to himself. Pretty soon, he'd get himself a shopping cart and start finding his clothes in trash dumpsters. The decline and fall of Byran Murphy.

With a sudden burst of anger, he wheeled out of the lot and headed for the freeway. What he'd do is make a complete break with reality. With the world of cops. With his own past.

He would go have lunch in Hollywood.

There was the usual pedestrian and auto traffic congestion in Tinsel City. Bryan managed after only ten minutes to find a spot where he could park the jeep and feel as if he stood a reasonable chance of finding it still there when he returned.

He set off on foot, in absolutely no hurry. For all the strange people and goings-on that he had seen as a New York City cop, and there'd been plenty, he still got a kick out of watching the freaks out here. For some reason L.A. weirdos seemed to be happier than those in New York. Maybe it was the weather.

They were shooting some television commercial on one of the corners, and he paused to watch. All the activity seemed a bit overdone since it was all merely in the service of selling toilet paper, but nobody except him seemed to feel that way. The women being questioned seemed really excited about the subject.

Toilet paper.

He shook his head and walked on.

A block or so later, he fell into step with a group of Japanese tourists, all heavily armed with Nikons, and wandered along with them. A petite and very pretty girl in a neat blue uniform was leading the tour. She seemed very efficient.

Bryan listened as she lectured the group on the Chinese Theatre and the footprints in the sidewalk. At least he assumed that was what she was talking about, because everybody pointed at the sidewalk and made admiring sounds. But it was all in Japanese, of course, so he couldn't be sure.

No one seemed to mind that he was tagging along. In fact, one of the group, a plump, smiling man in a neat blue suit, insisted on taking a picture of Bryan standing beside the Hollywood and Vine street sign.

When the group trooped into an expensive restaurant on Sunset for lunch, however, he parted company with them—amid some farewell waves—and kept walking until he reached Hamburger Habit on Santa Monica.

Because he knew so few people in Los Angeles, it was a real surprise to see a familiar face in the restaurant. He walked over to the table and sat down without being invited.

Tray Detaglio looked up from a hot dog he was smearing with too much mustard. After a few seconds, recognition flickered across his face. He set the mustard down. "A cop at lunch. Wonderful."

Bryan grinned. "Ex-cop, Tray, ex-cop, remember?"

"Uh-huh. So you keep saying. That's not how you act, though."

Bryan ordered a hamburger and 7-UP, then returned his attention to Detaglio. "I'm not following you, if that's what you're thinking. This is just a happy coincidence."

"Serendipity?"

"Right."

"My lucky day, is that it?"

"That's it." Bryan sipped the soda, then sat back to study his lunch companion. Detaglio still needed a shave. A haircut wouldn't have hurt, either. "You taking in the Hollywood sights?"

"Sort of." He finally picked up the hot dog and took a bite.

"If you don't mind me asking, what'd you do time for?"

"What if I do mind you asking?"

"Then I guess it's your constitutional right to tell me to fuck off."

"Bryan, fuck off," Detaglio said pleasantly.

They sat in a silence just short of companionable until Bryan's burger arrived. Detaglio had coffee now. He added two packets of sugar, tasted it, then added one more. Stirring it, he glanced at Bryan. "I stopped for a drink one night," he said carefully. "This was back home in Spokane. A little neighborhood bar. You know, the kind of place where everybody looks sort of familiar. Like maybe you know them, even if you don't."

Bryan picked up the salt shaker, held it over his fries, then remembered what the new rules were—and that he was already violating them sufficiently with the fries and the burger—and set it down without using any. "I know the kind of place."

"Well, there're these two guys. Ed Something and Something

Jones. Familiar faces, like. We talked politics or sports or whatever over a couple of beers. Pretty soon, I'm ready to leave and they ask me for a lift. I say sure thing. They ask me to stop at a store down the block so they can pick up a six-pack. I say sure." He almost smiled. "See, the joke was, I didn't know that while I was sitting out front with the engine running, they were inside robbing the place and shooting the owner to death."

"Great."

"Yeah, it was great. They came out, cool as you please, and I took off. Must've got three blocks or so before the cops stopped us. So Mrs. Detaglio's favorite son spends five years inside for being a dope."

Bryan finished chewing a bite of the burger and swallowed. "Kind of a stiff term," he commented. "Considering the way it happened. That you were sort of an innocent bystander."

Detaglio wiped his mouth with a napkin. "Well," he said.

Bryan just looked at him.

"Okay. It just happened that the car wasn't mine."

"It 'just happened'?"

Detaglio crumpled the napkin and threw it down on the table. "It used to be sort of a hobby of mine. Borrowing other people's cars."

"Without their permission?"

"Of course."

"I see."

"But that's a lot different than robbing and killing, you know."

"It is, yes." Bryan finished his burger. "So what are you doing these days?"

Detaglio frowned, looking for a moment as if he might say something important. Then he just shrugged. "Nothing much. Mostly just trying to pick up the pieces."

"Good for you. That can't be easy."

"Sure as hell isn't."

"Well, hang in there." Bryan reached for both checks. "Lunch is on me."

"Why?" Detaglio said suspiciously.

"Call it my contribution toward your rehabilitation."

The only response was a grunt that was probably intended to convey thanks. "See you on the beach."

"Maybe."

Bryan paid for the food and left the restaurant.

Since lunch had ended up being free, Tray decided to spring for some dessert, a piece of pie. As he ate it slowly, he tried very hard to figure out what the hell kind of game that damned cop was playing.

No way did he swallow that crap about this meeting just being a coincidence.

Serendipity, my ass, he thought.

That bastard Murphy was up to *something*, for sure. Even if Tray couldn't for his life figure out what it was.

He, after all, was nothing but a dumb car thief. Ex-car thief, he corrected himself. Certainly nothing for a big-deal cop to be interested in.

It was a nagging worry that he definitely didn't need in his life right now.

The new sander was a Rockwell. Bryan sat on the front porch and read the operating instructions carefully, trying to absorb the exact nature of things like paper clamps, shoe, and trigger switch. He was a complete beginner at all this stuff. The most he'd ever done back in his New York apartment was a little painting once in a while. That, and hauling his rubbish out to the trash chute in the hallway once a week.

But he was a homeowner now and that carried certain responsibilities. So he sat and read through the booklet about the sander.

It was hot and dirty work. By the time he had the porch smooth and ready for painting, Bryan was sweating and so tired that it was a little scary. He checked his pulse with some trepidation. Did it seem a little too fast?

But when nothing bad happened, he went inside and made himself a glass of iced tea. He took it out by the pool and sat in the hammock. The cold drink helped.

Now, however, there was something else to worry about. He was seriously starting to regret that he'd finally given in to Ann Hamilton when she'd called earlier and agreed to go to her place for dinner. Between the sanding business and what she undoubtedly had in mind, he'd probably be dead by morning.

When he knocked on Ann's door that evening, though, he was feeling a lot better. He had showered and dressed in a blue-striped sport shirt and blue slacks. At the last minute, he'd stopped at a liquor store for a bottle of white wine. It seemed like the polite thing to do.

Ann seemed to appreciate it. She met him at the door wearing flowing white trousers and a lacy top. There were the usual few minutes of awkwardness, but most of it had passed by the time she announced that dinner was ready.

They sat at a small table on the balcony and watched the Pacific as they ate the thin pasta with shrimp. It was all delicious.

"You never talk much about your marriage," she said as they waited for the coffee to brew.

"Nothing to say about it," he responded.

"Any children?"

"No. It didn't last that long."

She got up and brought a silver tray to the table. It held coffee cups and dessert plates. "You don't sound bitter."

Bryan shrugged. "No reason to be." He took a bite of the fresh strawberry shortcake. There was a great deal to be said for being a dinner guest, he decided. "She was a nice girl. An actress. We lived in Greenwich Village. Carol was all tied up with the theater and her friends in the business. Always looking for the big break."

"And what about you?"

He gave a rueful smile. "I was all tied up with the department and my friends in the business. Always looking for the big bust."

"That doesn't sound like the formula for a successful marriage."

And it hadn't been. He'd known it even on the very day they tied the knot. But goddamn, Carol had been beautiful. And in bed . . . For years after the divorce he'd had wet dreams, just thinking about it.

But when Bryan looked across the table at Ann, he put that thought aside quickly. Sex wasn't what he should have going through his mind right at the moment.

When the meal was finished they went inside to her studio, a surprisingly neat room with a vast skylight. Ann painted large canvases, mostly in primary colors. When she stepped out to answer the phone, Bryan moved around the studio for a better look. None of the pictures looked like anything real, as far as he could tell, but he liked them. They were cheerful. Maybe one of them was just what he needed to brighten up his living room.

Except that he had made the mistake once, in a gallery where some of her work was on exhibit, of asking the price for one painting that he especially liked. Twenty grand, he had been told. The amount had stunned him.

No wonder she could live in this wood-and-glass box overlooking the ocean. The question now became: What the hell could she want from a pensioned-off ex-cop?

On one wall there were some photographs, all of a blond girl, chronicling her growth from infancy to about age fifteen. He was looking at them when Ann came back into the studio. "My daughter," she said.

"Very pretty girl."

She stared at the pictures for a moment. "I haven't seen her in two years."

Her tone left no room for questions.

They went back out to the balcony for brandy. It would have been so easy. She obviously wanted to go to bed with him. And he could feel himself responding—who the hell wouldn't?

But he just finished the brandy, thanked her for the meal, and left.

He couldn't sleep.

Maybe it was the rich food or maybe it was unsatisfied lust. Or the vague pains in his chest. The meal, he told himself, that was all. Just indigestion.

He got out of bed, poured himself a glass of skim milk, and

went outside. It was a hot night, just like all of the nights lately. Was this weather ever going to end?

Bryan drank the milk slowly, watching the distant lights. They reminded him a little of the stars he used to see when he was a little kid. The family spent a lot of time on the road with the Holy Way Crusades, which were led by his evangelist father. Most of that time seemed to be spent out in the sticks, and the stars were very bright in the country. Sometimes, instead of staying inside the tent to listen to the whole sermon, he would slip outside and lie on the ground to watch the stars.

They used to make him strangely sad, the way these lights did now.

He had a weird thought suddenly. Maybe he really had died on that sidewalk back in Manhattan. Maybe this was limbo. Or hell. One hand massaged his chest restlessly.

He just hoped with all his being that it wasn't heaven.

5

Tray Detaglio sidestepped—politely—a tall, thin black man who was selling drugs and—insistently—a girl about fourteen in cut-off jeans and a halter top who was selling herself. Jesus, but Hollywood was such a zoo. It sure wasn't anything like the movies. He stopped underneath the pale light of a flickering marquee to read from the sheet of notebook paper in his hand. There was one more place he had scheduled to check out tonight. Although he was tired and increasingly irritated by the stone walls he seemed to be running into everywhere, he decided to stick to the schedule.

The Pink Pussycat Club looked, from the outside, like all of the other places he'd visited over the last several evenings. There seemed to be a notable lack of originality among the people who ran such businesses.

Of course, Tray conceded wearily, there wasn't a whole lot new that could be done with tits and ass. Although if there was, he was sure they'd know about it here.

More than a little bored by it all by now, he stood on the sidewalk and smoked his way through two cigarettes, watching the constant parade of weirdos passing by on Sunset. Most of them seemed to have either shaved heads or purple hair, or, in some cases, a strange combination of both. They made the cons he'd been hanging out with for the last five years look like candidates for the frigging Chamber of Commerce.

It was kind of funny, really. Who would have thought when he was sitting in that damned cell, thinking about sex, that he could ever get bored looking at naked broads? On the day he got out he had the usual hooker, although what with everything going on in the world, he made sure to use a rubber. But now, well, after all the stuff he'd been viewing, he sort of felt like the rest of the Trojans could stay right in his wallet.

When the second cigarette was gone, he dropped the butt into the gutter and reluctantly entered the strip joint. Inside was the usual mix of noise and sweat and the stink of something else he couldn't quite identify. Sometimes he thought it smelled like desperation. Men in the joint had that same smell. He'd given it off himself more than a few times over the years.

Tray shook off the past impatiently and shoved his way to the bar for a whiskey. One drink at each place was all he allowed himself. Even so, he was starting to feel the alcohol. The music from a bad four-piece band was so loud that he couldn't even hear himself swallow.

On a platform above the bar three bored and tired-looking women gyrated, not necessarily in time with the music. Tray looked at each one carefully, but there was nothing even vaguely familiar about any of them.

He waved the bartender down and took a battered photograph out of his pocket to show him. "You know her?" he asked.

The fat man looked at him, not at the picture. "What?"

Tray pushed the photo closer. "Does she dance in here?"

Finally, the man glanced down. Then he shrugged. "Could be. Maybe. Ask the boss."

"Where's he at?"

A plump finger pointed toward the back. Tray went through the door, down a dark hallway, and stopped at another door, this one marked PRIVATE. He knocked.

There was no response.

He knocked again, using his fist this time.

Someone yelled for him to quit the fuck banging on the door and come in, for chrissake.

He opened the door and went in.

A man in an ill-fitting tux sat behind a messy desk. He had a very bad toupee planted on his head and thick, horn-rimmed glasses from behind which he peered irritably at Tray. "Not hiring," he said. "Don't need another bartender and the band is filled."

Tray closed the door. "Too bad. They all stink and I'm a helluva bass player."

"Yeah, that's what they all say."

"Well, in my case, it happens to be true. But I'm not here looking for a job." As he spoke, the thought did occur to him that looking for a job was probably not a bad idea. His money was going fast. But this had to be done first.

"So? If you ain't looking for work, what'cha bothering me for?"

"I'm looking for a woman."

The man behind the desk laughed, but not like there was anything funny. "So is every other asshole out there. Take your pick. The broads ain't all that selective."

Tray held out the picture again. "Her name is Kathryn Daily. I heard that maybe she danced here."

The prescription-magnified eyes darted over the photo. "They all look alike to me."

Tray was really tired. And a little drunk. He kept getting hassled by all these creeps when all he was doing was asking a simple question. Didn't they even know how to be civil, for God's sake? "Look again, why don't you?"

The man looked instead at Tray. "Who the fuck are you and why the fuck are you asking me questions?"

"I'm just a guy trying to find a broad, that's all."

"Try the classifieds, why doncha, and quit bothering me?"

Tray put the picture away carefully. "You know, sir, it seems to me that you have an attitude problem."

"Take a flying fuck outta here."

There was a battered coffeepot sitting on one corner of the desk. Tray swept it aside with his arm. They both watched as it crashed to the floor, spilling cold coffee. "What the hell ever happened to good manners?" Tray said. "Christ, a man goes away for a few years and then, when he comes out, everybody in the country has this *attitude*."

The creep must have pushed a hidden button or something,

because suddenly the door swung open and another man came in. This one looked like a biker, lots of leather and chains. No smile.

Tray gave a weak grin and took two steps backward. He reached behind him with one hand, searching the desktop for something, anything, to use as a weapon. An Uzi would have been nice. Or a grenade. But all his frantic fingers found was a paperweight. He gripped it.

There used to be a time when they would have beat the shit out of him and then thrown his ass out into the street. Not anymore. Now they beat the shit out of him and called the cops. They must have been fucking Republicans.

The beating he could stand; nothing was broken and the nosebleed didn't last long. But when the cops showed up to bust him, he got a real sick feeling in the pit of his stomach.

He stared at the floor as they went through the routine of cuffing him and reading his rights. Big deal. He had rights. Somehow, that wasn't much comfort at the moment.

When they took him out through the bar and shoved him into the backseat of the squad car, he huddled in the corner, sniffling to keep his nose from bleeding again. He closed his eyes.

Damndamndamndamndamn.

Was he going to end up back in prison? Tray felt as if he were going to throw up. But he didn't want to make the cops mad at him, so he just swallowed hard. He didn't think he could handle going back inside.

Where he ended up right then was in the drunk tank.

Almost immediately, somebody threw up on his shoes. Wonderful.

He went to the farthest corner of the cell and crouched there, trying to make himself invisible. It didn't work. An old man in a suit that smelled like he'd had it on since the Depression shuffled over. "Don't I know you?" he said hoarsely.

Tray shook his head.

But the elderly bastard didn't buy it. "Sure, sure. I know you. You're the son of a bitch who ran away with my wife. Back in '52."

Tray tilted his head back a little and looked up at the drunk. "Man," he said softly, "I wasn't even fucking *born* in 1952. How the fuck could I run away with your wife?"

"You're the son of a bitch, all right." Two vague, watery eyes studied him. "Maybe you done had some kind of plastic surgery to keep you looking young."

"Go away, willya?"

After a moment the drunk wandered off, still muttering under his breath about his runaway wife. Tray closed his eyes again.

"Detaglio?"

He almost didn't register that the cop was saying his name. Belatedly, he stood and went to the bars. "Yeah?"

"You want your phone call now?"

Tray started to shake his head—who the hell could he call, anyway?—then, suddenly, he had an idea. Maybe it was a bad idea, but it was all he had at the moment. It was a hope, no matter how slender. "Yeah," he said. "I'll make my call. You guys got a phone book?"

If that damned cop was going to be hanging around all the time anyway, he might as well be fucking useful. Besides, maybe now Tray could find out what his game was.

They let him call Information. He wrote the number on the back of his hand, then dialed it quickly, forgetting that by now it was close to three A.M.

It took eight rings for somebody to pick up the receiver on the other end. "H'lo?" said a voice heavy with sleep.

"This Bryan Murphy?"

"Yeah, yeah, who'd you expect when you dialed my number?"

Tray leaned his forehead against the cool tile of the hallway, afraid to hope too much. "This is Tray."

"Who?"

"Tray Detaglio. Remember?" How could the jerk not remember, when he'd been on Tray's case for days?

There was a pause, during which Tray thought he might die. Then Bryan said, "Sure, I remember you, Tray."

No frigging kidding.

"What's wrong?"

He took a deep breath. "I got busted."

"Steal a car?"

"No, no. Nothing like that, I promise. But I can't . . . If you could go bail for me, I'll pay you back. I swear. See, I don't want to spend the rest of the night in the drunk tank. You were the only person I could think of to call."

"Uh-huh. Lucky me." There was another silence before Bryan spoke again. "Where are you?"

"Hollywood."

"Okay. Hang tough. I'm on my way."

"Thanks," Tray said, meaning it more than he'd ever meant it before in his whole misbegotten life. What a shame all this heartfelt gratitude had to be wasted on Murphy.

It seemed to be a whole lot longer than it actually was before the cop came back to the tank and let him out again. He was taken to a room where Bryan stood at the counter, just putting his wallet away.

Tray stopped next to him, suddenly aware of how he must look, what with the blood and the vomit and his three-day-old whiskers. "Bryan, I really appreciate this."

"You damned well better. Come on."

They left the police station and walked to a jeep parked nearby. Bryan got behind the wheel. "Get in," he said to Tray, who was still standing on the sidewalk.

"Where we going?"

Bryan started the engine. "I'm going home. And you're coming with me. Otherwise, how will I get my money back?"

Tray climbed in. "You'll get it back, don't worry."

"You've got blood all over your face," Bryan said. "And somebody puked on your shoes."

Tray just sighed. Maybe he'd been better off in the drunk tank. Neither said anything for the rest of the ride.

Bryan hit the wall switch and the light came on. Tray followed him into the kitchen. "Wash your face," Bryan said. As Tray bent over the sink and splashed water on the dried blood, Bryan made some instant coffee. "Hope you don't mind decaf," he said. "I'm supposed to cut back on the caffeine."

"Fine," Tray said from behind a paper towel. "That better?"

"Marginally."

They sat at the table and tasted the coffee. "Okay," Bryan said. "Tell me about it."

Tray didn't speak right away. He lifted the lid on the sugar bowl and dropped three lumps into the cup, then stirred for a long time. He sighed again. "Okay. It's like this. Up in Spokane, before I got sent away, I was living with a girl. Kathryn Daily. This wasn't like the big romance of the ages or anything, understand, we just sort of drifted into shacking up. You know how that goes."

Bryan just grunted.

"Well, two days before I get busted, she breaks the news that she's pregnant."

"Great."

"Yeah. Wouldn't you think she'd have been smart enough to be more careful than that?"

Bryan looked at him.

Tray shrugged. "Or me."

"It does take two, last I heard."

"Okay, so we were both stupid." Tray glanced around the kitchen. "You got anything to eat?"

Bryan pointed. "Some crackers in the cupboard."

Tray got up and found the box of cinnamon grahams. He brought them back to the table and ate one quickly. Then he took another and started on it. "Anyway, I got sent up and she was pregnant. I got one letter from her, right after I was put inside. Said she was trying to think of names for the baby. But that was the last I ever heard. She never even let me know when the kid was born or what it was."

"Uh-huh."

"I mean, it's my kid, you know? Shouldn't I at least have the right to know whether it's a boy or a girl?"

Bryan shrugged. Then he said, "Are you sure she even *had* the kid?"

Tray finished the second cracker. "I think so. Anyway, I hope so. Kathryn was never any kind of saint, but I don't think she could kill her own baby." His voice was firm, but his eyes showed doubt. He didn't want to think about the possibility—probability—that the broad had had an abortion, so he just didn't think about it. Except, Bryan figured, sometimes on long nights inside.

Tray took a deep breath. "When I got out, I started looking. She has an aunt in Seattle I found. The old lady told me Kathryn had moved down here a couple years ago."

"Couldn't the aunt tell you about the baby?"

He shook his head. "She didn't even know Kathryn had been pregnant until I told her. They weren't close."

"I guess not."

"So I came down here and started looking. She used to dance at some bars at home, so I figured she might do the same thing here. I've been looking every damned night. That's what I was doing tonight. I even got a nibble, from the bartender, that I might be getting close. But then things got a little out of hand, I guess."

"A little, yeah." Bryan got up for more coffee. When he was sitting again, he said, "Maybe I can help."

Tray looked at him through narrowed eyes. Oh, yeah, he thought, cops were famous for helping people, especially ex-cons. "Why should you?"

"Why not?" Bryan took a cracker. "I don't have anything pressing to do at the moment. And, hell, I can't stand too many phone calls in the middle of the fucking night. After all, I'm a man who's had a heart attack."

"You did? Shit, I'm sorry."

"Forget it. But remember something else. I'm a cop. Ex-cop." They both smiled fleetingly. "We're good at finding people."

Tray set his coffee cup down. "I don't have much money. No money, really."

"Don't worry about it."

He shook his head slowly. What the *fuck* was going on with this guy? Whatever he was trying to pull had to be good. Tray just couldn't think what it might be.

Bryan was quiet, then he said, "How about you work it off?"

"Work it off?"

"Sure. I've got a lot to do around this place. You could help, pay me off that way."

Tray thought about it. Maybe it might work. He wasn't all that hot on hanging out with a cop, of course, even one who wasn't one anymore, but Murphy almost seemed like an all-right kind of guy. And he sure as hell wasn't making much progress toward finding Kathryn on his own. Besides, this would give him a chance to find out why Murphy seemed so hot on cozying up to him. "I guess we could give it a shot," he said finally.

Bryan held out his hand. "Sounds like a deal to me."

Tray wiped crumbs on the front of his shirt, and they shook hands firmly. "A deal," he said.

For as long as necessary.

6

The lobby of the building was almost too cool. Dwight paused for a moment, feeling and enjoying the prickle of chilling sweat against his skin. Then he headed for the elevator.

As usual, he only had to wait a moment before the receptionist ushered him into the office. Schaefer ran a tight, well-scheduled ship here.

She was sitting at her desk, which, as always, was empty except for a spiral pad that had his name neatly printed on the cover. He often wondered what she actually wrote down in that damned mysterious pad. Sometimes he suspected it was her grocery list. While he sat across from her, spilling his goddamned guts, she looked serious as she scribbled *one head cabbage*.

Now, he sat in the chair directly in front of the desk.

"How are you today, Dwight?" she asked, flipping open the notebook. Schaefer was a tall redhead with great tits. But cold. She seemed so cold.

"I'm okay."

A silence fell between them, which was nothing new. Sometimes they didn't say anything for the whole damned hour. But today, for some weird reason, Dwight felt like talking. Maybe if he just told her the whole damned story, once and for all, it would be better for him. Talking it out might kill the nightmares.

"I was raped in jail," he said abruptly.

"Were you?" She was always so completely noncommittal and nonjudgmental. It made him crazy.

"I was *raped* in jail," he repeated. "I think that deserves more than just your usual comment."

"Do you?" She made a note.

One gal. ice cream.

"Sure I do."

"What do you think would be the appropriate response for me to make?"

"How the fuck do I know from appropriate? You're the expert, right? Or what am I doing here?"

"Would you like to talk about the incident?"

He almost laughed; this was one cold bitch, all right. "The *incident*? Is that doctor talk? According to you, rape is an incident?" He shook his head. "Jesus, lady, do you ever get in touch with the real world?" When she made no response, only looked at him like she was trying to decide whether or not to add him to the shopping list, Dwight sighed. "Well, I guess maybe I do want to talk about the *incident*, right? Or else why would I have brought it up after all this time?"

Another note. "That's a very good point."

He leaned back to stare at the ceiling. "It happened after my first week inside. I walked into the metals shop and this guy grabbed me. Great big bastard. He'd been looking at me, watching me funny, since my first day on the block. He came from behind and grabbed my arm, twisted it practically out of the goddamned socket. Dragged me into the hall. Nobody was around. Thousands of cons in the joint, not even to mention the goddamned screws, and there wasn't anybody in this hallway but him and me." He glanced at Schaefer quickly. "You want the graphic details here? It's pretty gruesome."

"Whatever you feel like saying, Dwight, I'm here to listen."

"Right," he said disgustedly. "Okay, lady. First of all, he made me suck him off. Then he rolled me over and fucked me in the ass. How does that grab you? Just for fun along the way, he beat the shit out of me."

She made a note.

Qt. skim milk.

Dwight gnawed on a thumbnail. "I tried to fight the creep, I did, but sometimes I think maybe not hard enough."

"That's a common feeling among rape victims," Schaefer said.

"I don't know what the hell would've happened next. But I think he might've killed me. Luckily, Chris came along."

"He did?"

"Yeah. Chris saved me."

"That was fortunate."

Dwight snickered; you had to laugh at the broad sometimes, with her chilly attitude. "Yeah, fortunate. And after that . . ."

"After that?"

"After that nobody bothered me anymore. Because the word went out that I belonged to Chris. So nobody touched me again. Just him."

"Did that disturb you?"

He was surprised at the question. "No. After all, I owed him for saving me like that. Besides, I like Chris. He never once hurt me. That's just the way it is inside. Some people are punks and some people own the punks." He lowered his gaze again fleetingly. She knew—and was the only one who did know—that he and Chris were still friends. With her, it was like with a priest or a lawyer. She couldn't tell anybody, not even the parole people. "In case you're wondering," he said, "we don't do it anymore. That was just inside." Although he doubted if she wondered about anything.

"I see."

"So, what do you think about all of that?" he asked. "And don't just turn my question around and ask it back at me. Just for once, why the hell can't you say something?"

She was playing with the damned silver fountain pen. "Whatever I might say, Dwight, wouldn't be terribly significant. The important thing is: How do you feel about all of it?"

It was hopeless. "How do I feel about the rape? I hate it, of course. Wouldn't you? It makes me sick even now to think about it. How do I feel about Chris? He's my friend. That about sums it up. But I'm very curious about something."

"What?"

"Do you ever commit yourself? To anything or anybody?"

She was watching him again. "Do you think that commitment is important?"

"Yes. Of course it is."

He wanted to explain it to her. The whole thing. About how he and Chris were committed to each other, like, and to the plans they had made together. He didn't think she would understand, though. Probably this cold fish never had a real friend, not like he had Chris.

It made him almost feel sorry for her.

But even if he thought she *might* understand what he was talking about, probably it was better not to say any more. It could get dangerous. Doctor or not, she could still betray him.

So he didn't say anything for the rest of the hour.

Chris gnawed on his lower lip thoughtfully.

There was something about Hal's Liquor Store that he didn't like. He tried to figure out what the problem was, but the outside of the place was just like all of the others they'd been hitting over the months—a little shabby, with windows that were grimy and a sign with peeling paint. But despite the appearance of the place, Hal seemed to do a good business; a lot of customers had come and gone while they'd been sitting here in the stolen Honda.

On the surface, anyway, everything appeared to be just like always. Chris couldn't figure out why his gut was telling him to pass on this job. A man should listen to his gut, probably.

But they were ready. It was late and he sure didn't feel like cruising Vermont Avenue trying to pick another target at the last minute.

So to hell with it. They were going to do Hal's and that was it. If his gut continued to bug him, he'd take an Alka-Seltzer.

Chris glanced at Dwight and decided to keep his feelings to himself. No sense making the other man more nervous than he usually was, anyway. Chris fumbled for his pack of cigarettes and lit one. "The broad starting to bug you?" he asked suddenly.

"She's okay," Dwight replied absently.

"I didn't know she'd keep hanging around like she is." It was almost an apology.

"It doesn't matter."

Chris glanced at the store as still another customer went in. Jesus Christ, was Hal giving away booze in there? "You sure?"

Dwight's voice was impatient as he said, "Chris, I don't care if you want to keep a fucking harem, okay?"

He gave a short laugh. "One is enough, thanks. Too much most of the time. She'll probably take off pretty soon, anyway. I just didn't want her getting on your nerves."

"My nerves are fine."

Chris patted him on the arm. "Good." He took another look at Hal's. Finally, there were no customers in sight. "Let's get in and out of here as fast as possible, okay?"

"Why?" Now there was worry evident in Dwight's voice. "Is something wrong?"

"Of course not. Don't go all paranoid on me. Just—" He broke off and opened the door. "Let's just do it and get it done."

They both got out of the car and walked across the street.

At the curb, Chris stopped for a moment. "Watch this guy, huh?"

Dwight looked at him, his eyes suddenly cloudy with anxiety. "What's the matter, Chris?"

Chris was mad at himself for being so damned antsy; he didn't know why the hell this was making him uneasy. The worry and the anger made him speak more sharply than he usually allowed himself to do. "I just said to fucking watch the bastard, all right? Is that so hard?"

Without giving Dwight the chance to say more or allowing his own fears to escalate to the point where he'd be unable to function, Chris stalked into the store. Dwight instantly followed him. There was a dark-skinned Hispanic man behind the counter. Close up, he looked younger and stronger than he had from across the street. "What you have?" he asked.

Chris took out the gun. "We'll have all the money, please. In a bag. And hurry."

The man nodded and moved toward the cash register. The baseball bat must have been right beneath the counter because he had it in his hands before either of them could react.

"Hey," Chris said. "Don't be dumb."

Dwight was reaching for a paper bag, seeming not to believe

that anybody could be stupid enough to go up against a Magnum with a goddamned Louisville slugger. But the guy did. The bat traveled in a rapid arc through the air and cracked across Dwight's arm. "Fuck!" Dwight yelled, his voice creased with pain.

Chris took one quick look at him, but that split second was long enough for the bat to swing again, this time at his hand. The gun flew across the room. What the hell was this asshole trying to prove?

As Chris scrambled to get the gun back, trying to ignore the burning pain in his fingers, the clerk turned back to Dwight, who had apparently recovered because he was already shoving money into the paper sack. He dodged one swing of the bat, swearing at the man in jailhouse Spanish.

Chris was down on his knees, fumbling beneath a display of wine coolers, trying to find the damned gun. At last he managed to close his fingers around it. He rolled over, firing once, hoping to scare the guy. The bullet smashed into the wall.

The clerk, maybe starting to get smart, ducked behind the counter.

"Come on!" Chris yelled.

But Dwight reached for the money again and the clerk jumped up, waving the baseball bat. He got lucky and his blow collided with the side of Dwight's head.

Dwight fell forward onto the counter.

Chris took aim and fired. The bullet hit the clerk in the face and he dropped like a stone. Still on the floor, Chris turned his eyes to Dwight. "Hey?" he said. "You okay?"

Dwight stirred a little, moaning.

Chris got to his feet and went around the counter, carefully avoiding the body and blood. Damned creep, having to be so fucking macho. What the hell did it prove? Chris put both arms around Dwight and pulled him up. "Can you walk, Dwight? We gotta get out of here."

Dwight looked at him and blinked a couple of times. "Yeah," he said slowly. "Yeah, I can walk." He clutched the bag of money to his chest.

Chris kept a firm grip on Dwight as they moved out of the store and across the street to where the stolen car waited. He shoved the limp man into the passenger seat of the Honda and got behind the wheel. He was shaking all over, from the massive dose of adrenaline pumping through his system and from the pain in his hand, and so it took him three tries to get the damned car running.

His hand was really throbbing by this time, but he tried to ignore it. The car squealed away from the curb and turned the corner. Chris glanced at Dwight, who remained slumped against the door. The side of his face was already swelling and changing color. "I got the money," he mumbled. "Got the fucker's money."

"Yeah," Chris agreed glumly. "We got the money."

He knew the bastard back in the store was dead and that meant they were in deeper shit than ever. The car turned another corner too sharply. Next time, he thought bitterly, I'll listen to my fucking gut.

Next time.

They dumped the Honda fifteen blocks from the store and got back into the VW. Chris drove again. Dwight mumbled a couple more times about the money, but beyond that it was a quiet trip back to Venice. They never even heard any sirens.

Chris parked in the alley, sat still a moment to give his wildly thumping heart a chance to calm somewhat, then got out of the car. He walked around to the passenger side to help Dwight out. It wasn't easy, as the other man was practically a dead weight.

Kathryn was sitting on the top step, reading the latest issue of *Playgirl* and smoking. She watched as they made their way slowly to the porch. "Lord, what the hell happened, Chris? You guys look like refugees from World War Three."

Neither man answered.

They went into the house, not stopping until they had reached the bathroom. Once there, Dwight leaned over the toilet and threw up. When the gagging stopped, he slid to the floor wearily. "Shit," he said. That seemed to sum up the situation pretty well.

Chris had been running cold water over his hand, trying to ease the pain. "You okay?" he asked.

Dwight just shrugged.

Chris took several aspirin from the bottle in the medicine cabinet and swallowed them. Then he filled the plastic cup with water again and shook four more aspirin from the bottle. He knelt beside Dwight. "Swallow these," he ordered.

Dwight did so. "And call you in the morning, right?" he said with a weak smile.

Chris touched his bruised cheek lightly. "Idiot. You should've just left the fucking money."

"No. We need it." Dwight reached out with one hand and flushed the toilet.

Chris helped him to his feet, and they went into the living room. Both of them more or less fell onto the couch. Kathryn stood there watching them, seeming vaguely amused by the sight. Chris looked at her impatiently. "Why don't you make yourself useful for a change and get us a couple fucking beers?"

Without a word, she disappeared into the kitchen, coming back a moment later with the beers and also with the bag of money that Dwight had dropped as soon as they were inside. As they each took a long swallow of beer, she opened the sack and peered in. "Not much here," she said. "For what it cost you."

"Tell us about it," Chris muttered.

"Gas station?"

"A liquor store, if it's any of your business."

"Uh-huh." She sat in the overstuffed chair and tucked her feet under her. "You guys are into this kind of thing, right? That's how you get by?"

Chris just grunted.

Kathryn seemed to be studying them thoughtfully, pulling and twisting a strand of her dark hair. "Let me ask you something."

Dwight was leaning back against the sofa, his eyes closed. He lifted the can of beer and took a small sip. "You could just shut the fuck up," he said. "Ever think of that?"

She looked at him angrily.

Chris sighed. "What's the question?"

She seemed to dismiss Dwight. "Would you be interested in maybe making a whole lot of money at one time?"

"Hell, no," Chris said. "We like doing this. We get off on being beaten to a pulp for a couple hundred dollars."

"Very funny."

"Yeah, well, I'm a stand-up comic in my spare time."

She made an impatient gesture. "You want to listen to my idea or not?"

Dwight spoke again, still without opening his eyes. "For chrissake, listen to her and her stupid idea. Then maybe she'll shut up."

"What's his problem, anyway?" Kathryn asked, angry again.

"He has a headache," Chris said. "So all right. How can we make a whole lot of money at one time?"

She leaned forward eagerly. "Remember me telling you about Michael?"

"The guy you were shacking up with? The one who threw you out?"

Dwight snorted.

She ignored him. "That's him. Well, what I didn't exactly say before is that he has a lot of money. A *lot* of money."

"I'm very happy for him."

Kathryn chewed a fingernail for a moment. "Michael's an importer."

"Of?"

She just smiled, but the message was clear. Very clear.

Chris nodded. "That's what I was afraid of. Those drug guys play rough."

She gestured at Dwight. "What you're doing now is *easy*?"

He gave her that point with a shrug.

"The thing is, I know where Michael keeps his money."

"You do?"

"Yes. And I'll bet we could get our hands on it." Her smile turned slightly mocking. "If you guys are up to something like this."

Chris stared at her for a moment. "We're up to anything we fucking want to do. If it's good."

"This is good. Michael is loaded."

"How good are you talking here?"

She just smiled.

Chris glanced at Dwight, who had finally opened his eyes.

They looked at one another. "She says it's good," Chris pointed out.

Dwight didn't say anything.

"What the hell is that?"

Kathryn sat straight up in the bed, her voice shaking as she grabbed his shoulder.

Chris rolled over and opened his eyes, listening to the sounds coming from the living room. "Oh," he said after a moment. "That's Dwight having one of his goddamned nightmares. Happens sometimes."

She relaxed a little. "Jesus H. Christ. It sounds like somebody's dying in there."

"He isn't."

"Well, do something about it."

"Shit." Chris got out of bed and went into the next room. Without turning on the light he perched on the back of the sofa, reaching down to put a hand on Dwight. "Hey, buddy. Wake up. Wake the hell up."

After one more shuddering moan, Dwight's eyes opened. In the pale light coming from outside, he looked white and damp with sweat. He shook his head.

"You okay?"

"Yeah."

But Chris didn't release him yet. "It was the damned nightmare again."

"I guess." After another moment, Dwight shook off the restraining hand. "I'm fine now. Sorry for bothering you."

"When the hell did you start apologizing? I've been listening to this for five years. I'm used to it by now."

Of course, the first time it happened, in the damned cell, it scared the shit out of him. Also woke up half the cellblock, which didn't earn Dwight any friends.

Chris walked around to the coffee table and pushed things aside until he found a pack of cigarettes. He lit two and handed one to Dwight, then sat next to him on the couch. They smoked in silence for a moment.

Dwight had never told him exactly what the bad dreams were

about, but he could make a pretty good guess. What had been done to Dwight in jail was certainly the stuff of nightmares. But it had been quite a while since this had happened. What, Chris wondered, had brought the memories to the surface again?

But he didn't ask. He didn't want to talk about all of that shit any more than Dwight did. Made him nervous.

Dwight broke the silence finally. "Are we going to do what she said?"

"You mean stealing that money from Michael the druggist?"

"Yeah."

"Well, I think so," Chris said thoughtfully. "I sort of feel like we have to. This town is going to be pretty hot for us before much longer. Especially after what happened tonight."

"Yeah, I know that." There was something in Dwight's voice that made Chris look more closely. Even in the dim light he could see Dwight's frown.

"What's wrong?"

"Nothing, I guess. It's just . . ." He exhaled noisily. "Maybe it's just that bringing in another person makes me nervous. It's always been only us and we've been doing fine."

Chris didn't know how this guy would define the word *fine*, but that wasn't exactly how *he* would have summed up their situation. He lowered his cigarette. "Hey, we're not 'bringing her in.' All we're doing is using her. Using her input so we can do the job."

Dwight leaned across him to crush out his cigarette. Then he sat back and stared at Chris. "So she won't be going to Mexico with us?"

"What? Are you kidding?" Chris was genuinely surprised.

"Well, how the hell was I supposed to know what you're thinking? You're shacking up with her. I thought maybe you wanted it to be permanent."

"Hell, no. Mexico is for us. You and me. And if she can help us get there sooner, then I'll put up with her. 'Sides, it's cheaper than paying for a whore, right?"

"I guess." Dwight seemed to relax. "Okay. I just wanted to get clear on that."

"We're clear." Chris dropped his cigarette into the overflowing ashtray. "So we're a go for the job?"

"Yeah."

Chris grinned. "Mexico, here we come," he said.

After a few seconds, Dwight returned the smile.

Chris had closed the door when he went back into the bedroom. Dwight got up after a while and went to get a beer from the fridge. He carried it back to the sofa.

He could still hear low voices from the other room. They were probably talking about him. Well, who cared? Now that he knew the bitch wouldn't be hanging around forever, as he'd begun to fear, he could put up with it.

He drank the beer slowly, wanting to put off for as long as possible the time when he would go back to sleep. God, he didn't want to have that dream again.

When the hum of voices from the bedroom finally faded away, Dwight stretched out on the couch and closed his eyes again. Maybe this time he could dream about Mexico, about lying on the beach and drinking margaritas. With nothing to worry about ever again.

And it would be just the two of them, him and Chris, the way it had been in jail. That was what he wanted. They didn't need anybody else. That was what Chris used to say when they were in jail. He kept them away from the shit that went on. "We don't need it," he'd said.

Now they didn't need anybody else, either.

He finally fell asleep again.

7

"The thing is," Bryan said over breakfast, "if you want to find someone, you don't just run around in circles and end up getting yourself arrested for fighting. There's a way to do this kind of thing."

"Well, a cop would know more about that sort of business than me," Tray said almost cheerfully. He seemed to have recovered from his experiences of the night before. Except, of course, for the bruised nose and a somewhat swollen eye. He was obviously pleased to be having—for free—a big breakfast out here on the patio. Not that Bryan had ever thought of himself as much of a cook, but his bacon and eggs had to beat prison chow to hell and back.

"No doubt," he said. "Cops know more about a lot of things than you do." He was disgruntled because while Detaglio sat there shoveling down food like it was going out of style real soon, he, himself—who had not only cooked, but paid for the meal as well—was having one egg, one slice of bacon, and some dry toast. Frankly, he was getting pretty damned tired of watching every frigging bite that went into his mouth.

Tray, oblivious to the bitter thoughts floating around the table, reached for and ate still another piece of bacon. He enjoyed it, too. "So? You're the man who knows the job. What's the scenario here?"

"The first step is to go back to the dump where you were busted and talk to the bartender again."

"So far, I'm not all that crazy about your idea. I mean, my last visit to the Pink Pussycat Club didn't exactly work out great. I'm a little reluctant to go back."

Bryan finished the last crust of his toast. "You'll be waiting in the jeep. Subtlety is obviously not your game."

"Whatever the hell *that* might mean."

"It means you should sit back and watch how the good guys do it for a change. You might even learn something."

"I've got nothing against improving myself," Tray said, still cheerful.

Bryan realized suddenly that this was starting to be fun.

Their first stop was the hotel downtown where Tray had been staying. Bryan had a clue to what kind of place it was when he realized that it had no name at all. Just ROOMS. The lobby smelled strongly of disinfectant. The odor, unfortunately, did not manage to waft up to Tray's room on the third floor.

Bryan stood by the single window and watched as Tray, after first changing into a clean shirt and a new pair of jeans, packed up his few possessions. It didn't take long, and then they went back down to the front desk.

The short, pimple-faced young man who seemed to be in charge of things tore himself away from the comic book he was concentrating on long enough to let Tray check out.

Most of the last few dollars in his wallet went to pay the room bill. He grimaced as he shoved the billfold back into his pocket. Poverty made him philosophical. "Does life ever turn out the way you think it will?" he asked, as they walked back to the parking space.

"I doubt it," Bryan replied. He climbed behind the wheel of the jeep. "And just how did you figure your life was going to turn out?"

Tray settled into the passenger seat. "Not like this, that's for sure." He beat a staccato on the dash. "I'm a musician, man."

"Uh-huh."

"Well, I used to be," he amended glumly.

And I used to be a cop, Bryan thought a little while later. He tried to quell the excitement he felt as he walked up the sidewalk toward the strip joint. It felt good to be working again. So what if this wasn't a real case and he wasn't a real cop? It was close enough. Even playing a game like this beat peeling one more fucking strip of wallpaper.

Maybe the Pink Pussycat Club looked better at night, although he was inclined to doubt it. The harsh morning light definitely wasn't flattering to the run-down interior. Nor was it to the weary woman propped at the bar sipping tomato juice from a small can.

She watched his approach with eyes too old for her face. As he got close, she adjusted the faded satin robe around her body more tightly. "We're not open yet," she said.

Bryan leaned against the bar. "I know that. Are you one of the dancers here?"

A faint smile played around the mouth. The eyes stayed old and wary. "Yeah, sure. I'm a dancer." She stuck one leg out from the folds of the robe. "Me and Ann-Margret."

He gave the leg a glance, then looked back at her face. She shrugged. "I'm trying to find a woman who might have danced here at one time. Her name is Kathryn Daily." He took out the picture that Tray had given him. "Maybe you recognize her?"

She took a pair of glasses with pink frames out of the pocket of her robe and put them on. There were rhinestones on the corners of the frames. He put the photo into her hand and she studied it.

Bryan was suddenly aware that someone else had come into the room. He turned around and saw a biker type decked out in leather and lots of metal studs; this was probably Detaglio's friend from the night before.

"You want something?" the man asked belligerently.

Bryan put on his best cop smile, which really wasn't a smile at all. "Just asking the young lady a few questions, if you don't mind."

"And what if I do mind? What if I mind a whole fucking lot?"

Bryan only shrugged. "We can discuss it, of course. Downtown."

One grime-encrusted hand rested on the bar. The ring he was wearing would have been classified as a lethal weapon in most states. It was almost possible to watch the act of thinking taking place behind the empty eyes. It was a slow and painful process. "You a cop?" he finally said.

Bryan continued to smile. "What the hell do you think, asshole?"

Indecision flickered over the dull, moon-shaped face for several seconds, then the massive shoulders moved in a slow shrug. "What the shit do I care?" he mumbled. "Ain't my job. Fuck her on the bar if you want to."

Bryan watched him lumber away. Christ, it was a wonder that Detaglio hadn't ended up with a broken body, tangling with that evolutionary throwback. It didn't show much smarts on the ex-con's part.

Then Bryan returned his attention to the woman. "Well?"

She nodded. "I know her. Katie. She was here for a couple months, is all." She held the photo out toward him. "Katie had too much class for a joint like this. And not enough up front to pull in the big tips. If you get my meaning." She straightened, displaying her own more-than-ample front.

"I get your meaning. So, did she quit? Or was she canned?"

"Oh, she quit. The Jew never fires anybody dumb enough to work for what he pays."

"Why'd she quit? Besides her lack of, uh, highly paying attributes?"

When the woman looked blank, Bryan looked at her boobs again. Her face cleared. "It wasn't that. Something better just came along, that's all." Her tone was wistful.

It was Bryan's opinion that almost anything would be better than the Pink Pussycat. "Would you happen to know what that something better was?"

She sipped juice delicately. "Well, somebody said that she went to live on some kind of commune. If that's the word."

"That's the word. But I thought all that stuff went out of style around the time Reagan went to the White House."

She shrugged. "Everything old is new again, like the song says."

Bryan returned the photograph to his pocket. "You wouldn't happen to have any idea where this relic of a bygone era is located?"

"You mean, where is the commune?"

"Right."

This required a little thought and some more juice. "It seems to me that somebody said it was out by Azusa. I think that's right, anyway."

"Okay. Thanks for your help." He slid a five-dollar bill toward her. "For your trouble."

She put the money into her robe quickly, then glanced at the door. "You really a cop?" she stage-whispered.

The smile he gave her was a real one. "Once upon a time, sweetheart, once upon a time."

She giggled and looked years younger all of a sudden.

"A *commune*?" Tray said. "Why the hell?"

Bryan shrugged. "You know the woman. Why do you think?"

Tray lit another cigarette, then asked, somewhat belatedly, "Hey, does it bother you if I smoke?"

Bryan shook his head. It wasn't exactly true.

"A commune, huh?" Tray said thoughtfully. "Well, Kathryn always was a little flaky, you know? She got a little crazy sometimes."

Bryan glanced at him. "You loved her?"

Tray leaned back and stared at the road ahead. "Oh . . . oh, hell, I don't know. Maybe. Actually, though, I just think I *wanted* to love her, because that's the way the world is."

"How is that?"

"You're supposed to love somebody. If you don't and if nobody loves you, there must be something critically wrong with you." He shot a fast smile. "Like maybe your deodorant isn't working the way it should. Or your mouthwash."

Bryan found this all pretty interesting. Love was not a subject he had ever given much thought to. He had loved his job, probably, and his ex-wife, maybe. Although that had probably just been hormones. And, come to that, maybe so was what he'd felt for being a cop. Hormones. It was an idea, anyway.

The jeep pulled to a stop at a light.

"So this thing with you and Kathryn wasn't exactly the romance of the century, that's what you're saying."

"Not even the romance of the decade." Tray thought for a moment. "Anyway, this isn't about her and me. This is about the kid." He glanced at Bryan. "You get that, don't you?"

"Sure."

That was all Bryan said, although he was far from sure that he got it at all. But maybe it didn't matter whether or not he understood Tray's motivations for all this. A cop didn't need to know everything. He just needed to know how to do the job. If he did that right, everything else would fall neatly into place.

Usually.

Before reaching Azusa, they stopped at a small café–cum–gas station. The fan inside the restaurant did little more than move the hot air around the booth they sat in. The girl waiting tables took only as much interest in their orders as was absolutely necessary, then wandered off vaguely in the direction of the kitchen.

Bryan shook his head and wiped the rim of his waterglass with a paper napkin.

Tray leaned against the wall, stretching out his legs the length of the booth. "So, you really had a heart attack, huh?"

"I did."

"But you're okay now, right?"

Bryan shrugged, although *okay* was probably the most ideal word. Okay was about as good as it got, it seemed.

"That's why you're not a cop anymore?"

"That's why."

"You miss it?"

"Most days."

"That's too bad." Tray sounded like he meant it.

"Well, you probably miss the music, right?"

"I guess so. But I'm not sure that I could go back to that life."

"Why?"

"I'm too different," he said flatly.

There didn't seem to be anyplace for the conversation to go after that, so they just sat in silence. After no more than twenty minutes or so, the girl wandered back, bearing a tray with two chili dogs and coffee. The burden seemed overwhelming and she sighed heavily as she put it down. Bryan tried to ignore the fact that a chili dog was definitely *not* on his diet.

The food didn't kill them, at least not right away. They went back out to the jeep and Bryan pulled up to the full-service pump. While the attendant—who must have been related to the waitress, judging by his enthusiasm for the job—filled the tank, Tray disappeared into the can.

Bryan stood next to the jeep. "You know anything about some commune supposed to be around here?" he asked.

The man, a rawboned hillbilly a long way from West Virginia, spat before answering. "You mean them damned hippies?"

"That's probably who I mean."

"Morningstar Ranch, they call the place. Ranch, my ass." He spat again.

"Can you tell me how to get there?"

"You don't look like no hippie to me."

"I'm not. I'm just trying to find someone."

"Uh-huh." He pulled the nozzle away from the jeep and replaced it. Bryan handed him a credit card and he disappeared into the station.

Tray came back and climbed into the passenger seat again.

Bryan waited where he was. When the man returned, Bryan signed the charge slip. "Well?"

The hillbilly carefully finished the business of selling gasoline before speaking. "Five miles the other side of town," he said then. "No-account dirt road. Half a sign left."

"Thank you."

"You might want to reconsider. Anybody what's been hanging around out there prob'ly ain't worth finding."

"I'll keep that in mind," Bryan said.

They missed the road completely the first time by and had to backtrack. It was Tray who finally sighted the broken, faded sign. Bryan turned the jeep off the highway. It was a bouncy ride, nearly three miles long, before they actually reached the house.

The whole place looked like somebody's faded memory of the sixties. Or maybe a shadowy drug flashback. Undoubtedly, there had been a day when the colors on the house and barn were gaudily psychedelic. Faint traces of flowers and peace signs were still visible even now, although the colors were washed-out and the paint was peeling away.

An old bus, its paint job in no better shape, was parked in the yard. On one side the words MAKE LOVE, NOT WAR were just barely readable.

"Jesus," Tray said. "Time warp."

Bryan didn't say anything. He parked the jeep next to the bus, and they got out. Three long-haired and completely naked children were playing in a mud puddle beside the porch. They watched the two of them approach with absolutely no curiosity on their filthy faces.

Tray stopped beside the kids, crouched, and carefully studied each face in turn.

"Well?" Bryan asked after a moment.

Tray stood, shrugging. "Beats the fuck out of me. All kids look alike as far as I'm concerned."

"I thought there might be some kind of psychic connection or whatever."

"Is that the way it's supposed to be?"

Bryan started up the steps. "How the hell do I know?" He had to knock three times before anybody appeared in the doorway. She peered at him through the torn screen.

She had probably been pretty, maybe ten years ago. Now, however, she was fat, dressed in baggy jeans topped with a ripped man's shirt. Two buttons were missing from the front of the shirt and her breasts threatened to break from inside the thin fabric. Bryan wondered if she had ever considered a career at the Pink Pussycat. She could probably haul in a shitload of tips.

"Yeah?" she said, sweeping a lock of gray-brown hair from her face. "If you're from the school people, them kids is too young."

Tray stepped around Bryan suddenly and opened the door. "We're looking for Kathryn Daily. Is she here?"

The woman took a step backward. "Who? And what gives you the right to know who lives here, anyway?"

Bryan took over, speaking in a reassuring voice. "Ma'am,

we're trying to locate a woman named Kathryn Daily. We were told she lived here."

Somewhere behind the woman, a kid started screaming and an adult female voice yelled in response. The woman glanced over her shoulder impatiently, then looked back at them. "Talk to Harry. Out behind the barn." She turned around and disappeared into the house.

They set off toward the barn.

"You know," Tray said, "I can't see Kathryn hanging around a place like this for very long. She likes the good life."

Bryan was inclined to agree with that. If she had been looking for a step upward from the strip joint, this didn't seem to be it.

They finally found Harry, who was sitting on an upended orange crate and smoking a joint. He looked up as they approached. "I have been giving this Star Wars thing a lot of thought," he said carefully.

"The movie or the weapons system?"

Harry seemed to like that; he smiled at Bryan. "Not the movie."

"What conclusions have you come to?" Bryan asked.

Harry was a short, thin man who'd lost most of his hair. Despite that, the eyes and the voice were oddly charismatic. Compelling enough, perhaps, to ensnare one Kathryn Daily— until she actually saw this place, anyway. He was wearing battered overalls with no shirt. "I think the damned thing might work." He gazed at them with slightly puzzled eyes. "Of course, that doesn't begin to address the moral issues involved."

"Of course. You have a woman here named Kathryn Daily?"

Harry inhaled loudly before answering. "Meadowlark."

"What?"

"When she was part of us, her name was Meadowlark."

"She *did* live here, then?" Tray said.

"Sure, Meadowlark and I shacked up for a couple months." Tray was lighting a cigarette. "What happened?" he asked. Harry shrugged. "She split."

"To where?" Bryan said.

Harry waved a hand vaguely. "The bright lights."

"Could you be just a little more specific?" Bryan urged.

"One day while she was soliciting funds in Hollywood, she met some actor and went off with him."

Tray shook his head and turned around to gaze off at nothing in particular.

"You have a name for the actor?"

Harry considered carefully. "Simon Black." His narrow face smirked. "At least that's what he calls himself now. But does anybody start off with a name like that?"

Tray turned around again suddenly. "Did she have a kid with her?"

"What? A kid?" Harry shook his head. "No."

"You sure?"

"That ain't a hard question. I'm sure."

Bryan nodded his thanks and then led the way back to the jeep.

Bryan was about halfway through his exercise routine by the time Tray wandered into the room, his hair still wet from the shower, a can of beer in one hand. He perched on a barstool and watched in silence.

Bryan, doing some push-ups, glanced at him. "Can I ask you something?"

"Sure."

"Where the hell did you ever get a name like Tray?"

He made a face. "My mother. From some old movie she loved. The hero was Traylane of something or other. *Traylane.* So Tray is better."

Bryan rested on the floor for a moment, then rolled over onto his back. "I guess it is." His legs began a lackadaisical bicycling motion in the air. "I have another question," he said after a time.

"Cops always have questions. That's all you people do is ask questions." Whatever friendliness that had been edging into Tray's voice during the course of the day was gone now; he sounded, once again, like the ex-con on the beach.

Bryan decided to ignore the obvious hostility. After all, cops *were* good at grilling the bad guys. "How come, considering what we know about Kathryn, you're so damned sure that the kid is even yours? If there is one."

Tray ignored that. He lit a match pointlessly. "I think that when we were together, she didn't fool around. I didn't. Besides, how does *anybody* ever know for sure? Some things you just have to take on faith, I guess."

"I guess."

Bryan, for one, wouldn't have wanted to wager his pension on the supposition of Tray's paternal claim to any offspring Kathryn might have produced. But in view of the dark glare he was receiving, he decided not to make a point of it at this particular moment.

The doorbell rang.

"Get that, willya?" Bryan said, panting a little.

"Sure." Tray went to the front door, returning a moment later with Ann Hamilton.

Bryan had quit his calisthenics and was sitting cross-legged on the floor. "Hi, Ann," he said, trying to catch his breath.

"Bryan. Hope this isn't a bad time for company?"

"No. You met Tray, I guess."

She glanced at him, curiosity clear in her eyes. "We met."

Tray took his place on the stool again, picking up the beer and taking a long swallow.

"I came by to invite you over to my place this evening. I'm having some neighbors for a cook-out on the beach. It would give you a chance to meet some of the locals."

Bryan used a hand towel to wipe his face, wondering glumly if maybe he'd overdone the exercises this time. Then he considered the invitation. It sounded safe enough, from the standpoint of Ann and him. She couldn't very well expect him to seduce her in front of the neighbors, right? "Sure, we'll be there. What time?"

She paused, glancing at Tray, who returned the look with a grin. "About eight?"

"Great. See you then."

She let herself out.

Tray wandered over to the window and watched her car disappear. "Maybe I better not go," he said when she was out of sight. "She probably wouldn't appreciate having an ex-con at her party."

Bryan got to his feet and started for the bathroom to shower. "Don't worry about it," he said.

Tray glared again. "Why should I worry? She's your broad. I don't give a flying fuck if she gets bent out of shape."

Bryan didn't bother responding to that.

It was a perfect night to be on the beach. The breeze coming off the water felt pleasantly cool after the heat of the day. In honor of the occasion, Bryan more or less forgot about his diet restrictions and ate whatever he wanted, washing it all down with a couple of beers.

And he had to admit that the people at the party were a pretty interesting bunch, a lot of artists and writers, with a few people from the Industry thrown in for good measure. Nobody seemed to mind that he was just an ex-cop.

He was finishing his peach shortcake when Ann came over and sat next to him. "Having fun?"

"Sure." He wiped his mouth on the linen napkin and set the plate aside. "Terrific food."

"Thanks." She leaned back against the bench. "Your friend Mr. Detaglio tells me that he just got out of jail."

Bryan stifled a smile. "He told you that, did he?"

She looked a little abashed. "Well, the truth is, I sort of asked him. He looks like . . . well, it didn't surprise me."

"He's okay."

"Are you sure? I mean, taking a man like that into your home might be dangerous."

Bryan shrugged. "Tray? No, I don't think so. What's he gonna do, run off with the family silver?" He grinned. "My car, maybe, but that's about it."

She didn't get the joke, of course. "Well, just be careful." She smiled and patted his hand. "I'm getting to like you, in case you hadn't noticed."

Bryan didn't know what to say to that, so he didn't say anything. It seemed safer that way.

It was not too much later when he looked around for Tray, but the other man seemed to have vanished. One of the guests said she thought he'd left.

Bryan said good-bye to Ann and headed for the jeep.

He had been driving for about ten minutes when he saw Detaglio walking along the side of the road. He pulled the jeep over. "You like walking?"

"Not especially," Tray replied. He got into the jeep.

"What happened?" Bryan asked, pulling back into the flow of traffic.

Tray shrugged. "Nothing. I don't know. It was just me, I guess. Maybe it takes time."

"What's that?"

"Fitting in. Getting back into real life." He smiled faintly. "Or what passes for real life in California."

"Yeah. It takes time. Some guys never make it."

"That's a cheerful thought."

"You're doing okay." Bryan was quiet for several minutes. "Tray, what are your plans if we do find Kathryn and the kid?"

"I don't know for sure. Maybe I could be like a regular father."

"Maybe," Bryan said.

Tray leaned back in the seat and stared at nothing. "I could try, anyway."

Bryan hoped that the mild pain in his chest was just a result of the meal. He'd really hate to die without knowing how all of this was going to turn out.

8

They drove by the house three times to get a feel for the territory. As far as Chris was concerned, the territory felt just fine. Kathryn's former boyfriend lived in a monster-sized house in what seemed to be the poshest section of Beverly Hills. The estate looked more like some national park than a place anybody actually called home. It was also surrounded by a high, black wrought-iron fence. Just inside the gate they could see a parked dark blue Ford. According to Kathryn, the car was always there and someone was always sitting in it.

Finally, Dwight slowed to a stop just down the street from the house, out of the direct line of vision of whomever was currently occupying the sentry car.

Kathryn leaned over the seat. "Some house, wouldn't you say?"

"I'd say," Chris muttered. "Be it ever so humble." He looked irritably at Kathryn. "You must've forgotten to mention that the place is protected like fucking Fort Knox."

She dismissed his words airily. "What'd you expect? Anyway, it won't be as hard as it looks to get in."

"Oh, really? And exactly how many fucking house jobs have you pulled in your life?"

"Well, none, of course."

"Me, either," said Dwight, unnecessarily.

Chris shook his head. "Wonderful. So that makes me the expert. I've done a lot of them. Maybe three hundred or so. And take my word for it when I say that getting into that place won't be so easy. And getting out alive will be even harder."

Kathryn pulled back a little. "You backing out already?"

"We're just studying the fucking setup, if you don't mind. I never go into a job cold."

She sighed impatiently. "This isn't exactly going in cold. I know the layout of the house. Jesus, I even know where the safe is."

"And where is that?"

"His office." She pointed vaguely toward the house. "In the east wing, third floor."

"Well, that's one point in our favor. You don't happen to know the combination, I suppose?"

She smiled at him. "If I knew that, honey, why would I need you?"

"Yeah, I see your point."

The smile took on an edge. "You know about that kind of thing, don't you? Getting into safes and like that? Or do I have to find someone else?"

Chris laughed softly. "You're no dummy, are you?"

"Count on that, lover. I've waited a long time for a chance like this."

"I know anything I need to," Chris said.

Dwight finally broke his silence. "Just how much money are we talking about here, anyway?"

"He usually has like half a million in there."

"Five hundred thousand dollars?" Chris said, almost reverently. He shook his head. "Damn." In this one job, there was more money to be made than he had scored in his entire career.

"You said 'usually,'" Dwight said, his tone uncharacteristically sharp. "And what about the rest of the time? Could we go through all of this, risk getting our asses burned, and then find nothing but an empty safe?"

She didn't seem to want to answer that question, but Dwight kept staring at her, and finally she shrugged. "Sometimes it's empty, yes. But—"

"But nothing," Dwight said flatly.

"So the first little problem comes along and you're ready to throw in the towel?" She looked at Chris. "Doesn't he know that you have to take a few risks when you're going after the big one?"

Chris couldn't help but agree with that, although he didn't say so out loud. But Dwight had a point, too. "Isn't there any way we could find out? Just so the odds get narrowed a little?"

Dwight sighed impatiently, but Kathryn nodded. "Of course there is. I've got this thing all figured out."

"Well, good. As soon as you decide to fill us in on everything you know, we can make a decision. In the meantime, let's get out of here before somebody notices us. We'll go talk about it."

They drove, mostly in silence, back to Venice and stopped at a sidewalk café. Sitting in the warm sun to share a pizza, they watched the roller skaters and assorted crazies. The pizza was gone and they were on a second round of beers when Chris brought up the primary subject again.

"Well?" he said. "You want to fill us in?"

"Sure." Kathryn took a delicate sip of the beer, then a drag from her cigarette.

"Jesus," Dwight said. "Don't keep us in suspense."

She just looked at him, then shrugged. "The money comes once or twice a month. It's always delivered in the same way. A guy named Don comes to the house driving a brown van. He goes into the office with Michael and stays about twenty minutes."

"How do you know he's bringing money?" Chris asked. He had taken a pencil from his pocket and was doodling on the tablecloth.

"I made it my business to know as much as I could about what went on at Michael's."

"Which maybe explains why you're not there anymore, right?" Dwight said with a nasty smile.

Chris leaned back and closed his eyes, tired of their verbal jabbing. He thought about the house, the safe, the half-million dollars. He'd done jobs harder than this before and sometimes he'd even gotten away with it. And if the broad was giving them the straight dope—a big if, he admitted—then this job was far from impossible.

It might work. It just might fucking work.

The sex between them had become routine already. Chris wondered how the hell people who were married for years and years kept from getting bored out of their freaking minds. He rolled off her and reached for the cigarettes.

Kathryn pulled the sheet up over her breasts. "We haven't discussed what kind of split we're talking about here."

Christ, and wasn't *she* a goddamned romantic? He had just finished fucking her and the first words out of her mouth were about money. They'd really have to keep an eye on this broad. She had a cold streak, a real cold streak.

Chris inhaled. "I guess we haven't. What did you have in mind?" He could hardly wait to hear what her calculating little brain had come up with.

"Fifty-fifty, of course."

Of course. "I don't think it's that easy."

"Why not?"

Chris flicked ashes onto the floor. "There are three of us in on the gig. That means a three-way split."

She stirred under the sheet. "That's not fair. You two are partners, so I think that should mean one share for you and the rest for me."

"Fuck that, Kathryn. In this business, things don't work that way."

"It's my idea, after all. I'm the one who knows the house."

"Fine," he said cheerfully. "You do the fucking job all by yourself."

She was quiet for a time; then she turned and propped herself on his chest, staring down into his face. "You know, there is one way we could simplify this whole thing."

He smiled without humor. If she was counting on sex to get her way, which was probably the way she got along in life, the lady was in for a very big surprise. No fuck in the world was worth a third of $500,000. "What's that?"

She lowered her head and nibbled on his neck for a moment. "We could dump him," she said, her voice muffled.

"Dump him?"

She looked at him again. "Dwight. We could dump Dwight."

The smile slowly faded from Chris's face. He shook his head. "No."

"I get the feeling that he isn't going to be much help on this thing. And by cutting him out, we make the split real easy. Or maybe we wouldn't have to split the money at all." Her body rubbed against his slowly. "You and I could have a lot of fun with that much money, Chris."

He put both hands on her shoulders and squeezed tightly, ignoring the wince of pain that crossed her face. "Listen, bitch, Dwight is in on this. He and I are partners. No way is that going to change. You understand?"

"You're hurting me, damnit," she said.

He let go and she pulled away quickly. They were both quiet for a long time. Chris lit another cigarette. "I didn't mean to hurt you," he said in a quiet voice.

"Well, you did." She reached for a cigarette as well. "He gives me the creeps. The way he watches me."

"Just ignore him. You don't have to bait the guy all the time."

"I don't. It's him. He hates me."

"So what?"

Kathryn sighed. "What was he in jail for?"

"Why do you want to know that?"

"Because," she said, her voice taking on an edge of hardness. It reminded him that there was more to her than her surface appearance would lead you to think. "We're about to do something that could be dangerous. You're the one who keeps talking about how damned tricky this job will be. If I'm going into it with him, then I have a right to know what he is. Don't you think?"

He gave a small shrug. It irritated the hell out of him when she made a point. But this time she was right and he couldn't deny it. He wouldn't ever work with an unknown quantity; why should she? Frowning, he leaned over to extinguish the cigarette. "Dwight was drunk one night. There was this woman he knew.

They left the bar together and went to his place. Later, they fought about something. I don't know what. He pushed her, she fell, hit her head. And she died."

"He murdered her?"

He shook his head. "They didn't call it murder. Manslaughter. He didn't mean to do it."

"But she died anyway."

"Yeah." He didn't tell her about the other incidents, the whores he'd had to pay off to keep them quiet about Dwight's violence. It wasn't really any of her business; Dwight wasn't going to hurt her. Sure, he was a little screwy sometimes, but so what?

"Well, that doesn't exactly comfort me. Sometimes, from the look on Dwight's face, I think he'd like to do something like that to me."

"Don't be stupid. Dwight is okay. He won't hurt you."

"He better not try," she said in the same hard voice. "I'll kill the bastard."

"Uh-huh," Chris said.

"Don't you believe me?"

"Sure I do. You probably would kill him." Chris patted her thigh. "Of course, I'd kill you then."

"Yes, I think you would."

"Count on it, sweetie." He wondered if he really would kill her. Maybe. Probably. The important thing, anyway, was that *she* believed it.

Kathryn moved a little farther away from him on the bed, although he had the feeling that she wasn't really all that scared. She seemed more excited than anything. "And there's something else," she said.

"What?"

"I don't want to . . . do it with him anymore."

Chris smirked. "Has he asked?"

"No."

"Then I wouldn't worry about it."

She didn't say any more after that, and in a few minutes, her breathing took on the even pattern of sleep.

* * *

The heat in the small living room was oppressive. Dwight rolled off the couch and, wearing only his shorts, went into the kitchen. He took a beer from the fridge and took it outside to the porch. Sitting there, he could feel a slight breeze coming from the water. It felt good against his hot, sweaty skin.

There was a party going on someplace nearby and the sounds of music and voices reached him like a dim memory. He tried to remember the last time he'd been at a party. A real party, anyway, not one of those things in jail, where everybody crowded into a hidden corner someplace and passed around a bottle of homemade booze. And where it always ended up with a fight or something terrible happening.

Not that he really wanted to be at the party he could hear. Having too many people around at one time made him nervous. He couldn't remember if it had always been that way or if being inside for so long had changed him. He thought that was probably it. Chris had been in and out of jail forever, though, and it didn't seem to have turned *him* into a flake.

And that's what Dwight felt like sometimes. A flake.

The screen door opened and he turned his head to see Chris come out. He sat on the top step next to him. "Hot," he said.

"Not too bad out here," Dwight replied.

Chris grunted. After a moment, he said, "Can I ask you something, Dwight?"

"Sure. What?"

"The other day you said you were scared of me when we first met. How long did that last?"

"Not long."

"No?"

Dwight sloshed some beer around in his mouth before swallowing. "Like you said, you didn't do anything to me. And then, after what happened in the metals shop . . . ." He stopped.

Chris nodded.

Dwight gripped the can tightly, denting the sides. That day in the prison metals shop was like a bad dream that never went away, even in the daytime. He never wanted to talk about it, even with Chris. Maybe especially with Chris, because he had been there. Even now that he had spilled his guts about the whole thing to Schaefer, it didn't make the subject any easier to deal with. So much for fucking therapy, right?

He never really knew how it happened that Chris was on the spot that day. Or even how long he might have watched before emerging. He had seen Dwight beaten and cut with a knife and raped.

Chris had saved him from even worse agony. Maybe even from death.

Nobody ever knew how the other inmate—Krell had been his name—died. Even Dwight wasn't real sure about that part. He could only remember looking up from the gritty concrete floor and, through waves of pain and tears, seeing the big man grab Krell and pull him away. While the fight went on, Dwight pressed his face to the floor and tried to die.

He had only a vague memory of being taken back to the cell, where Chris had tried to patch him up as best he could with pilfered medical supplies. They couldn't let anyone know what had happened, Chris had whispered to him. If it came out that he had killed Krell, even under the circumstances, it would be very bad for him. The first thing that would happen is, he'd be put into another cell. They didn't want that, did they?

Dwight had agreed because he was scared. He didn't want to be left alone, or at the mercy of another cellmate.

Nobody else ever touched him again, because the word went out that he was under Chris's protection and there wasn't anybody dumb enough to fool with *him*. Dwight St. John was Chris Moore's punk. Private property. But that was okay. Chris never did anything to hurt him. Most of the time, Dwight could even forget that he was only a jailhouse punk. They seemed to just be together because they wanted to be.

Sometimes now he almost missed those days. Not the prison itself, of course, but the closeness they'd had then.

Dwight looked up to find Chris watching him. He smiled and shrugged. "To hell with that," he said.

Chris seemed to know what he was talking about. "Yeah," he said. He leaned back and crossed his arms. "What do you think, Dwight? Is this whole idea a big mistake?"

"Going after the money, you mean?"

"Yeah, that's what I mean."

Dwight thought about it. "I don't know. We need the cash."

"I know we do." Chris shook his head. "It still bothers me, though."

"Then maybe we shouldn't do it."

But Chris grimaced. "Hell, Dwight, we might never get to Mexico otherwise."

"So we go for it," Dwight said flatly.

"I guess we do."

The smiles they exchanged were rueful.

"We ought to get some sleep," Chris said after a moment.

"Right."

They both stood and went back into the house. Dwight tossed the empty beer can into the wastebasket and sat on the couch again. Chris started for the bedroom, then paused. "Dwight."

"What?"

"Try to lay off the broad a little, will you?"

Dwight felt a surge of white-hot anger. "I haven't done anything. I haven't touched her."

"I know, I know. But she's . . . skittish. We could still blow this."

Dwight swallowed down his feelings. "Well, I'll try to behave myself. Wouldn't want to do anything to offend your girlfriend."

"She's not my girlfriend. She's just a business associate."

"Whatever."

Chris smiled and slapped his face lightly. "Hang tough. This won't take so long. Then we'll be lying on that beach in Mexico."

"Drinking margaritas."

"Right." Chris went back into the bedroom.

Dwight stretched out onto the couch again. He had to be careful about Kathryn. She made him crazy, but that didn't matter. If he blew this deal, Chris would be perfectly right to split. So no matter what she did, he just had to stay cool about it.

Stay cool. Stay cool. Stay cool.

It took him a very long time to fall asleep.

9

It only took a couple of phone calls for Bryan to track down the whereabouts of an actor named Simon Black (which really was a terrible name, he decided). Black's agent had a brief flurry of excitement when he thought that Bryan was looking for his client in order to offer him a job. He was ready to talk money instantly. When Bryan gently disabused him of that notion, there was a pause of palpable disappointment over the phone wire. He sighed, as if this kind of heartbreak were an old friend, and gave them Black's address, anyway.

The address turned out to belong to an aging pink stucco apartment building on Melrose. Bryan parked the jeep in front, and they sat looking at the shabby building and unkempt yard.

Tray made a face. "I may be wrong," he said, "but this doesn't look like the kind of a place where Kathryn could be happy for very long. Even if it does beat the hell out of the Pink what'sit or hippie heaven."

"Now, now," Bryan cautioned. "Don't be such a cynic. Maybe it's true love this time."

Tray looked at him in disbelief, but said only, "Uh-huh."

They climbed down from the jeep and walked into the lobby of the building. A very fat woman, with hair the color of a fire engine, was there polishing a mirror. She didn't seem to have much enthusiasm for the job.

Bryan, a little bemused by how easy it was to fall right back into the role he'd played for so long, asked her about Black.

"Apartment 104," she said, still moving the rag in a circle on the mirror. "He in trouble, is he?" The thought obviously tickled her.

"Why would you ask that?"

"You're a cop, ain'tcha?"

Bryan only smiled. So it still showed. Tray shook his head in apparent despair, and they turned away, heading down an ill-lit hallway, trying to read the numbers on the doors.

When they arrived at 104, Bryan had to knock twice before there was any response.

Simon Black looked like a TV star.

Or, more to the point, he looked like *every* TV star. Glossy and manicured to perfection, with about as much personality as a grapefruit. But he sure was pretty.

He smiled a pretty smile at them. "Yes?"

"Excuse us, Mr. Black," Bryan said smoothly, "but we're looking for a woman named Kathryn Daily. We've been told that you know her."

"Katie? Sure, I know her. You might as well come in."

He stepped aside, and they entered the apartment. Black had only a few pieces of furniture, none of it anywhere near new, but everything was clean. There were a number of eight-by-ten glossies hanging on the walls. All of them were of Black. It was a little hard to tell the difference between the photographs and the real man. Maybe there wasn't much of a difference.

He gestured them to the worn plastic couch and then dropped into the matching chair facing it. "Why are you asking about Katie? Has something happened to her?"

"Not that we know of. We're just trying to find her to talk to."

"Well, I can't say that it comes as any big surprise that the cops are looking for her."

Tray sighed audibly.

Bryan just nodded. It didn't hurt to let people believe what they wanted. "I guess she isn't living with you anymore?"

"You guess right." Black picked up a glass of orange juice from the end table and took a sip. "Katie didn't stick around too long. Just until something better came along." He looked around the dismal room. "This isn't a palace, you know?" Then he shrugged and visibly straightened his spine. "Someday I'll have it all, but she isn't the kind of woman who wanted to wait around for a break."

Tray seemed to agree with that.

"What was that something better?" Bryan asked. What they were dealing with here was obviously a woman who took the concept of upward mobility very, very seriously.

For the first time, Black looked at him with doubt. A single worry line creased his forehead. "Don't you already know? I figured that's why you're looking for her."

Bryan shifted a little. "We know a lot," he said. "But some of it needs independent corroboration."

Always let them think you knew more than you did. Nobody, even the best of citizens, wanted to be accused of being too helpful to the cops. It came a little too close to violating the playground code against snitching.

Black seemed to think about what he should say. As he thought, his hand strayed to his face, felt the worry line, and smoothed it out. "She fell for Mike Stanzione, moved in with him. And I don't have to tell you about Stanzione."

Bryan wished to hell that he *would*, but if he asked too many questions, it would blow their cover. "Why did she do that, do you think?"

"Hell, man, that isn't hard to figure. He has that big house in Beverly Hills. All the fucking money in the world. They talk about life in the fast lane; well, Katie likes to travel at supersonic speed." The smile that he wore now looked smug and maybe he was entitled. "I warned her about getting tied in with a man like Stanzione. And now she's in trouble, right?"

They managed to get out of the apartment without ever actually answering that question. The woman was still polishing the mirror as they passed through the lobby. She seemed a little disappointed that they didn't have Black, cuffed, in tow.

Once they were back in the jeep, Tray turned to him. "Who the hell is Mike Stanzione?"

"I have no idea. But we'll find out."

"How?"

Bryan smiled at him. "We'll go to the experts."

After a moment, Tray groaned. "Tell me you're not talking about the cops, please."

Bryan just stuck the key into the ignition and started the jeep.

"He's talking about the goddamned cops," Tray muttered. "Christ."

Tray suggested that maybe he should stay with the jeep to keep anyone from ripping it off while Bryan was inside Parker Center.

Bryan thanked him for his concern but said that it wouldn't be necessary. So they both walked into police headquarters. Tray was visibly less than thrilled to be there.

"Relax," Bryan said. "Remember, you're a law-abiding citizen now."

Tray punched the elevator button. "Yeah, I know that and you know it. But do all these guys with guns know it?"

"Just try to look honest."

The effort of that kept Tray occupied until they reached Blank's office. He kept them waiting only a couple of minutes as he finished a phone call, then waved them in. The cop stared curiously at Tray as Bryan made a cursory introduction.

Tray stayed close to the door, as if ready for instant flight, but Bryan settled comfortably into the visitor's chair. "What can you tell us about a guy named Mike Stanzione?" he asked, skipping the small talk.

Blank lowered the cigar he was about to light. "Stanzione? What the hell is your connection to him?"

Bryan shrugged. "No connection. Exactly. His name just came up in our investigation."

"Your what?" Blank still hadn't got the stogie burning.

"We're handling a missing person case."

"You and—" He gestured toward Tray.

"Right."

"Uh-huh," Blank said. He didn't seem real impressed. He did put the cigar down.

"You've been after me to work again," Bryan said with some defensiveness.

"Yeah, well. Maybe I should have minded my own business."

"No, you were right."

"Then listen to me now, because I'm sure as hell right again. If this so-called investigation is bringing you anywhere near Stanzione, I suggest that you drop it now and go back to painting walls and washing windows."

Bryan frowned. "Why?"

"You really don't have any idea who he is?"

"I'm a stranger out here, remember?"

"Well, Stanzione is not anyone a virgin wants to tangle with, believe me."

"Can you give me any fucking specifics?"

Blank looked at the cigar, then, instead, took out a cigarette and lit it. "Michael Stanzione is numero uno in this state when it comes to crime of the organized variety. At least that part of the business that deals with the import of certain pharmaceuticals."

"Like white powder?"

Blank aimed the cigarette at him. "You got it, buddy."

"That's interesting."

"You might think so. But remember, you're just a retired cop now."

"I'm too damned young to retire."

"Maybe. But that doesn't change the facts. How's your heart?"

"What're you all of a sudden, my mother?" Bryan put one hand to his chest. "For your information, it's still beating." He smiled. "Anyway, Tray here is a whiz at CPR. If I keel over, he springs right into action and brings me back from the edge of death."

"Wonderful. Unfortunately, CPR won't help much when Stanzione's gorillas start shooting."

"Buddy, are you going to give me a hand on this or not?"

"If I say no?"

"There are other ways for me to find out what I need to know."

Blank nodded glumly. "Most of which will likely get you killed." He stood. "Wait a minute." He left the office.

Tray stopped propping up the wall and came closer. "Hey."

"What?"

"You're not really planning on keeling over, are you?"

"You don't really know CPR, do you?"

"No."

"Well, then, I better stay on my feet, hadn't I?"

The door opened again and Blank came back into the room. He handed Bryan a single Xeroxed sheet. "These are the basic facts on Stanzione."

"Thank you very much."

"But if you want my advice—"

"I'll ask for it."

Blank was obviously not happy. "Who are you looking for, anyway?"

"Woman named Kathryn Daily. Mean anything to you?"

"Nope."

Bryan stood, slipping the paper into his pocket. "Well, thanks for your help."

"Please don't thank me," Blank said. "I feel like I just put a loaded gun into the hands of an idiot child."

"Hey, I was a cop for twenty fucking years. Don't forget that. And I was good, damnit."

"I've seen your citations. Very impressive. But you're not a cop now. Just don't forget that little fact."

The three of them had left the office and were walking toward the elevators. Tray moved ahead of the other two.

"Who is this guy?" Blank asked in a low voice. "He looks like trouble to me."

Bryan watched the slouching figure ahead. "He's okay. Mostly. Ex-con."

"I guessed that."

"Stress on the 'ex,' he'd like me to add."

"What's your interest?"

"I'm just helping him find the Daily broad."

"And that's it?"

"That's it. Simple, right?"

Blank sighed and shook his head. "Well, watch your back." Bryan just smiled and Blank headed back to his office.

When Bryan reached the elevator, Tray was leaning against another wall, studying a colorful poster hanging there. He looked up at Bryan's arrival. "Now I know."

"Now you know what?"

Tray pointed at the poster. It was a Red Cross diagram showing the procedure involved in cardiopulmonary resuscitation.

"Great," Bryan said, pushing the down button. "I feel much safer now."

"You want me to do what?"

Bryan carried his plate to the sink, rinsed it thoroughly, then put it into the dishwasher. "I want you to stay home and paint the porch."

Apparently that job didn't jibe with Detaglio's new image of himself. *"Paint the porch?"*

"That's right. The sanding was the hard part and that's all done." Bryan wiped the counter with a paper towel. "You're supposed to be earning your way around here, right?"

"Yeah." Tray poured himself more milk. "Meanwhile, what will you be doing?"

"I want to check out Stanzione a little."

Tray frowned. "But shouldn't I be along? Just in case there's trouble?"

"No. First of all, there isn't going to be any trouble. I know how to do a fucking surveillance. And second of all, if there *were* going to be any trouble, you should be right here painting the porch. The last thing an ex-con needs is trouble."

Tray still wasn't very pleased, but he didn't argue anymore. "Where's the paint?"

He got tired of painting pretty fast.

After dunking the brushes into some cleaner and abandoning the whole mess until another time, Tray went back into the house. A search through the refrigerator rewarded him with a can of 7-UP. Drinking it, he wandered out of the kitchen and began a tour of the house.

In a small office on the second floor he found a desk. He sat down and started opening drawers. There wasn't much of interest. Some bills. A few personal letters that he skimmed quickly and replaced. Stamps. Travel brochures. Paint color samples.

Could this guy be as boring as all of this made it seem he was?

He continued to push through the debris, not knowing what the hell he was looking for. Maybe what he hoped to find was some kind of answer to the puzzle of Bryan Murphy. What was the *real* reason behind this buddy-buddy scam? There had to be more to it than showed on the surface.

There just had to be.

Well, maybe so, but he couldn't find any evidence of a plot in the desk.

Just as he was about to give up, he found an envelope shoved in the very back of the bottom drawer. When he opened it, a small wad of bills fell out. Seven hundred dollars. Household money, maybe. Tray fingered the money.

After a moment, he replaced it in the envelope and put the envelope into his pocket. Then he took it out again. Too obvious, ripping off the whole thing. He counted out two hundred bucks, put *that* into his pocket, and replaced the rest in the drawer. With luck, he'd be long gone before Murphy was even aware the dough was missing.

Tray ran his sleeve along the edge of the desk, just in case. For all he knew, the bastard had a fingerprint kit hidden someplace.

Then he got up and left the office.

Bryan parked on a side street from which he had a good view of Stanzione's house. The size of the house and the wealth of the neighborhood did not surprise him in the slightest. He knew that in some cases there was very little truth to the old saying about crime not paying. Sometimes it paid very well, indeed. Sometimes it beat the hell out of what a cop made.

He pried the lid off the cup of coffee and settled back in the seat. Just like old times. Well, sort of. The coffee was Sanka and he didn't have a cigarette hanging from his mouth, but those were minor differences. Here he was, on a stakeout. It had been a long time. Since the day of his heart attack, in fact.

Right now, he felt terrific.

* * *

Five hours later, he was feeling somewhat less terrific.

It was nearly midnight by that time, and his body was protesting the enforced stillness. He was out of practice.

It hadn't been an entirely boring time. A lot of people had come and gone from the Stanzione estate during the course of the evening. The fact that he didn't have an idea in hell who any of the visitors were or what the possible implications of their connection with Stanzione might be only slightly dampened Bryan's curiosity.

But now he was tired and he decided to wrap it up. Go home to bed.

Just as he made that decision, however, a taxicab pulled to the front gate and stopped.

He recognized the woman who got out immediately, although it had been at least five years since the photo had been taken. She leaned back into the taxi, apparently telling the driver to wait. Then she went to the gate, spoke briefly to the man there, and went inside.

Bryan considered it for a moment. Then he started the car and drove around the corner, stopping next to the cab. "Whew," he said cheerfully. "I made it."

The driver looked at him with only a minimum of interest.

Bryan continued the good-buddy act. "I'm here now, so she won't need you after all. What's the damage on the meter?"

"Lady told me to wait."

"Yeah, because I wasn't here like I promised. Got held up." His grin was full of implication. "You know how it goes."

The driver grunted.

"But I'm here now. She's probably gonna bitch at me good, so maybe it'll help if I pay the fare."

The man hesitated briefly, but when he saw the bill that Bryan was extending, he shrugged. "That'll cover it."

Damned well should, Bryan thought. Aloud, he said, "Keep the change."

The cab left.

Bryan leaned against the jeep to wait.

It was nearly thirty minutes later before Kathryn Daily

emerged again, carrying a small brown suitcase. When she saw that the cab was gone, she stopped in obvious dismay.

"Kathryn," Bryan called.

She looked at him. "Do I know you?"

"Not exactly. But I'd like a few minutes of your time. Just to talk."

"About what?"

"I'd rather not stand here in the street and shout about it." He saw her glance back toward the gate. "It has nothing to do with Stanzione, don't worry. Why don't we go get a cup of coffee?"

She checked her watch. "I have to meet some people at Denny's. We could go there, I guess."

There wasn't much more conversation until they were sitting in a booth at the coffee shop. Kathryn ordered a cup of tea and then eyed him.

"So, who are you and how do you know me?"

"My name is Murphy. I was hired to find you." Which was close enough to the truth.

Her forehead creased. "Hired by who?"

"Tray Detaglio."

She looked surprised. "*Tray?* Jesus, I thought he was in jail."

"He's out now. And he'd like to talk to you."

"Why? After all these years?" Her bewilderment seemed genuine.

Bryan didn't feel up to getting into the whole thing at the moment. Besides, it wasn't really his responsibility, was it? "That's for Tray to say. Can we set up a meeting?"

He watched her think about it. This woman wasn't stupid; he could see the intelligence clicking behind her blue eyes. "I guess it would be all right." She had apparently decided that there might be something for her in it.

Bryan finished his coffee. "How about tomorrow night at eight?"

She nodded.

"You know Roscoe's on Gower?"

"I can find it."

"Okay. Tray will be there."

She was looking through the window. "Okay. I have to go now."

He stayed where he was, watching her cross the restaurant and go out to the parking lot. A battered yellow VW had pulled in and was sitting there. The driver, a big guy with a mustache, got out to shove her bag into the back. Then they both got into the car and drove away.

Bryan, reaching for the check, took absentminded note of the license number.

Tray was already in bed by the time Bryan got home, but he figured this was worth waking him up for. He went into the guest room and turned on the light.

Tray sat up quickly. "What?" he said in a startled voice. When he was awake enough to realize where he was, he relaxed a little. "Shit, you scared the hell out of me."

Prison nerves, Bryan figured.

"Sorry," he said without much sympathy. "Thought you'd like to know I found her."

"You did? Did you ask her about the kid?"

Bryan shook his head. "That's for you to do, I think. Tomorrow night."

After a moment, Tray smiled slightly. "You're a pretty good cop, aren't you? As far as cops go."

"Haven't I been telling you that?" Bryan turned the light off again. "See you in the morning."

"Uh-huh."

Bryan had the door almost closed before Tray spoke again. "Thanks" was all he said.

Bryan didn't answer as he pulled the door closed the rest of the way. Having met Kathryn, he wasn't altogether sure that finding her had been a favor to Tray. That was a woman worth watching. Pretty, smart, and, unless he had lost his feel for people entirely, she could be dangerous.

He almost opened the door again, wanting to echo to Tray Blank's advice to *him* earlier: "Watch your back."

But he didn't do that. People had to run their own lives. So he went to bed.

* * *

When the house was quiet, Tray slipped from the bed. He fumbled through his pants until he found the wad of bills. Walking on tiptoe and too nervous to turn on a light, he slowly made his way through the house to the office. Kneeling on the floor, he carefully slid the drawer open and took out the envelope.

He put the two hundred dollars back.

Then he paused.

After a moment, he opened the envelope again. This time, he only took fifty dollars. That could hardly even be called stealing, could it? Fifty lousy fucking bucks was hardly a crime.

Clutching the money in his fist, he went back to his room.

10

Kathryn returned from her visit to Stanzione's not only with the remainder of her belongings, which had been the pretext of the visit, but with the information they needed as well. Chris didn't ask her exactly how she had managed to ferret out the dope—he already had a pretty good idea about how Kathryn Daily got what she wanted from people—but it wasn't important.

She sat at the kitchen table and drank a Coke against the sticky night. "This is going to work out perfect," she said. "The money will be coming any day now. It goes right into the safe."

"And then?" Chris prompted.

"The cash stays there for a couple more days before it disappears."

Going, no doubt, into whatever particular pipeline Stanzione used to clean up such matters. So they had only a little time to get this thing together.

There was, apparently, an inviolable routine to the way Stanzione handled such things. Chris had often thought about crime and about those who committed crimes, and in prison, he'd read a lot about human psychology. It had not escaped his attention that a pattern of behavior could usually be detected among the criminal elements of society. So many times that very pattern brought about the downfall of the bad guys. It was personally satisfying now to realize that an observation of his was about to be proved true—and to his great advantage.

But right now he had more important things to think about.

Like just when a brown Ford van was going to make a drop at Stanzione's.

He was parked back on the side street again. This time, though, he was alone and driving a stolen Lincoln—a flashy car that fit right into the neighborhood. At the moment, however, the car didn't appear to be running. He was standing beside the open hood, pretending to fiddle with the wires and things inside.

The cop car looked at first as if it might go right by. Which is what Chris was fervently hoping. But then the car slowed and pulled to a stop just behind him. A young blond patrolman got out and walked up. "Trouble, sir?" he said politely.

Chris pulled his head out from under the hood. He wiped his hands on the front of the faded blue work shirt—the same shirt he'd worn in prison. "Think I've figured it out," he said. "Hope so, anyway. My boss is waiting at the airport for me. Should have it all wrapped up in a few minutes."

"You want a tow?"

"Nope. Thanks, anyway."

The cop nodded. Chris grinned and stuck his head back under the hood. After a tense moment, he heard the patrol car drive away.

Well, something better happen pretty damned soon, because he couldn't afford to be here when the patrol came by again—which would happen, no doubt about it. All he could do was hope the damned cop didn't decide to call in the license number.

For once, luck was with him. It was only about two minutes later when a shiny brown van pulled up and went through the gates. Chris felt a real physical kick to think that so much money was so close. And that it would soon be his.

But he didn't have time to think about it. He slammed down the hood of the Lincoln, got in, and drove until he spotted a bus stop. He dumped the car a block away and caught a bus five minutes later.

Kathryn was sitting alone in the living room when he got back to the house. She was playing solitaire and listening to a soap opera on TV. "Well?" she demanded, not looking up from the cards. "Did it come, like I said?"

"It came." He got himself a beer and returned to the living room. "It came, yeah. So maybe this is going to happen after all."

"It'll happen."

Chris sat down and drank about half the beer in one long gulp. "Where's Dwight?"

She shrugged.

"That doesn't fucking tell me much."

Now she looked up. "I don't know where he is. He just left. Took a walk."

"He just left?" Chris repeated. "Why?"

"Why? How should I know why?"

"Damn," Chris said quietly. He got to his feet again and walked over to the window. As he finished the beer, he tried to fight off the worry edging into his gut. Surely Dwight wouldn't go off and do something *now*, just when they were finally in sight of their fucking dream.

Would he?

He turned around quickly. "I better go look for him."

Kathryn gave a soft laugh as she flipped another card down. "Doesn't he know his way home?"

"Lay off, willya, please?"

She only shrugged again, her full attention back on the cards.

Once, a long time ago, when he was about twenty, Chris had gotten involved with a bunch of political crazies. Looking back, he could never quite remember how it had happened; certainly not because he had given a damn about the "causes" they had forever gone on about. What difference had any of that shit made to him?

Anyway, what had happened was, this bunch of looney tunes decided that what they wanted to do was blow up a bank. Not even one of the biggies, but some backwater bank in a backwater New Jersey town. Chris was never quite clear as to why they had chosen this particular symbol of the military-industrial complex to attack, but he suspected it had something to do with the fact that one of the members of the group was the daughter of the bank president. He didn't want to try to figure out what kind of weird emotional junk she was trying to deal with.

He met up with the group in a bar and one thing led to another until pretty soon he had agreed to apply his expertise to the job. He didn't exactly tell them that he'd never pulled a bank job before; with this bunch, he decided it wouldn't be hard to fake it. So he faked it. And he got them into the bank, just like they wanted. He even helped them set the dynamite. Then he took the money from the vault, just as promised. They were only interested in making some kind of fucking statement, so the money was supposed to be just his. Payment for his services.

As far as he was concerned, that was the end of his political life.

Except that as they were leaving the bank, the leader of the group came over to him. There was a funny look in his eyes and Chris realized at that instant what he had never realized before: The guy was dangerous. Never mind all the dumb talk and the funny clothes or even the damned beads he wore. This guy was a predator.

They took the money. Every damned penny of it and so much for idealism.

Chris had learned a lesson from that. A couple of lessons, actually. He stayed away from people with causes. And he looked out for the predators.

The look in Kathryn's eyes was why he didn't dare underestimate her. She would go for the jugular, if the opportunity arose.

And the same thing was true of Dwight. Maybe he wasn't much good as a thief or an armed robber, but he had something of the predator in his eyes, too. He hadn't always; when he first came into the joint, he was okay. Prison changed him.

What worried Chris was that when you took a predator and added it to the fact that Dwight had this problem getting along with broads, it might get really dangerous.

It might get deadly.

He started off by hitting a couple of the bars that they sometimes went to, but nobody had seen Dwight. It was almost two hours later before he reluctantly came across with his ten bucks and went into the Blue Angel Cinema on Hollywood Boulevard.

Pushing through the ratty velvet curtain, obviously left over from better days, he stepped into the darkness. He paused for a few moments, to give his eyes time to adjust themselves, then surveyed the sparse crowd. The back of one head was familiar.

He carefully made his way down the sticky aisle and dropped into the seat next to Dwight. "Here you are," he whispered.

Dwight glanced at him, surprised. "Yeah? So?"

"So I've been looking for you all fucking afternoon."

"Why?"

Chris realized that he had no good answer for that, at least not one he wanted to tell Dwight at the moment. How could he? Should he just admit, "Hey, I was looking for you because I was afraid you might flip out and do something stupid, like beating up on a broad and messing up all my plans"?

No, that didn't seem like a good thing to say.

Instead, he just muttered, "How come you took off like that?"

"The woman was making me nervous."

"Why?"

"How the hell do I know why? It was just too hot in there. Too small. She was watching me and I was getting nervous. So I thought it was better if I just split."

"That was good. You did the right thing. Don't let her get to you."

A voice from behind them said, "Shut the fuck up, assholes."

They both watched the screen for a moment. A man was in bed with two women, one white and one black. He didn't seem to be having much fun, but he was trying.

Chris sighed. "Come on," he said. "Let's get the hell out of here."

Dwight followed him up the aisle and out of the theater.

They had a strategy meeting early that evening, sitting at the kitchen table and drinking ice-cold beers in the lingering heat of the day. Although he tried to keep everybody's attention on the subject at hand—how to get Stanzione's money for themselves—

Chris kept finding himself, uncomfortably, in the role of peacekeeper. He was forced by the circumstances to keep an even tighter rein than usual on his own impatience.

"So, did you draw a map of the house like I told you to?" he asked Kathryn finally.

She pushed a sheet of notebook paper across the table toward him. The pencil drawing was neat and specific. He studied it for several minutes, then looked up. "What about alarm systems?"

Another sheet of paper. "I wrote down whatever I know. I can't promise it's complete."

This sheet held his attention for a longer time.

"He also has some of his men there all the time. Sort of like guards."

"Wonderful," Chris muttered. Alarms and armed men.

Dwight was brooding over his beer. "This whole thing seems pretty risky to me," he said suddenly.

Kathryn looked at him scornfully. "If you don't have the balls for this job, Dwight," she said in a soft voice, "why don't you just stay home?"

Dwight slapped her across the face.

It was so fast, so unexpected—although it probably shouldn't have been—that she couldn't evade the blow and Chris couldn't deflect it.

Kathryn fell backward, just managing to catch herself before landing on the floor. The chair landed on its side. "You bastard," she said.

"You've got no right to talk to me like that," Dwight said. "I should just go after the money myself and forget about you two. I couldn't do any worse."

Chris slammed one hand down onto the table. It cracked, loud as a gunshot. "Stop!" he said. "Shut the hell up, both of you."

They fell silent.

Chris stood. He took Kathryn by one arm and pulled her into the living room. There, he pushed her down onto the couch and stood over her. "Why don't you just leave him alone?" he asked in frustration. "You know that Dwight is sort of on the edge right now."

She was rubbing the side of her face, which was bright red from the slap. "I hate him."

"Fine. I don't think he's all that crazy about you, either." He leaned closer to her and spoke in a near whisper. "But none of that matters one fucking bit, understand? We want that money. That's *all*. We need each other to get it. None of us would stand much chance alone. You got that straight?"

"I've got it," she said sullenly.

"You admit it's true?"

"All right. It's true, damnit." She looked up at him coldly. "But you just keep that son of a bitch away from me. You got *that*?"

"Yeah, yeah. And *you* keep your fucking cool."

She leaned back and closed her eyes.

Chris went back into the kitchen. Dwight was still sitting at the table, working on another beer. "That was really stupid," Chris said. "It was a fucking dumb thing to do."

"Yeah, well."

"Forget that shit. Goddamnit, Dwight, I have enough to think about without having to play mother to you. Shape up, willya?"

"Or?"

Chris frowned. "Or what?"

Dwight almost smiled. "What you really mean is, shape up or else, right?"

"I didn't say that. There isn't any 'or else.'"

Dwight turned the beer can in his hands, kept turning it as he spoke. "Maybe you and her should just take the money and go to Mexico."

Chris stared at him. "Stop talking crap like that. You and I are going to Mexico."

"You sure that's the way you want it?"

"Dwight, we shared the same fucking cell for five years. Don't you know me by now?"

After a moment, Dwight nodded. "I'll keep it together, Chris."

"You damned well better."

Chris crushed one of the beer cans. Boy, maybe what he should be thinking about doing was dumping both of these losers and counting on nobody but himself. That was probably a real smart idea. Between the bitch and all her problems and Dwight, he was likely to lose his mind before very much longer.

Kathryn stuck her head into the room suddenly. "I'll be back later."

"Where are you going?" Chris asked.

"Just some personal business." She looked impatient. "It has nothing to do with this. I'll be back before it's time to do the job, don't worry."

They listened to her leave.

Chris got up for two more beers. He lifted one toward Dwight. "Here's to getting fucking rich," he said.

Dwight nodded and drank.

11

Whistling softly—some old Beatles song that he could not remember the title of—Bryan opened all of the cardboard cartons, put some plates and silverware on the table, and hunted up the bottle of soy sauce. When all that was done, he yelled that dinner was ready.

After a few moments, Tray came into the kitchen and looked glumly at the table crowded with rapidly cooling Chinese carryout. "Looks great," he said, his lack of enthusiasm obvious.

"Hey, just don't forget that you could be eating jailhouse cuisine," Bryan replied unsympathetically.

"I'm not so hungry, anyway." Tray sat at the table and took a little of everything.

Bryan filled his plate, and they ate in silence for several minutes. "Nervous, are you?" he asked finally.

"I guess." Tray looked up, as if suddenly struck by a brilliant thought. "Hey, why don't you come along?"

"Because what you two got to talk about is none of my business, that's why."

Tray tasted the shrimp in lobster sauce. "I used to think a lot about Kathryn when I was inside. Believe me, you have a lot of time to think, under those circumstances."

"I can imagine."

"I was always wondering what had happened to her. And to the baby." He washed down a bite of egg roll with a swallow of Pepsi. "She never showed up at the trial or anything."

"Well, she's been busy, apparently," Bryan said dryly.

Tray almost laughed. "That's true." He took some more egg foo young. "The thing about Kathryn is, she always had such big dreams. She *wanted* things. It wasn't like she was greedy, exactly. It was more like she thought she just deserved to have it all. Just because."

"Nobody deserves anything for free," Bryan said shortly. "People who think life owes them a damned thing are the ones who end up in trouble."

Tray stopped eating and looked at him. "Like me, you mean."

Bryan shrugged. "I never said that. But you did steal cars, right?"

"I did."

"So you must have felt that life owed you that much at least. Even if the car did belong to somebody else. And you did get into trouble."

"Yeah, well, that just about wraps it all up into a nice neat package." Tray picked up the bottle of soy sauce, read the label, then dumped the brown liquid all over his plate. "The way you understand human nature, you musta been a shrink as well as a cop, huh?"

"I just know what I've seen."

"Don't be so modest." Tray smiled at him faintly. "I ripped off my first car when I was ten. Actually, it was my old lady's Rambler. And I didn't really steal the damned thing; I just took it for a joyride one morning before school. She went crazy, called the cops. Squad car pulled me over a few blocks from home. I was sitting on the fucking phone book so I could see over the steering wheel."

"Bright boy."

"You better believe it. That was the greatest day of my entire fucking life. The cop took me to school in the squad car and everybody heard about what I'd done. I was a hero."

"I suppose you were."

"If it's any comfort to you, Bryan, it was a short-lived fame." Tray pushed the plate away. "I didn't even want the damned car, really. I just thought that if I did something that bad, maybe my folks would notice me." He wiped his mouth with the paper napkin from the Chinese Peacock. "I suppose that proves your point from before. Guess I just fucking thought the world owed me that much. I thought that a kid deserved to be *noticed*, for chrissake."

Bryan kept his eyes on his plate. "Sometimes," he said, "cops tend to sort of simplify things."

"And ex-cops, too," Tray added.

"It's an occupational hazard. Otherwise, things get too confusing."

"Well, not being a cop, maybe I don't quite understand that. But it seems to me that making things *too* simple might be dangerous. Maybe life should be a little confusing."

Bryan looked up. After a moment, he nodded.

The jeep handled easily—in fact, it was fun to drive—and Tray made it into Hollywood more quickly than he had thought he would. He had to drive around for several minutes, however, looking for a place to park. Instead of getting out of the jeep immediately and heading for Roscoe's, he lit a cigarette and stayed where he was.

Part of him wanted to just turn the damned jeep around and drive back home.

Then he snorted.

Home?

Who was he trying to kid?

Face it: He had no home. No place to go. He had nothing at all in his life, unless this worked out right. Oh, he didn't mean the thing with him and Kathryn. That really was stone-cold dead, just like he'd told Bryan. But with a kid . . . well, it would give him a purpose. Even if he could just see the kid sometimes, that would be okay. These days, a lot of fathers did that. He could do it, too. On weekends, they could go to Disneyland. And ball-games. Maybe Bryan would even come along. Being an ex-cop like he was, Bryan would be a good influence on a kid. It would be fine.

Finally, he tossed away the end of the cigarette and headed for Roscoe's House of Waffles and Chicken.

He saw Kathryn and recognized her immediately. She hadn't changed much, except maybe to get a little thinner. She was drinking a cup of coffee and didn't notice him until he stopped beside her.

She looked up.

"Hello, Kathryn," he said.

She smiled faintly. "Tray. You look good."

"Thanks. So do you." He said that and it was mostly true, even though this close up he could see the five years reflected more clearly in her face. There were tiny lines around her eyes and mouth. Something in her face made him think of desperation. He sat down across from her.

"I thought that being in jail all that time would have changed you," she said, still studying him.

"It did. But most of the changes are the kind that don't show on the outside." He ordered coffee.

"I felt really bad when you were sent away," Kathryn said.

"Did you?"

She had the grace, at least, to turn a little red and not meet his eyes. "Well. You know how it goes."

"I sure do."

With a familiar toss of her head, she dismissed that line of thought. "How come you hired that private detective to find me?"

He smiled. "He's not a detective, really. Bryan's just an ex-cop. A friend of mine."

That notion seemed to amuse her. "You have a lot of cops for friends these days, do you?"

"No, just Bryan."

"That's funny. I remember how you used to talk about the police."

"Well, like I said, things change."

She paused to light a pastel cigarette. "So, okay. He said you wanted to talk to me. Why?"

"I wanted to find out about the kid."

She lowered the cigarette slowly. "The what? The *kid*?"

Tray took a quick swallow of coffee, burning the roof of his mouth. "After I was busted, you never let me know anything. Even if it was a boy or a girl."

"Christ," she whispered. "I'd forgotten all about that."

He stared at her. "You *forgot*? How the hell do you forget a baby?"

Kathryn didn't say anything for a long time. She played with her lighter, a yellow Bic. When she did speak at last, she did not look at him. "There isn't any baby. I had an abortion not long after you were busted."

"What?" Tray wasn't sure that he'd heard her correctly.

She looked at him this time and spoke the words crisply. "I had an abortion. It was my right."

That possibility had occurred to him while he was in prison, of course, and even more so during the last few days. Now he realized with painful clarity that it was, in fact, the only thing that made sense at all.

But still . . . but still, damnit, she had written to him that she was picking names, for chrissake. Why pick a name for a baby and then kill it? That was crazy.

"It was your right?" he repeated. "Yeah, I guess it was, but why did you do it?"

"*Why?* Well, Jesus H. Christ, Tray, think about it. I didn't want a kid. You were in jail. I had to think about making a life for myself."

Tray knew that when he spoke, the bitterness would come through in his voice. "Yeah," he said. "I know something about the great life you've made."

Her lips tightened. "Is that any of your business?"

"No, I guess not." He tossed a dollar onto the table between them and stood. "That about takes care of that, I guess."

"You don't really care so much, do you? About the abortion?"

He shook his head. "It was a long time ago."

"Take care of yourself, Tray."

"Yeah. You, too."

He left the coffee shop without looking back.

Before he could get into the jeep, he heard her running after him.

"Tray! Wait!"

He thought about just ignoring her, but something made him stop. "What?"

"Can't we talk?"

"What about?"

She smiled in a way that was suddenly familiar. "Old times."

He gave a soft laugh and shook his head. "I'm not so sure that our old times are worth talking about."

"Wasn't so bad, was it?" she asked.

He just looked at her for a long moment.

He hadn't intended to end up in a motel room with her.

They stopped for a bottle of rum and a six-pack of Coke, which they took into the room of the Surfside Motel with them. The place was on Hollywood Boulevard, and there wasn't any surf in sight, but this was Hollywood after all and so a little fantasy was allowed.

Kathryn bounced lightly on the bed, which was covered with a worn chenille spread. "Sort of like our bed back in Spokane," she said with a giggle that seemed a little too girlish for a woman with lines around her eyes. "God, that apartment was such a dump."

He looked around the shabby motel room. "Well, we've sure come a long way in five years, right?"

They were drinking rum and cola from plastic cups. Kathryn downed hers quickly. "But it was good between us, even in that place, Tray."

"Yeah? Was it?" He tried to remember, but the years inside were like a wall, blocking off that part of his life.

"You haven't forgotten, Tray, I know you haven't."

He shrugged.

After staring at him for a moment, she set the empty cup aside and slowly unbuttoned her blouse. "I bet I can make you remember."

Skipping the Coke this time, Tray poured more rum into his cup and watched her undress.

Bryan turned off the television and checked the time again. Just after twelve. Things must be going good for Tray and the

Daily woman. It irked him to realize that, because his gut feeling had not predicted such an outcome to the reunion. Maybe sometimes there *were* happy endings.

He had just decided to go on to bed and hear the details in the morning, or whenever the hell Tray came back, assuming that he ever did, when he heard the familiar sound of his jeep pulling into the drive. It was, he noted, pulling in rather too quickly.

He went to the window and looked out. Tray had parked and was climbing down. It was obvious from the way the man moved that he was drunk. Bryan turned around as he entered the house.

Tray slammed the door.

"Hey," Bryan said. "Take it easy, willya?"

"Oh. Sorry."

Bryan took in the sight of the weaving man. "You've been out celebrating, have you?"

Tray laughed. "Sure. Sure. Celebrating, that's what I've been doing. Bry, old pal, you have any booze around here?"

"Maybe you've had enough already."

"No way. I have not yet begun to drink." He giggled.

After a moment, Bryan went to the cupboard and took out a bottle of bourbon. "This is for medicinal purposes."

"Right." Tray took the bottle from him and wandered out to the deck.

With a sigh, Bryan followed him.

Tray took a drink, then passed the bottle to him. "Have one on me."

"Well, maybe a swallow." He took some into his mouth. It tasted damned good. "So? What happened?"

"Not much. Did you really expect her to show up with a cute five-year-old in tow?"

Bryan took the bottle from him again and had another drink. "No, I didn't expect that to happen, Tray. Did you?"

Tray shrugged.

"If I had to make a guess, it'd be that she never had any kid at all."

Tray grinned. "Bingo. You win another drink."

Although Bryan knew damned well that he shouldn't, he did

take another swallow of the bourbon. It wasn't the last, either. Over the next hour or so, they kept passing the bottle back and forth. Since his heart attack he'd become unaccustomed to the effects of booze, and it made him feel more light-headed than it should have.

"Tray," he said finally, interrupting the other man's monologue. "You want to know something about me? Something that nobody else knows?"

"What?" Tray replied warily.

"My old man was a Baptist preacher. An evangelist."

"A what?" Tray seemed to make a real effort at thinking. "You mean, like those guys on TV?"

"Yeah. Except not on television." Bryan paused, wondering why the hell he was talking about this. "We went all over the country in this old bus. He used to have these giant prayer meetings in a tent."

"That's pretty funny."

Bryan leaned toward him confidentially. "You want to hear something even funnier?"

"What?" Tray stage-whispered.

"I used to do some preaching, too."

"No shit."

"No shit. Hell, I was baptizing people when I was four years old. Dunking the bastards and saving their fucking souls."

"That is funnier," Tray agreed with another giggle.

"Yeah. *Now* it's funny."

"God, a preacher and a cop." Tray shook his head. "You wanna hear *my* funny story?"

"Sure. Lay it on me."

"She says she still loves me. What she thinks is that we should make a new start. Can you beat that shit?"

Bryan was determined to be fair about this; he didn't always want to come across like a cop. "Well, I guess anything is possible."

Tray looked at him with bleary skepticism. "You think?" Suddenly, he stood. "I got an idea, Bry."

"What?"

Instead of answering, Tray walked over to the pool and jumped in.

Bryan stared at him. "That was a dumb idea," he said.

"Baptize me!"

Slowly, Bryan pushed himself to his feet. He walked over to the side of the pool and stared down at the man treading water. "You're crazy."

"My soul needs saving. Come on in and fucking baptize me."

Bryan shook his head. Then he slipped off his loafers and lowered himself into the tepid water of the pool. It felt good.

"Well, you gonna do it or not?" Tray said, kicking and splashing.

Bryan grabbed Tray and dunked him, pulling him up almost immediately. "How's that feel? This is supposed to wash away your sins," he explained. "Washing you in the blood of Christ." He dunked Tray again and held him under this time, until the other man forced his way up, struggling and gasping.

"You trying to fucking drown me or what?" he managed to say finally.

Bryan released him and they dog-paddled over to the side of the pool. Tray climbed out first, then gave Bryan a hand. They sat on the cool tiles. "Well," Tray said, "I'd probably be a crummy father, anyway."

"Probably," Bryan agreed cheerfully.

"After all, I'm a criminal."

"Used to be."

"Right." Tray tried to squeeze some of the moisture from his shirt. "You wanna know what?"

"What?"

"I don't even think I really wanted a kid, anyway. I was just looking for *something*. Does that make sense?"

"Sure it does." Bryan stood with an effort, then reached down to pull Tray up as well. Then he stopped to check his pulse. "Hope you still remember that CPR shit."

"Yeah, I remember. Don't worry."

"I'm not worried." Bryan patted him on the back. "I've got all the faith in the world in you, Tray."

Which wasn't exactly true, but why kick a man when he was already down?

And who the hell knew? Maybe the broad really did love him.

Bryan didn't believe it for a minute, of course. But he'd been wrong before.

He patted Tray again as they headed for the house. Surprising as it was, Bryan actually felt pretty good as they went inside.

12

Chris parked nearly a block away from Stanzione's place. He turned off the engine and it was suddenly very quiet. "Well," he said unnecessarily. "I guess this is it."

Kathryn was sitting alone in the backseat of the stolen Renault, smoking one more in an endless chain of cigarettes. "Michael is going to be so totally pissed," she said.

"And you think that's funny?" Chris asked.

"Sure I do. In a way. That bastard thinks he owns the world and everybody in it. This will teach him a lesson."

"Right," Chris said. Under other circumstances, he might have found such innocence—or was it stupidity?—touching. Or sad. As it was, he just got impatient. It was his experience that men like this Stanzione didn't learn their lessons. They mostly just got even.

Dwight, who had been sitting back with his eyes closed since they'd left Venice, spoke finally. "When I was a kid, there was a dog that lived at juvie hall. Big fucker that looked more like a wolf than a dog. But he was okay. As long as you played his games. The thing you didn't want to do was cross him. Because that made him mad. If you were stupid enough to piss that dog off, he turned into a fucking beast."

"So?" Kathryn said. "What's that got to do with anything, I'd like to know."

Dwight only shrugged.

"God," she said helplessly.

Chris was glad when they both shut up. He could feel a

familiar tension rising inside his chest, a feeling he always had before a big job. It had been a long time since he'd felt this way, though; the shitty little jobs they'd been pulling didn't feel the same. The difference, he thought, was a little like jacking off compared to a really good fuck. A difference of degree.

But no job had ever been as big or as important as this one. Chris knew, perhaps instinctively, that what happened tonight was going to determine how the rest of his life went. He didn't know if either Dwight or Kathryn really understood what was happening here.

Probably not. Kathryn was off on her own trip, which was partly lust for the money and partly revenge for whatever Stanzione had done to her. And Dwight . . . well, Dwight was full of dreams of Aztec gold and pirate treasure, as well as still fighting against the nightmares of the past. That didn't leave a whole lot of room for anything else in his mind.

All in all, this wasn't exactly the greatest collection of criminal minds since the Barker gang. But it didn't have to be. All they had to do was hang together a little bit longer.

They just had to keep cool for a little while and do this job. Then it would be over.

Chris opened the car door. "Come on, people," he said briskly. "Let's fucking do it."

Kathryn giggled as she slid out.

Dwight just got out and closed the door quietly.

The two men lingered in the shadows as Kathryn approached the gate and spoke to the man inside. After a moment, the gate slowly opened. Kathryn joined the man in the driveway. She moved very close to him and he bent down, apparently to hear her better. Chris wondered what line of bullshit she was feeding the dumb bastard. A woman like that was dangerous; for just a flashing moment, he was sorry that they'd ever gotten mixed up with her.

But he brushed off that thought quickly and touched Dwight on the arm. "Come on," he whispered.

The man was facing away from the still-opened gate now and Kathryn was almost on her knees in front of him. How far was she willing to go to distract him? Chris thought it would be fun to watch. Would she go all the way and blow him? Probably. But there was no time for fun now.

He took one more step toward them and shoved the barrel of the Magnum into the man's spine. "You can live or you can die," he whispered. "The choice is up to you."

The man straightened slowly.

"You don't make any more moves until I tell you to." At a nod from Chris, Dwight came forward and disarmed the guard.

"You're a couple of dumb fuckers," the man said. "Dead dumb fuckers. You know who it is you're messing with here?"

"Shut up," Chris suggested.

Kathryn was standing back, watching, a look of delight on her face. "Sorry, Ralph," she said.

Ralph, who had quickly lost what looked like a respectable hard-on, barely glanced at her. "Oh, you're dead, too, cunt," he said.

"Wanna bet?"

"Could we please can the shit here?" Chris said. "What we want you to do, Ralph baby, is take us to the place where the alarm system is anchored."

"Fuck off. He'd kill me."

"Maybe. But with me there's no doubt." Chris increased the pressure on the gun. "You got very little choice here. Let's move. One mistake and you're a memory. I think you'll agree we'd have very little to lose at that point."

Ralph seemed to think about it for a moment, then he slumped a little. "Okay," he said in a barely audible voice. "I'll show you."

"Good boy. You might just live through this after all."

The sigh he gave seemed to indicate that Ralph had his doubts. But he started moving toward the house.

He used a key to open the back door. Chris waited, not even breathing, because maybe the creep really was some kind of fanatic, like one of those crazy Arabs, willing to die for a cause. But no alarm sounded. They moved single file down a narrow, dark hallway until the man stopped. "Behind the panel there," he said.

"Dwight," Chris said. "Check it out."

Dwight slid the panel aside and, sure enough, there was a black box.

Chris smiled to himself. This system was one he knew. Someone inside had drawn a diagram of it a couple of years ago and given lessons in how to incapacitate it. Luck was maybe starting to turn their way.

He raised the gun and crashed it down on the back of Ralph's skull. The man started to drop to the floor, but Dwight caught him and lowered him quietly. He took out the roll of adhesive tape Chris had given him earlier and used some to bind the man's ankles and wrists, then to muzzle his mouth.

"One down," Chris mouthed.

Even though the alarm system was out, he knew they were far from being free and clear. Kathryn had explained the layout of the house and the other security measures Stanzione had taken. There would be four or five of his lackeys sleeping throughout the house as well, of course, as Stanzione himself. And every one of them had a gun or two nearby. Probably under the fucking pillows.

Dwight switched on the pencil-thin flashlight, keeping the narrow beam low. Kathryn took the lead now. They moved out of the hallway and up a winding staircase. It was on the third floor that they stopped climbing and started down another long hall.

She stopped finally, indicating a closed door. Chris stepped forward and turned the knob. When it clicked, all three froze. Nothing happened, though, and after a moment Chris pushed the door open.

It was Dwight who saw the man sitting on the leather sofa in the middle of the dimly lit room. He was resting back against the plush cushions and his eyes were closed. There was a gun in his lap.

Chris stared at him for several moments, then was convinced that the man was sleeping. Which was probably not what Stanzione was paying him to do—no more than he paid the creep at the gate to get his rocks off with Kathryn. Chris felt a vague sympathy for the men. But then he stepped over to the couch and brought the gun butt down across the dozing man's forehead. The man gave a soft grunt as he fell over, but nothing more.

Again, they waited, but there was no sound to indicate that anything was going wrong. Chris handed the gun to Dwight and then followed Kathryn to the safe in the corner. It was hidden behind a bad painting. Dwight, meanwhile, went to stand by the door.

Chris had to grin. His luck was really fucking turning. The safe was a Meilink, a damned good make, actually. But it was one he knew. It was one he could goddamned get into. Not everybody could, but Christopher Moore was not just anybody. He was a fucking genius.

He took out his tool kit and got to work.

Kathryn stood right behind him, watching.

He wanted to tell her to move the hell away, but that would take time and besides she probably wouldn't do it, anyway.

Each soft click of the lock sounded as loud as a gunshot.

Suddenly, the man on the couch stirred a little.

Immediately, Dwight moved toward him. He hit the man with the butt of the gun once and then, unnecessarily, again. The final blow was a soft, dull thud that echoed in the room.

Chris figured that the guy was dead; just one more additional complication. He gave Dwight an angry look.

Dwight just shrugged, smiled sheepishly, and went back to his post at the door.

Chris returned his attention to the safe.

Finally, after a little longer than it should have taken, the door swung open.

Inside, there was only one thing: a steel briefcase. Chris took it out and Kathryn nodded. "That's it," she breathed against his ear, touching the case with her fingertips.

Chris closed the safe door and they walked back across the room, not even wasting a glance at the man on the couch. Dwight quietly opened the door and led the way back into the hall.

Chris could feel the sweat that was running down his body. There was something else, too; another familiar sensation. It was a sexual charge going through him. He always got excited at times like this. A job done right was a turn-on.

Of course, the job wasn't done yet.

None of them could really breathe easily until they were out of the house, down the long drive, out the gate, and back in the car.

And still, nobody said anything even as Chris started the car and they glided away.

Their first stop was the Greyhound bus terminal downtown on Sixth Street. Parking the stolen car for the last time, they all went into the terminal, where Chris stashed the briefcase in a locker. Then he put the key into an addressed, stamped envelope and dropped it into a mailbox.

Now nobody could get to the money until they got the key back, by which time they'd have all the other details taken care of and so be ready to leave town. That was the safest time to make a cash split. It was an old trick, one he had used before. Of course, had it been just Dwight and him on the deal, such caution wouldn't have been necessary. But with a third person involved, he didn't intend to take any chances. Dwight, he trusted, though he could not have said why, if asked. But nobody else in the world. Certainly not Kathryn.

They retrieved the VW from the nearby parking lot and headed for Venice. On the way, they made one more stop, this time at an all-night store for some champagne.

Kathryn was giggly and flushed, but whether it was from the champagne or the excitement wasn't clear. She sat close to Chris on the couch and, when the last of her champagne was gone, gave him a meaningful look and disappeared into the bedroom.

Chris and Dwight exchanged a glance. "What the hell," Chris said. "That looked like an invitation to me."

The sexual charge he'd gotten from the successful foray into Stanzione's private kingdom hadn't left him. Dwight just smiled and shrugged, sipping champagne from a coffee cup.

Chris went into the bedroom and closed the door. Kathryn was already stretched out on the bed, naked. "No wonder you're a thief," she said in a husky voice. "That was the most fun I ever had."

"I guess fun is a good word. If you don't get caught."

"But we didn't."

"No. We didn't."

She was slowly massaging her breasts. "When you do something like that, does it make you feel like going to bed with somebody?"

"Sometimes."

"This time?"

Instead of answering, he undressed and stretched out on the bed next to her. She was all over him immediately, obviously as turned on as he was. Almost immediately, he plunged into her, making her cry out.

The sex between them was better than it had ever been before. Amazing, he thought, that so much was made of love and how important it was for good sex. He sure as hell didn't love this woman, didn't even like her very much, but that didn't seem to hurt this part of it. Love (whatever that was) was love and fucking was fucking.

Although it might be that if the two were combined, things might be even better. But that didn't seem likely.

They were both left panting and sweaty.

She spoke without opening her eyes. "If Dwight wants to come in, what the hell. It's a celebration, right?"

Chris got up, pulled on his jeans, and left the room.

Dwight was still sitting in the living room, drinking a beer now and watching television. Chris sat down on the arm of his chair. "Her majesty says you can go in if you want to," he said. "Crime apparently excites her."

"Uh-huh."

Chris touched Dwight on the thigh. "Does it excite you?"

"I guess." He got up and went into the other room.

Chris stared at the news channel for fifteen minutes or so, ignoring the sounds from the next room. He just hoped that Dwight wouldn't get carried away. Although now that they had the money, that didn't matter quite so much.

Finally, he took a beer and the last joint from the stash Dwight had given him several days earlier and went outside. It was still warm and muggy, even down here by the water.

By the time Dwight appeared, Chris was already floating a

little, the champagne and the dope and the thought of all their money lifting him. He smiled up at Dwight. "Well, buddy, we did it."

Dwight knelt next to him. "Yes, I guess we did."

"All those years in that fucking cell. Remember how we used to talk about making a big score?"

Dwight seemed to weary of crouching and leaned against Chris. "I remember. But did you ever really mean any of that talk?"

Chris shook his head. "Hell, no. I never even thought we'd see each other again, once you got out."

Dwight took a hit from the joint, then replaced it in Chris's mouth. "Well, it worked out okay."

"Sure did." Chris thought about bringing up the subject of the creep Dwight had killed when it hadn't been necessary. But then he decided to just let it go. He was feeling pretty mellow and, anyway, what good would it do to make an issue of it now? What he'd just have to do is keep a tighter rein on Dwight.

That and maybe pray a little.

"A couple days, huh?" Dwight said. "And then we'll be on our way to Mexico?"

"You got it." Chris wrapped one arm around him and squeezed. "The fucking world is ours now, buddy."

Dwight seemed about to speak again, but then he just smiled a little and got up. "Good night," he said.

"Night."

Dwight went inside.

Chris stayed where he was. Although he still felt good, there was a small twinge of sadness that he didn't understand at all, so he just ignored the feeling. Life was perfect. So fuck it. He would be happy, damnit.

13

Bryan was working on his second cup of Sanka. So far it didn't seem to be doing much for his head, which felt, somehow, vaguely wrong. How quickly, he decided, a man could forget the special agonies of a hangover.

It was only a very small consolation that Tray, when he finally managed to put in an appearance, didn't look to be in much better shape. Tray poured himself a glass of orange juice and sat at the table to drink it tentatively. Neither man spoke for almost five minutes.

Finally, Bryan stood to get himself another cup of coffee. He poured one for Tray as well.

"Thanks," Tray said in a raspy voice.

"Sure." Bryan let him get about half the coffee down before he said, "I think that porch is going to take another coat of paint."

Tray blinked at him. "Okay. I'll take care of it today. Then I'll get out of your hair. If you think that settles the account."

Bryan thought that over. "Well," he said then, "there's no rush, you know. I mean, there's a lot left to do around this place. You could stick around and help me out for a while. If you want."

Tray frowned. "What is this? National Rehabilitate A Con Week?"

"Who the fuck gets offended when somebody offers him a perfectly good job?"

Tray didn't answer.

Bryan set his cup down with a crash that made both of them wince a little. "Look, goddamnit, you're perfectly free to go. I just thought that you'd like to stay." He shut up at that point, not quite willing to admit out loud, at least to this asshole, that he sort of liked having some company around. Instead, he only shrugged. "Fuck it, if that's your attitude."

Tray rubbed his eyes with the heel of one hand and sighed. "I'm sorry, Bry. Christ. I shouldn't be dumb enough to alienate the only friend I have in the world." He paused then, looking bewildered at his own words. Then he shrugged and went on. "It's just that I feel so shitty this morning, I don't know what the hell I want to do."

Bryan nodded. "I sympathize."

"And it's not just because of all the booze, either. It's the whole thing." He stared down into the coffee cup, perhaps trying to see something meaningful reflected there. "Probably I just had my hopes built up."

"Hope can be a fucking killer."

"You ever have a kid, Bryan?"

"No."

"Ever wish you did?"

He tried to remember. "Sometimes, I guess. When I was married. But life is what it is."

Tray grimaced. "Gee, is that original? Maybe I should write it down to remember."

"Maybe what you should do is stop being such a wiseass."

"That, too." Tray looked at him sharply all of a sudden. "You shouldn't drink like that, should you?"

"Probably not."

"You okay?"

"My heart is still beating, if that's what you mean."

"Okay." Tray stood carefully. "Maybe a shower will help." He headed for the bathroom.

Bryan decided to make some toast. He was standing at the counter when his gaze fell upon the wall calendar. Shit, tonight was the opening of Ann's new show. And he had promised, weeks ago, to attend.

He didn't think that he would ever feel comfortable trying to fit into that circle. Arty types. Not what he was used to back East. In New York, Bryan Murphy was a cop. All of his friends were cops. He socialized with cop families, and most of the women he dated were the sisters or ex-wives of cops. It was all very safe.

It wasn't easy trying to fit into a whole different world. Especially when he wasn't sure that he wanted to. The toast popped up finally and he reached for it. The hell of the whole thing was, he still felt more comfortable with an ex-con like Tray than with any of Ann's friends.

But since Tray was apparently on his way out of here, he might as well get used to the idea of being an outsider once and for all.

Glumly, he chewed on a slice of dry toast.

14

Dwight burned the scrambled eggs he made for breakfast—again—but nobody seemed to have much of an appetite, anyway. Although Chris didn't know what the hell they were all so antsy about now, for chrissake. The hardest part was over; they had gotten away clean as could be. At this point it was just a matter of waiting. Waiting for the key to show up. Which might happen this very day, except that, given the lapses frequently shown by the post office, that was far from a sure thing. Chris figured the next day was a better chance.

Anyway, they had no problems left. Except, of course, for the fact that Michael Stanzione would be *very* eager to get his hands on whoever had his money. But Chris didn't want to think about him right now.

"We still haven't settled it about the split," Dwight said suddenly.

Kathryn, who had been glumly pushing the eggs around on her plate, looked up. "I still think that fifty-fifty is fair."

"Well, I don't," Chris said flatly. "Three people pulled this job and the money is going to be cut three ways. That's the way it is."

"Oh, to hell with it," she said with sudden agreeability. "All right, split the damned money three ways."

Chris had been expecting more of an argument. When he looked at her suspiciously, all he got was a smile in return. "Good," he said. "I'm glad we're all clear on that."

She shoved the plate away impatiently. "So when are you guys heading for Mexico?"

God, Chris thought, she hadn't decided to tag along, had she? "As soon as we can," he said. "There're still some details to be taken care of."

Which brought him inevitably to the second problem, the one he had been careful to avoid so far. Well, there came a time in life when even the most unpleasant truths had to be faced.

"Dwight," he said, "we need to talk about the car."

The blue eyes darkened. "What about it?"

"You know damned well that heap of yours will never make it to Mexico. I think we should take the money from the box this morning and buy something else. So we'll be ready to go."

Dwight didn't say anything for a moment, then he nodded. "You're right." It was said grudgingly, but it was said.

"Thank you," Chris replied.

"What're those other details you were talking about?" Dwight said after a moment.

Chris wiped his mouth with the back of one hand. "That's a little more complicated. I've been thinking that with a man like Stanzione on our tails, we better disappear real good."

Dwight looked puzzled. "But we're going to Mexico. Isn't that enough?"

Chris shook his head. "It's not good enough for Chris Moore and Dwight St. John just to split. Not when Stanzione is looking for blood. Our blood. When I say disappear, I mean we better not leave any kind of a trail for that bastard to follow. I used to know a guy, a real genius, who specializes in making new IDs for people. He can create a whole new person. I think that's what we need. I'm going to track him down today."

Dwight shrugged. "Whatever you say." He glanced at Kathryn. "What about her?"

"I really love it when you talk about me like I'm not even here," she said.

Chris shoved his plate aside. "Up to her. If she wants to spring for the cost of being a new person, I'll tell him."

But Kathryn shook her head. "No. I don't need anything like that."

"Suit yourself."

She smiled faintly. "I usually do."

Although he knew damned well that there was really no way the key would arrive this morning, all three of them were sitting on the porch when the mail carrier strolled up. Kathryn grabbed the small stack of envelopes from him and riffled through them quickly. Disgusted, she threw the whole pile down. "Nothing," she said. "Why isn't it here?"

"Don't worry about it," Chris said, although he was a little concerned himself. "Tomorrow for sure."

"We hope," she said.

Dwight leaned back against the steps and looked up at her. "He just said it'll be here tomorrow. Just chill out a little, will you?"

"Go fuck yourself," she replied cheerfully. "I'm going out for a while."

"Another secret mission?" Chris asked.

She didn't answer as she grabbed her purse and walked away, humming.

Chris watched her go.

It took Chris nearly three hours to track down the man he was looking for. He finally found Henry Talese living in a tidy bungalow in Whittier, of all places.

Talese had to be pushing seventy by this time, but he was still ramrod-straight, wearing a spotless white shirt and bright green tie when he opened the door. His trousers held a perfect crease.

He remembered Chris and let him in. They walked through a living room that smelled nauseatingly of lemon furniture polish. A white-haired woman sat in the room watching a soap opera on television. They ignored her and she ignored them.

It wasn't until they were in a basement-turned-workshop that Talese spoke again. "I heard you were out," he said.

"I'm out," Chris agreed. "And I'd like to stay that way."

Talese gave one of his almost smiles. "Which is why you're here, I guess."

"You got it. Also because I'd like to stay alive."

"Okay."

"I need a couple new IDs. The whole works. One for me and one for a friend of mine. Including some passports."

The old man gave a low whistle. "Sounds like you're in a lot of trouble."

"Not yet. And I want to keep it that way. You're still in business, right?"

"On occasion." Talese brushed some imaginary dust from the top of his worktable. "What you're asking for, it isn't going to be cheap, you know."

"That doesn't matter."

Talese raised a brow at him but didn't say anything.

"How fast can you have the package ready?"

"You want fast, go to McDonald's."

Chris sighed. "I'm under some pressure here, Talese."

"Thirty-six hours," the old man said flatly.

"Too long."

Talese shrugged. "So go find somebody else. I hear there's a spic broad on Alvarado that does the work. She can maybe suit you."

Chris grimaced, tapping the top of the table. What fucking choice did he have? "Okay. But if you can, make it faster, okay?"

"I'll do my best."

He took out his wallet and handed over two passport pictures he and Dwight had taken that morning. "All the vitals are written on the back."

Talese was already looking at the photos and didn't answer.

Chris walked back upstairs, through the living room, and let himself out.

Michael Stanzione was not in a good mood. He didn't have to say that out loud because his posture behind the desk conveyed the message all too clearly. Ralph was getting the message; the hapless sentry had avoided this meeting for as long as he could. But this morning his luck had run out.

"So you just let that bitch and her two friends come strolling in here like they was on a guided tour, is that right? You let them take my money and kill Rizzo."

"I'm sorry about Rizzo."

"Sure you are. We're all sorry about Rizzo."

"And about the money," Ralph added quickly.

Stanzione waved a well-manicured hand. "Ah, the money. You know, Ralph, of course I'm pissed about the bread. But that's really secondary. You know? That's secondary to me at this particular moment. The important thing is not the money itself, but just the fact that a couple bums took it. You know what happens, word gets out that some stupid cunt and a couple jerk-offs can steal from Michael Stanzione?"

Ralph just stood there. One hand reached toward his head and poked gingerly at the white bandage there. The lump still hurt and he was hoping for a little sympathy from the boss.

"What happens, Ralph, is people will lose their respect for me. And when that happens the whole picture falls apart, because a man doesn't have respect from his peers, he doesn't have anything. That's maybe old-fashioned, but it's goddamned true."

"I guess so," Ralph mumbled.

Stanzione stared at him for a full minute in silence, then, still without speaking, dismissed him with a curt nod.

Ralph gave a sigh of relief and left the office.

As soon as he was alone, Stanzione picked up the desk phone. "Two things," he said to the voice on the other end. "First, Ralph made it too damned easy for those bastards. He's too stupid to be around. Take care of that for me. Second, find Kathryn Daily and whoever she pulled the job with. Turn over every fucking rock in this city and find them. I want them and I want them now. You got it?"

Apparently the answer pleased him because Stanzione was smiling as he hung up.

15

Tray was eating a bowl of cornflakes and thinking about getting started on the porch when the front doorbell rang. The sick-cow sound reminded him he had to replace the bell, too. Bryan looked up from the *Times*, but Tray stood. "I'll get it," he said.

Bryan nodded.

He was surprised as hell when he opened the door and saw Kathryn standing there. He had sort of figured that, despite the words of undying love, she had finished with him the night before. Surprise and caution made him defensive. "What the hell do you want?" he said flatly.

"Well, you don't have to bite my head off before I even say anything. Can't you at least say hi, after all the trouble I went to trying to find you here?"

"Hello, Kathryn. What the hell do you want?"

"Just to talk."

"I think everything got said last night, didn't it?"

"Not by a long shot, sweetheart. Can I come in?"

He hesitated, then stepped to one side. "I guess so. But make it fast. I have work to do." He didn't know, exactly, why he was so mad at her. They had parted on fairly friendly terms the night before. And they had made love for several hours. Or they had done something that passed for making love.

"Can't we go someplace a little more private?"

With a sigh, he looked toward the kitchen. "Come on."

Bryan glanced up as Tray walked in, then raised his brows when he saw Kathryn.

"She wants to talk," Tray said. "Can we go into my room? Into the guest room?" he amended quickly.

"Go ahead," Bryan said.

"Thanks."

The door was hardly closed before she had her arms around him. He was startled, although he shouldn't have been. Nobody ever accused Kathryn of being shy. And after last night, she had no reason to think he wasn't hot for her as well.

"Last night was so good," she whispered damply into his ear. "Just like it used to be. We go together fine."

Tray was bothered to realize that, despite his hangover and his mixed-up feelings about Kathryn, he was responding to her voice and to the slow rubbing of her body against his. "Hey," he said in protest. "Bryan is right out there."

"I won't scream if you won't. He'll never know." She drew away and pulled the pink T-shirt over her head. She wasn't wearing anything underneath it. Or, it was soon clear, under the tight white shorts. "Tray?" she said softly. "Let's do it. Last night made me love you all over again."

He stared at her for another moment, then unzipped his jeans and stepped out of them and his shorts. "This is a mistake," he said.

She laughed softly and pulled him down onto the narrow bed. "You always were the best, Tray."

Even he wasn't dumb enough to believe that, but by now it didn't matter.

"You ever do it with another guy in prison?" she asked. "I heard a lot of cons do."

He ignored the question, working instead on getting his fingers between her legs. This was no time for finesse.

It was only about five minutes later when he lit two cigarettes and handed her one. "How would you like to make a lot of money, Tray?" she said suddenly.

Postcoital conversation had changed in the years he'd been away. "Sure," he said sarcastically. "Why not?"

"I'm serious. I know where we could pick up half a million dollars."

"Right. Let me ask you something."

"What?"

"Is this legal?"

Her hand was tangled in his hair, slowly massaging his scalp. "Well, let's just say it's not exactly illegal."

He reached up and removed her hand from his head. "In that case, let's just say that's not good enough. I have no intention of ending up back in Boys Town."

"There's no danger of that happening."

His gaze was skeptical.

She smiled sheepishly. "Well, there's not much chance, anyway."

"Any chance is too much."

"Will you at least listen to me for a minute? There's some money that was stolen recently. Stolen from a drug dealer, so he can't very well go to the cops, right? And to make it even better, the money was ripped off by a couple of parolees, two real losers, so what the hell could they do about it?"

"This drug dealer who got ripped off, that wouldn't happen to be a guy named Stanzione, would it?"

She pulled back a little. "You know him?"

"Only by reputation. And his reputation says he's a very dangerous man to fool with."

She bounced once with eagerness. "But that's the best part, baby. We don't have to mess with him at all. All we have to do is take the money from the two losers."

"Like ripping off a Tootsie Roll from a kid, right?"

"Right."

"It can't be that simple. Nothing is."

"But *this* is. That's what I'm saying."

"Uh-humm."

"The only thing is—"

Tray gave a sharp laugh. "I knew there was a thing. There's always a thing."

"It's no big deal. We just have to move fast because they're on the way out of the country in a couple of days."

"So what you're saying is, we rip off the money they ripped off from Stanzione."

"Right."

Tray felt that things were moving too fast here. He got out of bed and pulled his jeans back on. Although he had thought that his head was hurting before, that was nothing compared to how it was pounding now. He pressed his temples. "I need to think about this."

"Fine. Sure. Think about whether you want to earn an easy fortune. But don't think too long or the chance will be gone. Just like all the other chances in your life."

He stared at her. "What the fuck does that mean?"

Instead of answering, she got up and started to dress again. That didn't take long, considering. "Just look at your life," she finally muttered, zipping the shorts. "I better get back. I'll call later."

He wanted to ask "Back where?" but then he thought maybe it was better not to do that. The answer probably wouldn't make him very happy. "Okay," he said instead. "Later."

He walked with her to the door, where she embraced him tightly. "It's great being together again," she whispered.

Tray mumbled something vague and watched as she hurried away.

Then he went back to the kitchen.

Bryan was fooling with some things in a toolbox.

"She's gone," Tray said.

"You know," Bryan said, hefting a hammer in one hand, "it's probably none of my business, but it might be a good idea to steer clear of that one."

Tray nodded. "You might have a point," he said. "I'll get started on the porch."

He could feel Bryan's eyes on him as he walked out of the room.

Tray still didn't know why the hell he had let Bryan talk him into coming here. He wandered around the gallery, looking at the paintings and listening to the conversations flowing around him. Bryan, the bastard, was nowhere to be seen.

Taking another glass of champagne from a passing waiter, Tray stepped out of the gallery and into the night. There were only a few people standing in the courtyard. He sat on the low brick wall and lit a cigarette.

He felt restless. And that scared him. It was like the old days, when the itch to jump into somebody else's car and take off was too great to resist. Except that this time he looked to stumble into something much more dangerous than just ripping off some damned car.

It kept coming into his mind, what Kathryn had suggested. Of course, there was always the possibility that she had been lying about the whole damned thing. The truth and Kathryn were no more than passing acquaintances, had never been more. But she *had* been shacked up with Stanzione and maybe, just maybe, it was as she had said.

But even so, did it matter?

Did he really want to get involved in *anything* that held even the slightest possibility of getting him sent back inside? Was even half a million dollars worth that risk?

Kathryn could afford to be offhanded about that part of it, because she had never done time.

But.

Yeah, just like there was always a "thing," there was also always a "but." And this time the "but" had to do with what Kathryn had said.

"But don't think too long or the chance will be gone. Just like all the other chances in your life."

Maybe, just for once, the broad had a point. Face it: His life hadn't exactly been a roaring success up until now. All of his dreams and plans seemed to have gotten derailed somehow. He had always blamed others for that. But maybe, painful as it was to admit, maybe he was at least partly at fault. Maybe because he hadn't been willing to take the big chance, he had never gotten the big break.

Damn.

"You look very serious," a voice said. "Don't you like the paintings?"

He looked up and saw Ann Hamilton standing there. "Oh,

no," he said. "They're very nice. I don't know much about art, though."

She smiled, as if he'd said something funny, although he didn't think he had.

"There was a guy inside who painted. I used to watch him sometimes. Once, he gave me a canvas and I tried, but it didn't look like anything."

"Most of my pictures don't look like 'anything,' either," she pointed out.

"Well, there's a difference."

There was a pause between them during which she seemed to be studying him. "Are you going to be staying on at Bryan's for a while?"

He shrugged.

"He says you've been a big help."

"Did he?" Tray tossed the cigarette butt over the wall. "I think he was exaggerating. I haven't done so much. Some painting, is all." Then he smiled. "Not pictures. Porches."

"Well, everybody has to start someplace."

"I'm no artist."

"What are you, Tray?"

He met her gaze. "Nothing."

"I doubt that."

"I used to be a car thief. I used to be a musician. Now . . . now I paint porches."

"You seem bright enough to do whatever you want."

"Is that what it takes to succeed? Brains?"

"Yes. And guts, I suppose."

"Guts?" He mulled the word over for a time. She waited patiently. "Does having guts mean being willing to take a chance?"

Ann nodded. "Yes, I guess so." She sat down next to him. "Bryan seems to think you're going to be okay."

"Does he?"

"Yes."

That pleased Tray in a way he couldn't really explain.

Ann put a hand on his arm. "I hope you won't let him down."

Tray realized suddenly that she was in love with Bryan. Well, that was fine. Maybe they would get lucky and it would work out. Maybe it was a sign that he, too, should grab on to something and just go with it. "Do you know CPR?" he asked suddenly.

She looked a little puzzled. "What?"

"Never mind." He set the plastic champagne glass down on the wall. "Hey, think I'll take off. Maybe get a bus or something. Tell Bry, will you, please?" He stood. "I really like the pictures."

He didn't wait to hear if she responded.

Bryan walked through the empty house and out to the pool. Tray was sitting there dangling his feet into the water. Bryan pulled one of the patio chairs over and sat down beside him. "You left before the party was over again."

"I had some thinking to do."

"Thinking is good. Anything I can help with?"

After a moment, Tray shook his head. "Not yet."

"Okay. Then I'll leave you alone to think about it." Bryan stood. "See you in the morning."

Tray nodded, still watching the water.

Bryan went into the house.

16

Dwight had his books piled around him on the couch. He was leafing through them, making a careful list of all the things they would need to buy before heading for Mexico. Now that they had the money from Stanzione—well, almost, anyway, if the post office didn't fuck them up—they could get everything and take off.

He stopped writing finally and looked back over the list.

Metal detector (induction balance type)
Two backpacks (18-inch baskets)
Snakebite kit

The last item worried him just a little. Not that he was scared of snakes, of course. But the thought of getting bitten by one was upsetting. Or, maybe even more worrying, was the thought that Chris might be the one to get bitten and then he would have to play the hero. Strangely, much as *that* concerned him on the one hand, it was also the subject of a not entirely unpleasant fantasy: Chris, suffering unbearable pain, maybe even on the verge of dying, and he, Dwight, the one who knew just what to do to save him. Chris would realize then what a good guy he was. Chris would be grateful.

With a sigh, Dwight returned to the list.

Two plastic ponchos
Waterproof matches

> *Compass*
> *Notebook and pens*
> *Insect repellent*
> *Flashlight*
> *Two canteens*
> *Pick*
> *Shovel*
> *Depth sounder*
> *Underwater metal detector*
> *Scuba equipment*

He stopped reading again as Kathryn came wandering into the room, waving her just painted fingernails in the air carefully. "Where'd Chris go, anyway?"

Dwight picked up one of the books at random and pretended to be deeply interested in what it said. "Shopping."

"What for?"

Dwight knew damned well what Chris was out getting. A couple of clean guns for their trip. But he wasn't going to tell her that. So he didn't say anything at all.

She perched on the back of the couch and poked at the piled books with one bare foot. She had also painted her toenails a vivid pink. "Are you still fooling around with all that treasure stuff?"

Again he didn't bother to answer her.

"Sunken ships and buried treasure. What a joke. You can't be serious about finding anything. Can you?"

"Somebody probably said that to Mel Fisher, too."

"Who?"

He just smiled.

She shook her head. "Well, I think it's a thoroughly dumb idea."

"Your opinion has been duly noted," Dwight said, turning a page.

"Gee, you sound like a real smart guy, Dwight."

He wished to hell that Chris would get back. Kathryn made him so nervous. He tried to concentrate on the book for real, but it was impossible to ignore her presence. The very smells coming off her body seemed to wrap themselves around him.

They sat that way, not talking, for nearly ten minutes.

Finally, Kathryn broke the silence. "What is it like in jail?" she asked suddenly.

"Why do you care?"

"Well, I guess we might go to jail for what we did, if we got caught. Maybe I should know something about it."

Dwight gave up and closed the book. "You might get sent up. I won't."

She tested a nail for complete dryness. "Oh, no? What're you, some kind of big shot or something?"

Dwight looked at her without blinking. "No."

"Well, then?"

"It's just that I'll die before I go back," he said flatly.

She gnawed at her lower lip. "It's that bad?"

"What do you think?"

She just stared at him. There was a new hint of fear in her eyes. Dwight smiled. Then he got up from the couch and walked across the room to the window. Where the hell was Chris? How long could it take to pick up a couple of pieces?

"Chris told me that you killed a woman." Her voice was very close.

"It was an accident," he said, not turning around.

"What does it feel like?"

"To die?"

"To kill someone."

"I don't know. It's not a major turn-on, if that's what you're thinking."

Suddenly, her arms were wrapped around him. "What does turn you on, Dwight?"

He closed his eyes. "I don't know. All the usual stuff, I guess."

Her hands were moving in slow circles on his stomach. "Maybe we got off on the wrong foot, you and me, Dwight. I think we could be friends."

"We're friends," he said.

"Think about all the fun you and me could have with all that money."

"What? You and me?"

"Think about it." She tightened her hold on him for just a moment, then, inexplicably, laughed, let go, and walked out of the room.

Dwight leaned his forehead against the window. His hands were shaking. After a moment, he heard the front door close.

The bitch. What was she talking about, anyway? He didn't want to have fun with her. She scared the shit out of him, that's what she did. Kathryn was like some kind of a witch and he was afraid of the spells she might cast.

Dwight wasn't really a Catholic—he had no religion if it came to that—but one of his foster families had been very devout. Now, from somewhere, a memory asserted itself. Quickly, he made the sign of the cross.

Then he did it again.

Maybe it would keep them safe.

Dwight pretended not to be pissed all the way over to the used car dealer—Honest Abe's Reliable Autos, on Melrose. When Mr. Moskowitz—aka Honest Abe—started to show them the great bargains in his inventory, Chris had to give Dwight a sneaky kick in the shin to get him moving.

It wasn't until Abe led them to the bright yellow Volkswagen Rabbit that Dwight showed any real enthusiasm. Chris didn't know exactly why his partner had such a thing for those dumb German cars, but since it didn't matter a damned bit to him, the deal was made.

Dwight was even whistling a little as he drove back to the house.

Again, they were all waiting for the mailman when he arrived and this time it wasn't in vain. He brought only one thing: the envelope with the key.

Without wasting any time, they climbed into the Rabbit and headed for the bus station.

Once they had the briefcase safely in the car, a sudden

giddiness seemed to overtake the three of them. The giggles they had successfully held in check while opening the locker came out in bursts of helpless laughter.

Chris held the case on his lap and pounded out a tune on it. "Fucking rich," he said. "You understand that we're now goddamned fucking *rich*?"

Kathryn was leaning over the seat, her eyes bright. "Open it," she said breathlessly. "Let's look at it."

Chris bent his head and examined the lock more closely. "Need my screwdriver. Let's go home."

Once back at the house, they made a ceremony of it. Kathryn got three beers from the fridge and set them on the table. They all sat down and just looked at the case.

"God," Kathryn said suddenly. "I just had a thought."

"What?" Chris asked, picking up the screwdriver.

"What if there was some kind of horrible, terrible mistake and there's no money inside at all?"

Dwight, about to take a swallow of his beer, lowered the can slowly instead. "Is that supposed to be a joke?" he asked in an icy voice.

"It was just something that came into my mind, is all."

Chris was trying to ignore both of them as he worked on the lock. "Well, I guess we just have to hope for the best," he said pleasantly.

Dwight was still staring at Kathryn. "*She* better hope that's not an empty briefcase," he said.

Kathryn shuddered with mock fear. "I love it when you talk rough," she said.

"Shut the fuck up, both of you," Chris said, almost automatically.

After another moment, there was a loud click and then he opened the case.

"Jesus," Dwight said.

Kathryn reached out a finger and touched the stacks of bills lightly. "Wow," she said.

Chris didn't say anything.

Dwight shook his head. "You know what actually seeing all this money makes me think?"

"What?"

"How completely crazy Stanzione must be right now. I mean, this was *his*. And now it's gone. If I was him, I'd be ready to kill."

"He probably is," Kathryn said. "But he doesn't know who to kill."

"He knows you," Chris pointed out.

"But he doesn't know where I am."

"Let's hope to hell he doesn't find out," Dwight said.

Chris took one stack of bills and hefted it. "Anyway, pretty soon we'll be gone from here for good. New names and everything. Just two more Yankee tourists heading for Mexico. We'll be gone before he has a chance to find out who we are."

Dwight nodded, although he didn't look altogether convinced. "What about you?" he said to Kathryn.

"What about me?"

"Are you getting out of town, too?"

"Why should you care?"

"I don't give a fuck what you do except where it concerns us. If Stanzione should happen to get his hands on you, I don't think it would be too long before he had our names, too."

She smiled. "Don't worry. He's not going to get his hands on me."

"Still," Chris said, "Dwight is right. It might not be a bad idea if you split, at least for a while."

"I might." She folded the bills. "Let's divide this, okay? I have things to do."

Chris nodded and began to count out the money.

She didn't hang around long once she had her share. She shoved the bills back into the briefcase, tossed the rest of her things into her suitcase, bid them a rapid and unsentimental farewell, and then was gone.

They stood in front of the house and watched her walk away. Dwight seemed to be frowning. "What's the matter?" Chris asked.

"Nothing. Nothing, I guess." He watched for another moment, although she was out of sight. "All that money," he said.

Their share was in a newly purchased duffel, which was locked in the front closet.

"Yeah." Chris punched him on the arm, then patted him. "All that fucking money. It's just you and me again, buddy. You and me and the dough."

Dwight nodded. Then he smiled.

17

Tray was drilling a hole for the new doorbell and didn't hear the phone ringing. Bryan tapped him on the shoulder and he turned the noisy drill off. "What?" he said, too loudly.

"Telephone. Your girlfriend."

Tray frowned. "Okay."

He had been hoping that maybe she wouldn't ever call. It would be like Kathryn to drop a bombshell about all that money and then just up and leave town to chase some other dream. But this could only be her. Or the whore he'd picked up on his first day out, and that was extremely unlikely. He didn't know any other women.

Bryan followed him into the hallway and stood there as he picked up the telephone. Tray didn't say anything, and after a moment Bryan turned around and went back out to the porch.

Tray dragged the phone as far away from the open door as he could. "Yeah?" he said softly.

"It's me," Kathryn replied.

"I know."

"Well, you don't need to sound so happy about it."

He swiped at the sawdust sticking to his sweaty bare chest. "It's hot. I've been working."

"Have you made up your mind about what I said?"

"Not yet."

She sighed. "Tray, there isn't any more time. We made the split this morning. And they're leaving the country any minute now. With their two thirds of the money."

He leaned against the wall. "That still leaves a helluva lot of dough. Why don't we just take that and be satisfied?"

"Because I want it all," she said flatly. "Those creeps don't deserve it. Are you in or not?"

He thought about it, rubbing the bridge of his nose. "I don't know, Kath. God, I don't want to get sent back inside."

"But wouldn't you like to get away from here and have the money to do something with yourself?"

"Yeah, sure, but . . ." His voice dwindled off.

"For chrissake, Tray, make a decision. For once in your messed-up life, make a damned decision."

Stung by her tone, he was quiet for a moment.

"Tray?"

"Okay. Okay, I'm in."

"You're sure?"

"Yeah."

She gave a soft laugh. "Good. I knew I could count on you."

"It's probably a mistake."

"No way. It's the biggest break either one of us have ever had. Look, I'm at the Bluebell Motel on Ventura. Meet me here."

"When I can."

"This has to go down tonight," she said in her commanding-general tone. "There won't be another chance."

"I know, I know. I just have some things to finish up around here, is all. I can't just split."

"Well, make it fast. I'm in room 102."

He jotted down the name and room number on the edge of the phone book. "All right. See you later."

He hung up slowly.

Well, he was in it now.

He walked into the kitchen. All he could do was hope that this wasn't one of the dumbest moves of his life.

The night he had first met Kathryn, it had looked like his life was finally starting to take off. He had been playing bass for a group called High Gear and they had had a pretty steady gig in a Spokane bar. He had been especially excited because they had started to do some of his original stuff. Three of his songs, in fact.

So it had seemed just right when, after the second set one night, this good-looking broad had brought him a beer. They had talked all during the break, and when the third and final set was over, she had still been there. They had had another drink during the last round and then had gone to her place.

Yeah, that night it had sure seemed like things were on the right track for him.

But then, two days later, the lead singer of High Gear had killed himself with a dose of bad smack and the group had fallen apart. Nobody else in town had seemed to need a bass player then, and before long he had gone right back to stealing cars.

And now here he was, five years later. About to rip off big bucks from some hardball players.

Well, this was probably a step up from heisting Buicks.

He took two swallows of a soda and went back out to the porch. Bryan was studying the paint job. "Yeah, that's definitely going to take a third coat," he said.

"I'll do it soon as I finish with the doorbell."

"Drink the soda first. The porch isn't going anywhere."

Tray took a long drink, not looking at Bryan. "Yeah, well."

Tray thought about it. The question was, would Bryan turn out to be a real friend or just another damned cop pulling some kind of scam? That was the really vital question here. If this was such a good idea, maybe Bryan would even like to be in on it. Never was a cop that couldn't be bent just a little, not in Tray's experience.

And if it was a bad idea, a dumb idea, a dangerous idea, then maybe Bryan would be a good friend and talk him out of it. He took a deep breath.

Bryan was quiet.

"The thing is, Kathryn has this idea. She and I can pick up some cash. Easy money."

"Easy money." Bryan made the two words sound obscene. It was like he was talking about child molestation or something.

"That's right," Tray said, already feeling defensive. "Enough money for a new start."

"You and the Hollywood Boulevard virgin?"

Tray shook his head. "Kathryn and me, that's nothing

permanent. I wouldn't want it to be. But I can come out of the deal with some cash. Maybe I could buy a new bass. Maybe I could start playing music again. I might make it work."

Bryan drank silently. He walked over to the railing and stared toward the city. "New beginnings that are based on so-called easy money usually don't last long, Tray. It's like building a house on a very shaky foundation."

"Hey, a law-and-order lecture is not what I need here."

"I'm not lecturing."

"Sure as hell sounds like it to me." Tray walked to the other end of the porch, then turned around and looked at Bryan. "Could be I'm entitled to one little slip from the straight and narrow. I already paid five fucking years for something I didn't do. This might be a chance to even things up a little."

Bryan looked at him with shadowed eyes. "So this is a crime, is what you're saying."

Tray half smiled. "Only technically."

"Damnit, Tray, technicalities are what the law is all about."

"If you're just going to yell, we can't talk about this."

"I'm not yelling," Bryan said in a much softer voice. "If you're going to commit a fucking crime, why the hell are you standing here telling me about it?"

"Beats the hell out of me." Tray was honestly puzzled. What the *hell* kind of dope was he, anyway? Here he stood, jerk of the world, telling a goddamned cop that he was about to commit a crime. And if he had ever had any doubt, there was none now. Those were cop eyes looking at him.

"Well, I wish you wouldn't."

"Let me try to explain." Tray was quiet for a moment. He desperately wanted to bring Bryan around. Maybe he wouldn't actually come in on the scheme, but at least maybe he could be convinced not to look at Tray like he was a piece of dog shit that somebody had deposited on the porch.

"Instead of committing a crime like . . . this is really more like . . . committing an act of justice. These guys who have the money now, they stole it in the first place."

Bryan still didn't say anything.

"And it gets better, Bry. The guy they stole it from is a bigger creep than they are. He's the worst of the bunch. This is drug money, see?"

"So that makes it okay for you and the broad to run around playing Bonnie and Clyde."

Tray winced. "I saw that movie. It didn't have a very happy ending."

"That should tell you something."

"It's not like that."

"So? I'm still listening. Why don't you just tell me what the fuck we're talking about here?"

Tray crushed the Coke can. "Damnit, Bry. I'm almost thirty years old. Once upon a time I had plans. I was going to be somebody. I'm a damned good musician, you know. Or I used to be, anyway. Before."

"And you also stole cars."

"Ah," Tray said in disgust. "Why am I wasting my breath? You won't ever understand, so why don't I just stop trying?"

"I understand you, Tray. Too damned well. That's the problem. The first time I saw you on the beach, I understood."

"So why did you bother talking to me?"

"I don't know." Now it was Bryan who sounded genuinely bewildered.

It was several moments before Tray spoke again. "Bry, you can't have a whole lot of money. Since I figure you for one real straight cop."

"Thank you."

"So maybe you'd like in. Pick up some bucks for yourself."

Bryan blinked at him. "Are you fucking serious? You're jerking me off here, right?"

"I'm serious. Why not?"

Bryan shook his head. "Because. Because I was a straight cop for all those years."

"Never too late." Tray wanted him to be a part of this, wanted it badly.

"I guess it is for me." Bryan straightened. "Fuck it. You just go find Lady Macbeth and play your stupid games."

Apparently, Bryan wasn't even going to try to talk him out of it. Which proved just how little he cared. "Well, if the whole thing blows up in my face, you can say 'I told you so.'"

"Uh-huh. Good-bye."

"Not leaving yet. I have to finish the doorbell and paint the porch."

"Forget it."

Tray's chin lifted. "No. I told you I'd paint the fucking porch and I will."

Bryan shrugged. "Suit yourself." He went into the house, letting the door crash closed behind him.

Tray stood where he was for a moment. Then he picked up the screwdriver and the doorbell and got back to work.

It was late in the afternoon before Tray finished both jobs. He carefully cleaned up the mess and then went around to the back door. At the kitchen sink, he splashed cold water on his face. He was drying with a paper towel when Bryan came into the room.

"Porch is done," Tray said. "I think that coat will do the job."

"Thank you." Bryan took out his wallet and put some bills on the table. "This seems like a fair amount for what you did."

Tray looked at the money and then frowned. "That wasn't the deal we had. I was working to pay you off, remember?"

"I'd rather just pay you for the job and be done with it."

"Why?"

Bryan didn't answer.

Tray picked up the bills. "Fine. If that's the way you want it. I'm gonna pack."

He went into the guest room and started throwing things into his duffel. This was a nice place, what with the pool and color TV. Too bad he had to leave. But that was the way it went.

It didn't take him long to pack. When the job was finished, he went back to the kitchen. Bryan was still there, leaning against the counter. Tray stopped, having made a decision as he packed. He took the money from his pocket and put it back down on the table. "I don't want your money."

"Why the hell not? You got something against taking money that you earned legally?"

Tray didn't think that he could explain the whole thing without sounding like an idiot, so he didn't even try. He just walked to the door, then stopped. "Thanks, Bryan."

"For what?"

"Well, everything."

"Yeah, sure." Bryan sounded disgusted.

"Bye."

Tray hesitated, waiting for the other man to say something more. But finally he just left.

Fuck it.

He was glad he'd kept the fifty bucks from the desk drawer. Now he didn't even feel the slightest bit of guilt about that.

Fuck it, that was all.

He had to walk for a long time before somebody finally stopped to give him a lift. Used to be a lot easier getting rides. Of course, used to be that if he needed to get someplace, he would just rip off a car.

Which he had briefly considered doing now, but then quickly decided against it. What an ass he'd feel like getting dropped on for taking somebody's Ford when real money was so close he could almost taste it.

The ride he finally got was from a young kid who looked like a surfer and who played the radio so loud that conversation was impossible. Which suited Tray just fine.

The kid dropped him five blocks from the motel and he walked the rest of the way quickly.

Kathryn opened the door on his first knock. "God, it's about time you put in an appearance."

"I told you I had some things to do first."

"You do realize that we don't have a whole lot of time here, right?"

"Right." The room was all brown and dirty white. And shabby. He dropped the duffel onto the floor. "Do we have a car?"

"Yes. I borrowed one from a girlfriend at this place I used to work at."

"Good. There's a couple things we need to get."

"Okay." She moved closer. "Of course, we do have a *little* time. For the important stuff."

Tray could see her nipples through the sheer gauze shirt she was wearing. He lifted a hand and touched one breast lightly, then when it responded, his fingers tightened. "Yeah? What kind of important stuff you have in mind?"

"I really think you were the best, Tray."

"Considering the numbers, I suppose that's very flattering." He still didn't believe it, of course.

She was standing even closer now, rubbing the front of his jeans. "Maybe I learned a few things over the years."

The TV was droning on with an early news broadcast. The woman reporter was talking about a scandal in the state highway department. Everybody was a goddamned crook, Tray thought. In one way or another.

He sat on the end of the bed and watched as Kathryn undressed.

He only wished to hell that he could figure out why Bryan had wanted to pay him for the work. That hadn't been the deal.

He knew damned well why he hadn't *taken* the money. That was easy. The deal they had made was sort of like an agreement between friends. And maybe things had gone wrong for them—okay, it was his fault. He'd screwed up by going along with Kathryn on this thing. But that didn't mean they hadn't been friends, before. Crazy as that sounded.

If he had taken the money from Bryan, it would have sort of canceled out the rest. It all would have been nothing but business.

He didn't want that to happen. He wanted to be able to go on thinking that Bryan had been his friend, at least for a while, even if he wasn't anymore. No matter that Bryan, when push came to shove, turned out to be nothing but a cop.

Dumb, but that was how he felt.

Kathryn was on her knees in front of him now, tugging at the zipper on his jeans. Tray stopped thinking about it and let his body take over. That was simple.

18

When they had all their clothes and the new treasure-hunting gear packed securely in the Rabbit, Dwight ran out to the nearby Burger King and brought back a couple of Whoppers and some fries for dinner. They ate sitting on the back porch.

"This place hasn't been so bad," Dwight said suddenly, looking almost nostalgically at the house.

Chris crumpled up the bag that dinner had come in. "It's okay." He was briefly quiet, finishing the last of his fries. "If you want the truth, it's been more like a home to me than any place has since I was a kid." He hadn't realized the truth of that until he said it aloud, and suddenly he felt sorry to be leaving the place.

"I'm going to miss it." Dwight got to his feet quickly. "Come on. Let's take a walk. One more time around the old neighborhood."

Chris nodded.

They walked along the water's edge, not even talking for long minutes. That was one thing Chris liked about being friends with Dwight; they never had to make stupid conversation just to avoid having those uncomfortable silences that sometimes came between people.

A young boy pushing an ice-cream cart approached and Dwight paused to buy two cherry Popsicles. He sucked on one for a few moments before saying, "What it is, I think, is that I feel like something is ending."

"Well, I guess something is," Chris said. He bit off an icy red chunk, chilling his teeth so much that he got a quick pain. "All the shit we been going through in this city is ending. I can live with that."

"What do you think will happen to us in Mexico?"

Rubbing his forehead, Chris just shrugged.

"Yeah, who knows, right?" Dwight said. "Well, I just hope to hell it's good stuff."

"Sure it will be. We've fucking earned it."

Dwight nodded as he licked the Popsicle thoughtfully. "It's just that when things change, it always makes me sort of nervous."

Chris stopped walking. He leaned against the railing and stared out at the water. "Sweetheart, fucking *life* makes you nervous."

"I guess that's true enough." Dwight gave a small, uneasy laugh. "Sometimes I wonder why the hell you put up with me."

Chris was watching the gulls fight over a soggy hunk of bread. "Sometimes I wonder that myself," he said absently.

The silence was so heavy suddenly, so different than silence usually was between them, that Chris turned his head to look at Dwight. Shit, he thought when he saw the expression on the other man's face. "Hey, that was a fucking *joke,* buddy."

"Sure. I know that." But he still looked like a dog somebody had kicked.

"Then smile, goddamnit."

Dwight smiled.

"That's better." Chris turned his gaze back to the gulls. It wasn't completely a joke, of course. But there was no sense in making a big hassle about things now. Now was the time to just coast along. It occurred to Chris that maybe this was the biggest flaw in his character: He hated to make hassles; he liked life to be quiet. "I read someplace once about some Indian tribe. Or maybe it was the Eskimos. Anyway, the rule was, if a guy saves somebody else's life, he's like responsible for that person. Forever."

"Yeah? So?"

"Nothing. I just thought it was interesting."

They walked on.

"You're not fucking responsible for me," Dwight said abruptly. "Even if you did save my ass inside."

"I know that."

"You better know it!"

"I *do*."

"You know what I think about Mexico?"

"What?"

Dwight finished the Popsicle and snapped the stick in two. "That it's going to be like a whole new world. A new place where the rules from this world don't apply at all."

"Which means?"

"I don't know for sure. Which means, I guess, that we can make our own rules."

Chris grinned at him. "What kind of rules should we make, Dwight?"

Dwight smacked him on the shoulder suddenly. "Whatever kind we fucking want to, buddy. And I like that. I like that a lot."

He took off in a slow jog toward home.

Chris watched him for a moment, then followed at a more normal pace. Personally speaking, he wasn't altogether sure that living in a world where all of the rules were made by Dwight St. John would be so great.

They saw the headlights of the car as it pulled up and stopped beside the house. The damned heavy metal music from next door had covered the sound of the unexpected arrival. Chris folded the map quickly as Dwight went to the window. "Big blue Olds," he said. "Mean anything to you?"

"Dwight, who the hell do I know?" Chris joined him at the window. "Shit," he said when he saw the man behind the wheel of the car. "What the fuck is that bastard doing here?"

"Who is it?"

Chris wiped the sudden sweat that had appeared on his face. "Whitson. Christ, it's fucking Whitson."

The parole officer was getting out of the car. Chris glanced around the room quickly, trying to shove down the fear that had suddenly taken up residence in his gut. He moved to stuff the map and travel books under the sofa cushions. "Get into the bedroom," he ordered Dwight.

"What does he want?"

"What do I look like, a fucking psychic? Just move your goddamned ass. And stay there."

Dwight went into the bedroom and closed the door.

Chris gave the room one more fast look, then went to answer the second knock. "Sir," he said. "This is a surprise." He hoped that his voice sounded normal.

Whitson stepped inside without waiting to be invited in. "It's supposed to be. I sometimes like to drop in unexpectedly on my parolees. Just to be sure." His small eyes were busily checking out the room.

"Sure of what?"

Whitson was seemingly preoccupied with his examination of the room and didn't answer.

Chris sat on the edge of the couch, resting both hands on his knees. He was determined to keep this cool and not let a simple annoyance turn into something else. Something much more dangerous. Not now. Not when the fucking car was all packed and ready to go. Not when they just needed to catch a few hours of sleep and then be on their way. Not fucking now. If he had to play kiss ass one more time with this bastard, then, by God, he could do it. He could do anything he had to do.

"Was there something special you wanted to know, sir?"

Finally, Whitson turned to look at him.

There was something in the small man's eyes that scared Chris. There had been a con once, years ago, who used to kill spiders in the cell Chris and he had shared. Well, everybody killed the fuckers, of course, but that guy, he enjoyed it. He used to practically get off on torturing the little bugs to death. That was what Chris thought of when he saw the look in Whitson's eyes.

Chris swallowed hard and clutched his knees more tightly.

"Yes, Moore, there was something special that brought me here tonight."

"Yes? What?"

"I heard a rumor about you. From one of my other parolees."

Some prick trying to make points with the fucking system. Chris wondered who. He wanted to kill whoever it was. "What rumor?"

Whitson moistened his lips with the tip of his tongue before answering. "That you were seen fraternizing with another parolee. With your former cellmate, in fact. That's a violation, and you know it. It's a violation that can get you both sent right back inside." Whitson stopped, his face reflecting clearly the pleasure he felt with this turn of events.

Chris thought carefully before speaking. Take it easy, he cautioned himself. Just take it fucking easy, because this can be saved. This can be handled. "Ah, man, come on," he said with an ease he was far from feeling. "Gimme a little slack here. Maybe I just ran into the guy on the street. And, okay, we had a beer together. I mean, hell, Mr. Whitson, is that a crime? We shared a cell for five years. What're we supposed to do when we see each other on Sunset? Just walk right by? Just ignore each other?"

"That's exactly what you're supposed to do."

"Okay. Next time I'll do that."

But Whitson shook his head. The look was still in his eyes, and Chris knew without a doubt that there was worse yet to come. He felt like throwing up.

"Not good enough, Moore. After I heard about this, I did some checking. I found out that this house is actually rented in the name of Dwight St. John. Your former cellmate."

Chris sighed lightly. "We don't have to make a big deal out of this, do we, really?"

"You screwed up, Moore. And you've been jerking me around all this time. I won't put up with that."

After a moment, Chris shook his head. He couldn't help smiling just a little. "So you've decided to show off your balls, right? Gonna show me what a fucking tough guy Emory Whitson really is?"

Whitson practically rubbed his hands together. The bastard was probably creaming in his shorts. "You might as well face it, Moore. You're going back. And when St. John's P.O. finds out about this cozy little setup, he'll probably find himself right back inside, too." The smile he gave was like the one the old con used to have at the moment he finally delivered the crushing, fatal blow to the spiders. "Though if I were you, Moore, I wouldn't count on being roomies again." He took another look around, then stepped toward the bedroom door. "St. John in there, is he? That the bedroom?"

Chris was still trying to maintain, still trying to salvage, the whole thing. "Whitson, I don't think we should get all excited here."

"Shut up, Moore. This is my game now."

The door opened suddenly and Dwight stepped into the room, the Magnum in his hands. "You bastard," he said quietly.

He fired once.

Whitson's body flew backward, a spreading red mass where his chest used to be. He never made a sound.

After the echo of the shot faded, the room stayed quiet for a very long time. The music from the house next door was so loud that Chris couldn't even hear his own soft profanity as he stared at the body. Neither of them even moved for minutes. Finally, Chris took a step toward it. Whitson looked like a broken doll flung aside by a petulant child.

"I think he's dead," Dwight said in a whisper.

"Oh, there's no doubt about *that*," Chris replied. "He's definitely dead."

Dwight took a deep breath, then exhaled slowly. "Well, I didn't have a choice, did I?"

Chris didn't say anything.

"Chris, I had to do it. He was gonna fuck everything up for us."

"Oh, shit, Dwight. We could've done *something* else. We could've stashed him in the goddamned closet and thought about it for a while. Dead is dead. Now we're in even deeper shit than before."

Dwight, bewildered, shook his head. "I was only trying to help. I thought he was gonna fuck us up."

"Well, we're fucked now, that's for damned sure."

"It's not so bad. Nobody has to know I killed him."

"Don't you understand? The best part about this whole deal was that the cops wouldn't be after us. Just Stanzione. That was the beauty of this deal. Now everybody in the fucking universe will be on our butts. Stanzione *and* the goddamned cops."

"So what do we do now?"

Chris poked the body with one foot, being careful to stay clear of the blood. "I better dump this somewhere. You stay here with the money."

They stripped the blanket from the bed and used it to wrap up the body. Dwight stood on the porch, to see when the coast was clear, and then Chris carried the bundle to the Olds and shoved it into the trunk. "I'll be back," he said, finding the ignition key in the bunch he'd taken from Whitson's pocket.

He got behind the wheel of the Olds.

Dwight watched the car until it was out of sight. Where the hell would Chris go? Where did you dump a body, anyway? He wiped his suddenly sweaty palms on the front of his jeans. Chris had seemed so cool about the whole thing.

He turned around and went back into the house. There was blood all over the linoleum floor of the living room. That made him mad. It was like a violation.

Dwight found some Comet and rags under the kitchen sink. He got down on his hands and knees and began to scrub the floor.

Chris parked the car behind a boarded-up restaurant on Santa Monica. He sat still for fifteen minutes. When nobody passed by during that time, he decided it was safe.

He wrestled the body out of the trunk, straightened the blanket around it, and managed to hoist the awkward load into the dumpster. With any kind of luck, they would be long gone before the stiff was ever found. Any parolees under Whitson's jurisdiction would no doubt be the first suspects the pigs would go after. He wanted to be out of the country by the time that happened.

He got back into the car and drove for about ten blocks before parking it again. Using the edge of his shirt, he wiped off the steering wheel, the door handle, and the trunk. No sense helping the bastards along. He left the bloody shirt in the car.

He walked until he found a bus stop and sat on the bench to wait. Actually, he was glad for the time, hoping it would help him come down from the nervous high he was on. This was not the time to get rattled. What he had to do was go home, relax, maybe have a beer, and then hit the sack. They would get some sleep, then, after picking up the shit from Talese, they would take off.

They would be safe in Mexico. He thought about what Dwight had said earlier. About Mexico being a new world, a place where they could make their own rules. Maybe it made more sense than he'd first thought.

And there was no law saying he had to stick with that fuck-up St. John forever. They weren't married, after all, or joined at the hip. If Dwight got any crazier, then, just out of self-preservation, Chris would dump him.

Hell, maybe life would get better in Mexico. Maybe they might even find a fucking treasure.

Dwight was just finishing his cleaning job when he heard Chris's footsteps on the porch. The door opened and Chris came in. He was tired and sweaty.

While he washed up, Dwight gathered the bloody rags and dumped them into the trash. Then he took two beers and went back into the living room. He sat on the couch next to Chris.

"You were afraid I'd fuck up and I guess I did," he said.

Chris shook his head. "We couldn't let Whitson leave. You only did what you thought had to be done. Why bitch about what can't be helped? It's all over with now, so don't worry about it."

Dwight nodded, glad that Chris understood. "Maybe we should just leave now," he suggested.

But Chris shook his head. "No. We need the damned papers from Talese. More than ever now. We'll just have to wait."

After a moment, Chris reached under the cushions and pulled out the map and travel guides again. Dwight moved closer, leaning against him as they bent over the map, tracing the route they were going to take to Mexico.

19

As the day ground slowly on, Bryan had thought the whole thing over and had come to certain conclusions.

One was that he'd gotten good and drunk the other night and it hadn't killed him.

Two was that he'd inhaled all of Detaglio's secondhand cigarette smoke and that hadn't killed him, either.

And last, but far from least, was that he had put up with all the aggravation the stupid ex-con had given him. All that in the past few days and his heart was still beating.

So, Bryan figured, why not get laid?

Just thinking about it gave him a sudden pain in his chest, but he ignored it. The hell with worrying about his mortality. If life wasn't worth losing, it sure as hell wasn't worth living.

He took a shower and, after splashing on some English Leather, dressed carefully. When he was satisfied with himself, he took a bottle of pretty good California chablis from the sparse supply he kept on hand and headed for the jeep. If he felt a small twinge of guilt about the cynical way he was approaching this, it didn't bother him much.

After all, wasn't that the way the world worked these days? Take what you could. Things like honesty and loyalty were just words in the fucking dictionary.

Bryan was mad without knowing why. Or even at whom.

Ann seemed glad to see him and she didn't appear to attach any sinister motives to his surprise visit. She poured the wine into a couple of expensive-looking crystal glasses that were too good for the vintage. They went out to the balcony and sat.

Bryan was quiet for a time, just staring at the view.

"Are you feeling all right?" Ann asked after several minutes of silence.

"I'm feeling fine. Terrific, in fact." He swallowed some wine. "It occurred to me a little earlier this evening that maybe I'm not going to drop dead right away after all."

"Well, that's good news." She was still studying him curiously. "Isn't it?"

"Oh, sure."

"You don't look exactly thrilled with the idea of living a long life."

"I'm thrilled." He twisted the wineglass carefully between his fingers. "When I was a cop," he said, "things were either good or bad. At least that was the way I saw them. Maybe it wasn't exactly *true*, but it was simple. That was for damned sure. It was simple."

Ann poured a little more wine into his glass and then into her own. "Does this mean that you're finding life more complicated now?"

"Oh, yeah."

"But doesn't that make it more interesting?"

"It should, I guess. But not for me."

"You miss the job?"

He nodded slowly. "I miss the job."

Ann seemed to understand that. After another pause, she changed the subject. "How's Tray?"

Tray is totally fucked up, is what he wanted to say. Tray is on the road to a major smashup and the stupid son of a bitch doesn't even know it. And why the hell should I care?

But Bryan didn't say that. He only shrugged and said, "Tray is gone. He got a better offer."

"Oh, that's too bad. You seem upset about it."

He snorted. "Why the hell should I care about how that asshole decides to mess up his life?"

She didn't say anything.

Bryan drained his glass. "After all, it's not like I haven't seen a lot of punks just like him over the years. Always looking for the easy way. The big score. I never made friends with any of them. To hell with him."

"I'm glad you don't care," she said with mild amusement.

After a moment, he shrugged.

Her bedroom was like the rest of the house: simple, not gussied-up. He approved. Bryan stood by the window and waited for her to come out of the bathroom.

She emerged wearing a plain white nightgown that was styled like a man's shirt. It looked good on her.

Bryan started to unbutton his shirt, feeling himself begin to respond to the sight of her endless tanned legs and dark nipples that showed through the cotton nightgown. As his gaze moved downward, he could make out the dark triangle of hair. His cock hardened.

That was definitely reassuring.

This might be just what he needed.

20

Tray drove Kathryn's borrowed old Chevy over to the K-mart. He parked it, and they both went in. He was trying to remember everything he'd ever heard in prison about the fine art of housebreaking. It was nice to know, at least, that the past five years hadn't been entirely wasted.

At this time of night, there weren't many shoppers in the store. He tugged a cart free from the huddle just inside the door and pushed it up the aisle. Just another young couple out shopping for the good life, cut-rate style. All they needed to have was a crying kid shoved into the cart and the picture would have been complete.

The first stop they made was at the men's clothing department, where they picked up two black sweatshirts and some black jeans. Kathryn made a face as she looked at the things, but Tray just dropped them into the cart. "All the best cat burglars wear black," he said. "Don't you ever watch television?"

She shook her head. "Great. I'm pulling a job with a *Kojak* fan."

Tray's only response was to push the cart into the shoe department and pick out two pairs of black Keds. He lingered in the housewares department for a few moments, looking at the rubber gloves.

Kathryn bumped him impatiently. "Hey, stupid, you know, we don't need these dumb gloves. Who cares if we leave fingerprints? Chris and Dwight sure as hell aren't going to call in the cops to dust the place."

"I guess that's right," he admitted, reluctantly dropping the gloves back into the bin.

Finally, they were in the toy department. Tray looked through a whole shelf of guns before he settled on one called the AVENGER MAGNUM! LOOKS JUST LIKE THE REAL THING! He deposited it into the cart with the other things.

Both of them realized that they were hungry, so he pushed the cart over to the snack bar.

Kathryn opened her purse to pay for the food.

"By the way," he said offhandedly. "You haven't said exactly what it is you did with your share of the money."

She only smiled and picked up the small plastic tray to lead the way to a booth in the corner.

"You're not gonna tell me, is that it?" Tray said as they sat.

"Later. When this is over." She smiled again. "Maybe."

Tray ripped the paper from his straw and shoved it through the plastic cover on his Coke. "Someday, honey, you're gonna push somebody just a little too far."

"And then?"

"And then he's liable to burn your ass."

"Well, don't let it worry you."

"Oh, I don't."

She squirted mustard from a little packet onto her hot dog. "That toy gun thing is really stupid, you know."

He shrugged. "Maybe in your opinion. I don't happen to agree."

"Well, you can take my word for it that Dwight and Chris are using the real thing."

"I don't like guns."

"Then maybe you should take up another line of work," she said around a bite of hot dog.

"I don't plan on making a career out of this," he said sharply.

"That's probably a good thing. If make-believe guns are your thing."

Tray crumpled the wrapper from his hot dog and threw it across the table at her. "Hey, sweetheart, like you said, your friends Chris and Dwight use real guns. If that turns you on, maybe you should've stuck with them."

Her only response to that was a shrug.

"In case you forgot, somebody used a real gun the last time I got caught in something like this. I ended up doing a nickel inside. I don't want that to happen again, thank you very much."

"I just hope it doesn't turn out to be a major mistake."

"I'll drink to that." He finished the meal and glanced at his watch. "It's getting late. We better move our asses."

Back at the motel, Tray sat on the bed and took the plastic Magnum from its wrapper. He hefted it and aimed it at Kathryn. "Does this scare you?"

"Scares the shit out of me."

He nodded, pleased. "Good."

"I mean it. The thought that just a dumb hunk of plastic is all that stands between me and Chris is scary as hell. As for Dwight, I don't even want to think about him. That is one very strange guy."

He set the gun down and started to unbutton his shirt. Time to dress for work. "Look, we're not even going to see them, right? Isn't that the way the plan goes?"

"That's the way it goes." She was undressing, too. For the first time, he noticed a small leather bag on a string hanging around her neck. He wondered what was in the bag but knew it wouldn't do a damned bit of good to ask.

"Okay, then."

He watched her as she took the black jeans from the bag. "Hey."

"What?"

"We got a few minutes. Come here."

"I'm not exactly in the mood for screwing right now."

Which was probably a first. He unzipped his jeans. "Just do me."

After a moment, she came and knelt in front of him.

* * *

Tray had a shot of cheap bourbon before they left the room, hoping it would work to calm his nerves, where the quick blow job had failed. Unfortunately, on top of the crummy hot dog, all it did was make him feel nauseated.

He wondered exactly when things had slipped so completely beyond his control.

21

Dwight couldn't sleep.

He rolled out of the bed carefully and went into the kitchen for a beer. Nerves, he told himself, it was just nerves. And that was only natural. Anybody finding himself caught in the middle of this whole thing would be a little on edge.

Except Chris, of course, he amended quickly.

Dwight took a gulp of cold beer, sloshing it around in his mouth for a moment before swallowing. Bastard Chris *never* got shook. That was one of the things Dwight admired most about him. That and his brains.

Once they were safely on the way to Mexico, Dwight figured that he'd calm down. He walked into the living room and sat down on the couch, opening up the treasure book. The volume reminded him of a book he'd had a long time ago. *Wonderful Treasures of the World* had been the title. One of his foster families had given it to him for Christmas when he was four. That damned book went with him to the rest of the fifteen or so foster homes he spent time in during the next thirteen years.

In fact, he'd had the book up until the time he went to prison. Then it disappeared. Dwight wondered what had happened to it. That battered old book had gotten him through a lot of rough days when he was a kid. And a lot of lonely nights, too.

Dwight let the beer slide down his suddenly dry throat. The days and nights of his past were much better forgotten. Things were okay now. He was out of jail. And he had Chris for a friend.

And they had a lot of money.

He kept turning the pages of the book slowly, trying to lose himself in the images. It worked almost like self-hypnosis.

So deep was his concentration on the gold and silver visions covering the glossy pages of the book that when Chris came into the room and spoke, Dwight jumped. "What?" he said, trying to calm his racing heart.

"I said, what's the matter?"

"Nothing. I just couldn't sleep, is all. So I decided to look at the book."

"You should be sick of that damned book by now." Still, Chris took the book from him and stared at the photograph of a gleaming Aztec artifact. "Maybe we'll find something like this, huh?"

"Maybe."

Chris sat next to him on the couch and turned a few more pages. Chalices. Jewelry. Coins. "Neat, isn't it? It would be great to uncover this stuff."

"Sure. We will." Dwight smiled a little sheepishly. "And even if we don't, it's going to be fun looking, right?"

Chris frowned as if the idea of not finding anything had never even crossed his mind. "Yeah, I guess so. It might be fun."

Dwight leaned toward him, eager to pass along all the feelings that were boiling inside of him. "You know what this seems like to me?"

"What?"

"Like we're setting off on a . . ." He fumbled for the right words. "A grand adventure."

Chris laughed. "You're a funny guy, Dwight." He lifted a hand and slapped him lightly across the face. "Bed, dummy. Or else you'll sleep all the way to fucking Mexico, and I need you awake riding shotgun."

"Okay."

Chris's hand slid down and rested on Dwight's neck. "Shit, you're wound up tighter than a clock. Come on, I'll give you a massage."

It had been a long time since Chris had offered to do that. Since the night before Dwight had left prison, in fact. Dwight stood quickly. "Okay."

They both went into the bedroom and he stretched out on the bed. Chris crouched next to him and started to rub his back. Dwight closed his eyes.

"This helping?"

"Yeah. Feels good." He gave a short laugh. "Only thing I miss about fucking jail, I think. The massages."

"Shit."

"It's true." Dwight was quiet for a moment. "Chris?"

"What?"

Again he hesitated, not sure what exactly it was that he wanted to say. Then he just said, "Thanks."

Chris's movements were becoming quicker, rougher.

"What for?"

He gestured vaguely. "Everything. You know."

"Don't be stupid," Chris said. He let his hands rest where they were for a time, then, abruptly, he moved away and stretched out. "If you want a fucking backrub," he said, "just ask for it."

"Okay."

"Sometimes you act like you're still scared of me or something, for chrissake. I can't help being big, you know. But I've never done a goddamned thing to hurt you."

"I know."

"Well, then, stop being such an ass."

"I will."

Chris just sighed, as if he didn't really believe it. "Good night," he said.

"Night."

Dwight rolled over and stared at the ceiling. Chris never seemed to understand what it was he tried to say. Probably it was his own fault; he just didn't have the words.

Maybe when they got to Mexico it would be different. They could make the rules there, like he'd said before. Like they had in jail.

He listened to the ragged sound of Chris breathing on the other side of the bed and finally the sound lulled him to sleep.

22

Tray took another swallow of the by-now lukewarm Pepsi. "Aren't those jerks ever going to bed?" he said, not for the first time.

"They will. Loosen up, for goodness' sake, will you, Tray?"

"No. I'd rather stay tight, thank you very much. All I keep thinking about is the possibility of going back to jail."

She released her breath in a sigh loaded with aggravation, playing absently with the damned little bag around her neck. What the hell did she have in there, anyway? "Be like me. I'm thinking about all that lovely money."

He grimaced. "There isn't a whole lot to buy in the prison store, take my word for it."

She just shook her head.

Tray lit a cigarette, thinking about the whole thing. It was starting to seem more and more like a big mistake.

A *very* big mistake.

But what the hell could he do about it now?

You could drive away, asshole.

He could almost hear Murphy's voice saying the words. Yeah, except where was good old Bryan when the chips were down? Not sitting here to help, that was for damned sure.

There was one thing that Tray was trying very hard *not* to think about. He certainly didn't want to remember that sitting in a car waiting was just how he'd gotten into trouble the last time.

He sighed.

"You know," Kathryn said suddenly, "I'd forgotten how cautious you always were."

"Cautious?"

"Yes. Sickeningly so."

Tray glanced at her. "Which is why I spent all that time in jail, I guess."

"I wouldn't be surprised."

He crushed the soda can and threw it out of the car window. It landed with a dull *thunk* in the gutter. Great, now he was a litterbug, too. "I really enjoy having you analyze my character like this," he said. "It brings back a lot of memories."

She flashed him a smile. "We never would have lasted even if you hadn't gotten busted."

"You've got that straight."

"I did the right thing."

He looked at her again.

"The abortion. It was the only thing to do. Can you imagine some poor kid living in the middle of all this?"

"I guess not. Yeah, it was the right thing to do."

"And as for us, well, all we have to do is hang in a little while longer, and then we can part company a little bit smarter and a whole lot richer."

"Suits me fine," he said.

There was just one thing. Tray wished that he could remember how to pray. Sister Mary Angela would have rapped his knuckles good had she known.

Even being fucking baptized a second time hadn't helped.

After waiting for nearly an hour after the lights had gone out inside the house, Tray and Kathryn got out of the car. They shut the doors carefully and walked side by side to the porch. Kathryn used the key she'd had made without Chris's knowledge.

They stepped inside and stopped, waiting to be sure that the sound of the door opening hadn't wakened the men in the other room. When there was no noise, Tray switched on the small flashlight, keeping the beam aimed at the floor as he followed Kathryn across the room to the closet, where, she'd assured him, the money was.

The door of the closet was locked, but even he had very little trouble getting it open. A *real* thief would have been able to do it in his sleep.

Kathryn was right, he decided, these guys were a couple of first-class losers. They actually deserved to have the money snatched away.

Despite how easy this all seemed to be, Tray still couldn't quite believe it when he reached into the closet and came out with the green duffel, just as Kathryn had described it. He exhaled.

Could getting rich actually be such a snap?

Kathryn tugged impatiently at his arm.

He nodded and turned around. They tiptoed back across the room toward the open door. They made it, with Kathryn right on his heels.

When the room light went on all of a sudden, Tray was surprised, not scared. This wasn't supposed to happen and somehow he thought that Kathryn had done it. He stopped, half turning, to confront her. The duffel was in one hand and the toy gun, almost forgotten, was in the other.

Standing in the middle of the room was the biggest fucker he'd ever seen close up. It had to be Chris. Not that his name mattered much at the moment. "What the hell are you doing?" Chris asked in a quiet voice.

That was when Tray got scared. When he heard that soft voice. The words seemed almost like a caress from a lover. Except that this caress sent an icy shaft of fear down his spine.

"Shit," Tray said.

Then they ran.

They were just off the porch, side by side again and moving like a couple sons of bitches, when the first shot sounded. It shouldn't have startled him, but it did. These guys were shooting at him, for chrissake. He'd never been shot at before.

They pounded down the alley toward the car. It seemed like a whole bunch of people were chasing them, shooting at them. Tray suddenly remembered how to pray.

He heard Kathryn gasp, then felt rather than saw her stumble and fall. He paused and looked down. She was sprawled on the ground a few steps behind him. "Kathryn?"

He moved back toward her instinctively. Close enough to see that the back of her head was now just a bloody mess. No way could she still be alive. Not for long, anyway.

Kneeling beside her, he spared an instant for a pang of something that might have been grief. Giving in to a sudden unshakable hunch, and risking way too much, he reached out with one hand, trying to avoid the blood, and yanked the small bag from around her neck. Kathryn had thought the bag was important and so maybe it was. He scrambled to his feet and ran again.

Suddenly, just ahead there was a low brick wall. He kept running, jumping over it. There was a house with a FOR SALE sign in front of it. Tray stopped running and dropped to his knees next to the porch. He pushed both the duffel and the small leather bag under the porch until they were completely hidden.

Jumping to his feet again, he headed down another alley. When he rounded a corner, a man with a gun stood directly in his path.

It wasn't the big bastard, Chris, but with a Magnum in his hand, how big did he have to be? "Drop it," he said. This voice was louder, a little panicked. But the gun didn't waver.

Tray glanced at the forgotten plastic toy he was still holding, shrugged, and let it fall to the ground.

"Kick it over here to me."

He did.

Still watching him, Dwight crouched to pick up the weapon. Now it was his turn to be surprised. "A fucking toy?" he said. "You're packing a toy gun?"

Tray swallowed, hoping to moisten his throat a little. "Pretty realistic though, don't you think?"

Dwight didn't seem to get the joke. "Where's the money?"

Tray tried to look stupid. The way he was feeling right then, it wasn't much of an effort. "Money? I don't know what you're talking about."

He realized that the line sounded like the dialogue from a TV cop show.

"I'm talking about the money that you just took from us."

Tray just shrugged.

The gun was still leveled at him. "You could be as dead as that bitch back there."

"Yeah, I know."

Dwight started to speak again, then instead gestured with the gun barrel. "Come on. Back to the house."

There didn't seem to be a whole lot of choice involved in the matter, so he went.

Bryan stopped at a Denny's on his way home from Ann's. He ordered a cup of coffee and a slice of apple pie. Was this supposed to be some kind of celebration? He wasn't quite sure.

And if it was, what exactly was he celebrating?

It was late, and the only other customers in the restaurant were a couple of uniformed cops taking their dinner break. They were talking baseball, arguing the merits of a certain hotshot young pitcher. The discussion was without real heat, although it was profane, in the absentminded way of two men who know one another well. Bryan half listened to their conversation, not caring a damned bit about the subject but nostalgic for something he couldn't quite define.

Over a second cup of coffee, he thought back over the evening. The sex with Ann had been good. Nothing fancy, which suited him just fine, at least for the moment. But still it had been exciting. She was obviously a woman of passion. If she had enjoyed it as much as he, which was the impression he'd had, then maybe this might become a regular kind of thing. That would be okay. Having a regular situation for this part of life made things easier.

And if he *was* celebrating something, maybe it was just the fact that his body had worked. As well as it ever had, at least.

The portable radio sitting on the table between the two cops squawked. They finished up in a hurry and left Denny's.

Bryan sighed, swiveling on the stool to watch as the patrol car raced out of the parking lot.

In a few more minutes, he finished the pie and left as well.

He still didn't go home. Instead, remembering a penciled note on the front of his telephone book, he drove to the Bluebell Motel on Ventura. The lot was only about half full of cars, most of which had local plates, but there was nothing parked in front of room 102. The room itself was dark behind the closed curtains.

Bryan parked there for a few minutes, the engine of the jeep still running. Nothing happened. And what the hell were you expecting, asshole? he asked himself impatiently.

Finally, he turned the jeep around and left the lot. To hell with it. He had more important things to do.

He went home.

The two of them sat in the shabby living room and waited for the big guy to come back. Dwight didn't say a word and Tray couldn't think of anything that might help the situation, so he kept quiet, too.

Finally, the door opened and Chris came in; the front of his clothes were bloody and he looked tired. He walked across the room silently and sat on the couch next to Dwight. "Oh, boy," he said with no particular emotion.

Dwight held out the plastic gun. "This is what he was carrying, Chris. Can you fucking believe it?"

Chris took the gun and looked at it, a small smile on his face. Then, watching Tray, he closed his hand into a fist, shattering the toy. He opened his hand and the pieces of plastic fell in a shower to the floor. "A fucking toy. You crazy, buddy, or what?"

"Maybe," Tray admitted. "But real guns, they can cause a lot of trouble."

"I'm glad you realize that."

"Oh, I do."

Chris was quiet for a moment, then he looked at Dwight. "I took care of that other little problem."

"Good. I never trusted her."

"Yeah, but you're a fucking misogynist, so your opinion doesn't count."

"I'm a what?"

"Misogynist," Tray said helpfully. "Means you hate broads." He glanced at Chris. "Prison libraries are a great place to improve your vocabulary, right?"

Chris smiled again. "You're a funny guy."

Dwight stirred. "Chris, what're we gonna do with this bastard?"

"Why, we're just going to ask him to give back our money."

"I already asked him. He won't do it."

Chris stretched his legs out and spoke almost companionably. "Oh, sure he will. We just have to persuade him in the right way, that's all."

Dwight didn't seem convinced.

Chris leaned over and patted Tray on the knee. "Where's our money, sweetheart?"

Tray took a deep breath, wondering why he had suddenly decided to play hardball. After a lifetime spent rolling over and letting things happen to him, maybe it was time, but, truthfully, this didn't seem like the best possible time in the world to get tough.

And if he was feeling so goddamned tough, why the hell was he so scared?

"I can't tell you that," he said, hating himself even as he spoke.

This Chris seemed to be a real smiler. "You will," he said with another pat.

The two words were said in the same quiet voice as before, and like before, it scared the shit out of one Tray Detaglio. Real tough guy.

He leaned back into the chair, wishing that he could just disappear.

Chris quit smiling finally and turned to Dwight. "You get your ass out there. Retrace his steps. Look for the goddamned money."

"Where should I look?"

Chris gestured impatiently. "Wherever. He stashed it someplace close by."

"Okay," Dwight replied with obvious reluctance. "I'll look."

With Dwight gone, the room got very quiet. Chris and Tray stared at one another.

* * *

Dwight carefully lifted the lid of the metal trash can and peered in, making a face at the smell. Would anybody really put all that money into the garbage? It didn't make much sense to him.

He'd been looking for over thirty minutes now, with no sign of anything to suggest where the money might be.

What would Chris say if he came back without it?

He stopped for a moment, considering his next move carefully. But before he could decide what to do or where to look next, he saw the headlights and the unmistakable shape of a squad car cruising slowly in his direction.

Shit.

He eased back into the shadows, waited until the taillights had faded, and then headed quickly for home.

23

Bryan slept badly and woke up in a rotten mood.

He put on his black swimming trunks and went outside. The day promised to be hot, smoggy, and thoroughly unpleasant.

Which suited him just fine.

He jumped into the lukewarm water and did five lengths of the pool without even thinking about it. So far away was his mind from that time and place that he wasn't even aware that he had company until Blank spoke.

"Hey, Mark Spitz."

Bryan pulled himself out of the pool and reached for the towel. "You want to race, wise guy?"

"Not in this lifetime, thank you, anyway." Blank glanced around in apparent admiration. "You've done a lot with the place since I was here before."

Bryan surveyed the freshly painted porch with disgruntlement. "Yeah." He poured himself a glass of juice from the pitcher on the poolside table. "Want some?"

"No, thanks. It might dilute the caffeine I'm running on."

They sat.

"This must be a slow day in Homicide."

Blank snorted. "There is no such thing. Not in this city. Especially in weather like this. Maybe a country cop has slow days. That's what I should be."

"Uh-huh." The juice was cold and just a little sour. "So, in that case, why are you taking time to socialize with me?"

"This isn't a social call," Blank said in a flat, cop voice.

Bryan just looked at him over the top of the glass.

"I have this stiff. One of many, of course, but this one is sort of interesting. Her name is—or was, to be more accurate, I guess—Kathryn Daily. Does that ring any bells with you?"

Suddenly the orange juice was even more sour. He set the glass down. "Damn."

"Damn? Is that all you have to say? This young woman has half her head blown away and all you can say is damn?"

"What would you like me to say?"

"Well, you might start by telling me where your good pal Detaglio is."

"I don't know."

Blank didn't look as if he bought that disclaimer completely. "You don't know?"

"You a fucking echo or something?"

"What I am is a real tired cop. Which is something you should know about, I think. I'm looking to clear this case in a hurry and then concentrate on all the other dead bodies piling up in this city. I don't want to waste a whole lot of time on Ms. Daily."

"And you figure Detaglio is your man?"

"That's what I figure."

Bryan shook his head. "I don't think that tracks."

Blank leaned back and crossed his arms. "You're kidding, right? Or did that heart attack fuck with your mind?"

"My mind is fine. I just don't make Detaglio as a killer."

Blank smirked.

"Okay, you lay it out for me. As you see it."

"Okay. I see it this way. Detaglio is an ex-con. He goes looking for an old girlfriend. Maybe wanting to rekindle the flame. Or maybe to settle a score with the broad. Whatever. He finds her—with your help, by the way—and something goes wrong. Or maybe this is what he was planning all along and it went right. Anyway, she ends up dead."

"That's all you have?"

"That's enough for me. And for the captain."

Bryan was quiet for a moment. "Well, it's not my place to tell the esteemed L.A.P.D. how to do its job, but this time you're going in the wrong direction," he finally said mildly.

"It wouldn't be the first time," Blank replied, sounding unconcerned. "But unless you can show me something to the contrary, I'm going to keep looking for your pal."

Bryan poured some more juice into his glass. "The reason he was looking for her was that when he got sent up five years ago, she was pregnant. Tray only wanted to find out about his kid."

"And did he?"

Bryan was already sorry he'd said anything. "Yeah. Well, it turns out she had an abortion."

"Uh-huh." Now Blank was smug. "That must have upset him pretty bad."

Bryan frowned. "I wasn't trying to feed you a motive here, for God's sake." There was no way now that he could mention the "easy" money the two of them had gone after. That would just sew the case up even tighter as far as Blank was concerned.

Blank just smiled. "I'll see you around," he said, standing.

"That's very possible," Bryan replied.

And just what the hell was *that* supposed to mean? Bryan wondered about his own words as he watched Blank leave.

Bryan finished the glass of juice before going back into the house. He rinsed the glass carefully, thinking as he did so, then picked up the phone and dialed Ann's number.

She answered on the second ring.

"Something's come up," Bryan said. "I won't be able to make lunch after all."

"Aha," she said. "I knew it. Just like my mother always warned. You don't respect me this morning."

He laughed a little. "That's not it. Something really has come up. Business." He wondered if she would ask what possible kind of business an ex-cop might have to concern himself about, but she didn't say anything. "I'll call you," he said at last.

"Well, if you don't, I'll call you. I'm quite shameless."

"Good. I like my women shameless." He hung up, his mood slightly improved.

After a fast shower and shave, he dressed, choosing his clothes with care. Beige linen suit, yellow pin-stripe shirt, baby-blue silk tie with matching handkerchief. Very classy. Like a well-dressed cop. Or, maybe, a high-priced private investigator.

Of course, looking the part was one thing. Knowing what the hell to do next was something else altogether. Although since this was Los Angeles, maybe just looking the part would be enough.

He strapped on a small gun, the first time he'd been armed since the day he'd turned in his official piece. Then, just in case and with a slight grimace, he tucked the honorary shield into his pocket. What the hell. It might come in handy and most people didn't look that closely at what was flashed in front of them, anyway.

Finally, just like a real L.A. private eye, he donned his shades and went out to confront the city.

The parking lot of the Bluebell Motel was almost empty; it was undoubtedly a little too early for the lunch crowd. Bryan went into the office, which smelled strongly of something he was glad he couldn't quite identify. The being behind the counter looked more like a child molester on the skids than a desk clerk. He didn't look up from the racing form.

Bryan leaned against the counter chummily. "Room 102," he said.

"Occupied."

"Anybody in there now?"

"How the fuck do I know? Maybe they went out for brunch."

Bryan lowered the sunglasses and looked at him. "You must be a graduate of the Hotel Management Institute, am I right?"

The man ignored that.

Bryan left the office and walked over to the room, which was still dark and shut up tight. He knocked, just in case, but there wasn't any answer.

He crouched to examine the lock on the flimsy plywood door. It was a joke. Even a man who'd had a heart attack, for chrissake, could get it open without breathing hard. There was something to be said, he decided, for operating outside the confines of officialdom. He didn't have to worry about screwing up the evidence or violating anybody's fucking rights. This was crime-buster's heaven.

The room was too cold because the noisy air conditioner was running at full blast. Bryan walked over and punched it off, then shoved the pea-green curtains aside so that the daylight could come into the room.

That might have been a mistake, he decided, surveying the dismal room. The bed was unmade, its gray sheets in a sweaty jumble, and the floor was littered with clothes. Several empty paper bags were also scattered around.

He walked into the bathroom, which was no bigger than most closets and which almost dripped with dampness. Bryan picked up a soggy towel and draped it over the sink.

When he walked back into the other room, something colorful mixed up in the dirty sheets caught his eye. He went over and picked it up. Bryan examined the empty package, reading the description of what it had contained. He shook his head, wondering what the hell Detaglio thought he was up to. Toy guns? Easy money? And corpses beginning to litter the landscape. This was starting to feel like home.

No doubt the next body the cops turned up would belong to an ex-con named Detaglio. And how hard would they pursue that case? He knew too damned well how a cop would view it. Just the death of one more creep, saving them the trouble of trying to get him sent back up.

There was one thing he thought they should remember: Detaglio hadn't blown the woman away with the *Magnum Avenger!*

He dropped the empty package back on the bed and walked out of the room, carefully closing the door as he went.

Roger Blank was having a bad day, even for a cop.

It was a shift that had started off with Kathryn Daily's body and was now ending (theoretically, anyway, although there was no way he'd be leaving on time) with two more stiffs.

He wanted to think that it was just a coincidence, finding first the body of a woman who had recently shacked up with Michael Stanzione, and then, a few hours later, being called to this abandoned icehouse. Inside the icehouse a couple of wandering kids had found the remains of two petty hoods, both of whom had been in the employ of that same Michael Stanzione. Blank really wanted to think that it was just an act of capricious fate, but the infamous cop cynicism was coming out again. This was no coincidence.

One of the deceased had a crushed skull and the other had been shot once through the back of the head.

Blank stared down at the bodies for a thoughtful moment—too much death made a man philosophical—then he lit a cigar and looked at his sergeant. "I don't know what the fuck is going on here," he said pleasantly. "But I know that Detaglio is up to his balls in the whole mess. I want that man. Put the word out that I want him bad."

Sergeant Montrose nodded.

Blank walked outside to where the air was at least a little cleaner-smelling. He saw a pay phone on the corner and strolled down to it.

There was no answer at Bryan Murphy's.

So where the hell was that bastard?

Bryan parked just outside the gate of Stanzione's house and sat there. This was probably not a smart move, but he was here now, so what the hell. He certainly didn't have any place else to go looking.

The place looked very quiet. Maybe he'd guessed wrong and Stanzione wasn't the key here. But Bryan still figured that the damned "easy money" had belonged to him. It made sense.

Finally, he climbed down from the jeep and approached the gate. There was a man standing on the other side of the fence and he didn't look especially friendly. Nevertheless, Bryan smiled. "I'd like to see your boss, please."

"He doesn't want to see anybody."

"This is important."

"So tell me. I'll pass the word along."

But Bryan shook his head. "No, I'd rather not do that."

The man shrugged. "So fuck off then. Unless you've got a warrant."

Bryan held back a smile; he wouldn't even have to flash the fake shield. He looked at the guard for a moment. This jerk looked more like a surfer than a hood: flowing blond hair, a great tan, purple muscle shirt. Crime in California was certainly more colorful than in New York. More laid-back.

He leaned against the fence. "Maybe you ought to check this out with him. He might be upset later to find out that I was here to talk about some valuable property of his that recently turned up missing and I couldn't get through you."

Two blue eyes surveyed him briefly. Then the beachboy walked back to a car that was sitting up on the drive and got on the phone. It was a fast conversation.

The gate slid open silently and Bryan stepped through. Efficiently, the young man frisked him, finding and removing the gun. "I'll want that back when I leave," Bryan said.

There was no response. With a gesture for Bryan to follow, the young man started up the drive toward the house. It was a short hike. At the porch, Bryan was turned over to a man dressed like an English butler.

He was, in fact, an English butler. Bryan was impressed.

They walked through the house, out to the pool. Stanzione was sitting there working on a martini and shuffling some papers. "You have a name, do you?" Stanzione asked. He was wearing a pair of tight white swimming trunks.

"Bryan Murphy."

"Cop?"

There wasn't any percentage in trying the bluff here. "Not anymore. Used to be, back East."

"Yeah, you sound like a home boy. I'm from Brooklyn."

He sounded like it. "We should get together some time and talk about home," Bryan said.

"Uh-huh." Stanzione didn't sound real interested. "So?" he said impatiently.

Bryan shrugged. "You lost something recently."

"Did I?"

"Maybe you want to play games, Stanzione," Bryan said flatly. "I don't have the time. Can we just cut through the crap here?"

Stanzione nodded and sipped his drink.

"There was some money that used to belong to you. Now somebody else has it. How am I doing so far?"

A grunt was the only answer. Stanzione picked up the papers again, then he said, "If you know the bitch, you ought to tell her that she's in trouble. Serious trouble." He finished the drink. "In fact, tell her that this kind of trouble is always fatal. Like AIDS."

"Kathryn, you mean, right?"

"Of course I mean Kathryn."

"Well, her trouble is fatal, all right. Maybe you haven't heard, but her body turned up a while ago. Somebody got to her."

Either Stanzione was in the wrong business—maybe he belonged in the movies—or else he hadn't killed the woman. Surprise flickered across his face. Then he picked up the glass, realized that it was empty, and frowned. "That's too bad. I was looking forward to talking to her again."

This *was* too bad. Stanzione pretty much had to be eliminated as a suspect. Which didn't help Tray any. "You don't have any idea who might have done it?"

"Unfortunately, no. But when I find him, I'll probably find my money, too."

"That's possible, I guess."

Stanzione looked up at him curiously. "Murphy, what the hell is your interest in this?"

He smiled faintly. "I'm not sure. Maybe I just got tired of sightseeing. Once a cop, you know."

Stanzione nodded. "Speaking as a fellow New Yorker," he said, "maybe you should find a hobby. Something safer than this. It isn't a good idea to stick your nose into other people's business."

"I'll give that some thought," Bryan said.

The English butler returned to show him out.

Stanzione sat still for a few moments after the nosy ex–New Yorker had left. Then he leaned across the table and picked up the phone. As usual, it was answered immediately. "Find out what you can about a jerk named Bryan Murphy. Supposed to be a former dick from back home." He listened for a moment, then sighed with mild annoyance. "How the hell do I know what the connection is? That's what I want you to find out, asshole."

He hung up with a crash, then pushed the button to summon the damned limey so that he could make another martini.

24

Chris sat up finally. He had been stretched out on the couch, staring at the ceiling, for over an hour. The small room, with all of its windows closed and curtained and the door shut as well, was stifling.

Dwight was still sitting in the chair, looking aimlessly through one of his damned *National Geographic*s. There wasn't a sound anywhere in the house.

Chris picked up the phone, thought for a moment, then dialed carefully.

Talese himself answered the phone.

"Moore here," Chris said. "How you coming on that job for me?"

"I told you how long it would take," Talese replied.

Chris sighed and rubbed a hand across his face. "Look, buddy, things are getting very tight on my end. Extremely tight. Couldn't you push it a little? Like, what's the absolute soonest I could pick up the merchandise?"

Talese was quiet for a moment. "Eight tomorrow morning. But it'll cost you an extra five."

"No problem. We'll be there at eight."

He hung up. No problem getting five hundred more dollars. Of course not. But if that creep in the closet didn't crack soon, things were going to get nasty.

Chris stood, feeling the sweat roll down the length of his body. "You want me to go get some burgers?" he asked.

Dwight didn't look at him. "Why not pizza?" he said. "Pizza sounds better."

"Fine. Whatever. I'll go get some."

Suddenly, Dwight slapped the magazine closed and turned to look at him. "What're we supposed to do about this fuck-up, Chris?"

"I don't know," Chris said wearily.

Dwight swiped impatiently at a fly buzzing near his head. "Shit, man, we're running out of time here."

Chris felt his smoldering anger blaze abruptly. "Go to hell, why don't you? I know we're running out of time. What the fuck am I supposed to do about it?"

Dwight looked startled. "What're you mad at me for?"

Chris didn't like to lose his temper. Take a deep breath, he told himself. Calm down, damnit. Don't blame Dwight for this. He made the effort to speak quietly. "I'm not mad. I just don't know what we should do. I just don't know. But how about this? How about if I get any ideas, I tell you about them right away? Okay?"

Dwight frowned and gnawed a hangnail. "Maybe we should just split. Forget the money and worry about saving our asses."

Chris wiped sweat from his face. "Maybe. We'll talk about it all later." He was more tired than he could ever remember being in his life. "I'm going for the pizza."

Dwight nodded and opened the magazine again.

Blank pulled to a stop next to the empty restaurant and got out of the unmarked sedan. He was getting pretty tired of corpses.

The uniformed officer came toward him. She was carrying her hat in her hand but put it on as she approached. "This way, sir," she said. "In the trash bin."

Good a place as any. He shrugged and followed her.

A second uniform was standing on a box peering down into the bin. He jumped to the ground. "Helluva thing," he said with no purpose.

Blank wondered if maybe he should be feeling upset about the lack of human dignity in the way this man's body had been disposed of. But all he could feel at the moment was tired. He stepped up onto the box and looked down.

The man inside was wearing a brown suit, the front of which was covered with dried black blood.

As Blank stepped down, a lab van pulled into the alley. Now he would just have to wait while they did their thing. Maybe he would know who the stiff was.

All he had to do was try to care.

Chris walked away from the house quickly. When he was safely around the corner, he stopped and took several deep breaths. God, he felt like a drowning man. A drowning man going down for the fucking third time.

What the hell was he going to do?

A roller skater whirled past. Chris watched her go, envying the girl her freedom. Had he ever been that free? Then, shrugging off the thought, he started walking again. A large pepperoni pizza. Double cheese. Maybe some onion. That was what he had to concentrate on now.

Dwight finally got an idea.

He remembered something that had happened in prison and decided that the same thing might work here. After a moment, he got up from the chair and went into the bedroom. When he pulled open the closet door, Detaglio, bound hand and foot, almost fell out. Dwight crouched down next to him. He took the cigarette lighter from his pocket, flicking it on and off several times.

Detaglio, his face already bruised and swollen from an earlier beating, watched in silence.

"Where'd you hide the money?" Dwight said, trying to sound cool about it, like Chris would have.

Detaglio was staring at the flickering flame. He moistened his lips with the tip of his tongue. "Ah, Dwight, we don't have to get nasty here, do we?"

"That's up to you."

Detaglio didn't say anything.

"I saw a con do this inside," Dwight explained conversationally. "He wanted another guy to turn over the dope concession on the block."

"Did it work?"

"Oh, yeah." Dwight moved around behind him and twisted Tray's arm until his hand was palm-up. "It worked real good." He flicked the lighter on again and moved the flame close to the palm.

Detaglio made a sound, an unintelligible grunt, then began to swear under his breath. It sounded, to Dwight, like what some of those religious freakies used to do inside. Their—what was the word?—mantras, they would chant over and over. Except that this guy was saying dirty words.

Dwight pulled the lighter away. "You see why this works so good?" he said. The reddened skin was already beginning to blister.

"Uh-huh," Detaglio said, sounding like he was close to tears.

"You want to tell me where the money is now?"

"I want to . . ." But then Detaglio shook his head. "I can't."

Dwight shrugged. This time he kept the flame to the hand even longer, until the smell of burning flesh was starting to fill the room. Detaglio's whole body writhed and shook, but he just kept up that same mantra of profanity, the words coming in an increasingly hoarse whisper.

"I wish I didn't have to do this," Dwight said, pausing for a moment. It was the truth. The burned hand was making him a little sick.

But then Detaglio went all limp and stopped talking.

Dwight checked him, saw that he was still breathing, and then pushed him back into the closet.

He was sitting in a rear booth, drinking a beer and waiting for the pizza to be ready, when a voice shattered his thoughts.

"Moore, that you? Chris Moore, you bastard!"

He looked up, thought quickly, and then recognized the face. "Jimmy Lee. How the hell are you?"

"Fine, fine." The lanky redhead dropped into the booth. "God, what's it been, like eight years?"

"More like ten," Chris said.

"Yeah, yeah. How're you doing? Heard you took another fall."

"Yeah, but I'm out now."

"Me, too. You're looking good." Jimmy Lee leaned across the table and spoke in a low voice. "This might be like fate, us running into each other this way."

"How's that?"

"I'm getting a deal together. We could use one more good man. You interested?"

Chris lifted the bottle and took a swallow of beer. "What kind of deal are you talking?"

Jimmy Lee grinned wolfishly. "Well, you understand that I can't be going into specifics here and now. But if you're interested . . ." He took a paper napkin from the holder and a pencil from his pocket. "Come on over," he said, scrawling an address. "About ten tonight. I think it'll be worth your while."

Chris folded the napkin and put it into his pocket. "I'll think about it."

The counterman called his number.

"I gotta go." He shook hands with Jimmy Lee and went to get a large pepperoni with double cheese.

The pain from his burned hand brought him around in only a few minutes. Nothing had ever hurt so much. Tray swallowed down the bile rising in his throat and tried breathing through his mouth for a while. The air inside the small closet was thick with the smell of his own body. Every few minutes, he would try to move a foot or an arm or maybe just his head, hoping to keep at least a little blood circulating. The ropes binding him were tight enough to make his nerve endings tingle. His hand hurt so much that he wanted to cry, but he didn't have the energy.

He could hear the muffled sounds of conversation beyond the door occasionally, but it was impossible to make out any of the words. Which was probably all for the best, considering. The last thing he needed right now was to know for sure exactly what the two creeps out there had in store for him.

He thought that he could smell pizza. His stomach growled. Logic told him that he shouldn't be hungry—fear and pain, he would have thought, should wipe out all mundane things like hunger. But, God, it smelled so good. Pepperoni, he thought.

Tray had, hours ago, made a conscious decision not to think about Kathryn and what had happened to her. It was too bad, but she was dead and he was still alive. At least for the moment. Surviving had to be his first priority. Surviving *with* the money, he amended.

If that sounded selfish, fuck it.

So he took Kathryn's advice and thought about the money instead of death. That cash was his now, damnit, and there was no way he would turn it over to those bastards. They didn't deserve it.

But, even more important, he had decided that this was where Tray Detaglio made his stand.

Without warning, the closet door was yanked open again and he was hauled out unceremoniously. This time, Chris dumped him on the floor. "You want some pizza?" he asked.

"Uh, yeah, guess so." He blinked at the sudden light and then saw two slices of pizza—pepperoni, by God—on a plate in front of him. "Need my hands."

Without speaking, Chris started to untie him. When he saw the burned palm, he stopped. "What the fuck happened to you?"

Now that he could see the blistered, seared flesh, the pain was even worse. "Dwight's not subtle," he mumbled.

Chris sat next to him.

Tray tried gingerly to get some of his blood flowing again. When he could manipulate the fingers of his good hand, he picked up one slice of the cold pizza.

"Lemme ask you something, Detaglio," Chris said.

"Sure, Chris, what?" he said, deciding to try friendliness. It had worked for him in jail. By making himself everybody's buddy and nobody's friend, he had kept himself out of a lot of trouble. "Great pizza, by the way."

Chris didn't smile; maybe he wasn't looking for a buddy. "You don't really want to die over this money, do you?"

Tray shook his head and wiped his mouth on the sleeve of the black sweatshirt. "No," he said. "I sure don't want to die for it." He took another bite and chewed thoughtfully, swallowing before speaking again. "But something inside won't let me give it up. I really need to have that money."

Chris seemed more depressed than mad. Which was good, Tray figured. "We need the money, too."

"I can understand that."

"And, believe me, we've got absolutely nothing at all to lose by wasting you."

"I guess that's true."

Chris shook his head. "Jesus H. Christ, man. Are you really such a cold bastard? Are you that tough?"

Tray started on the second slice of pizza. "Not that tough. My hand hurts like hell. But I won't back down. I can't. Hey, Chris, I know it's crazy. Shit, I'm a man who'll walk a mile to stay out of trouble, usually. I can't explain this, even to myself."

"You've done time, right?"

"Oh, yeah, we're all just ex-cons together here." He finished the slice and wiped his hand on his jeans, eyeing Chris. "You probably didn't have many problems in the joint."

"Not many."

Tray nodded. "So what happens next? If you don't mind me asking."

"I don't mind. It's your ass. But I don't know what to tell you. Something has to give here, sooner or later. And since we don't have a whole lot of time left, it pretty much has to be sooner."

"Yeah, I can dig that."

Chris started to tie him up again.

"Chris, can you understand at all what I'm doing here?"

The other man stared him in the face, then nodded. "But it's stupid. It's just so stupid."

"Yeah, you're probably right about that."

"You said that hand hurts, huh?"

"Sure as hell does."

Chris yanked his head back by the hair and stared at him. "It's gonna get worse, buddy. A lot worse."

"Yeah, I guess so."

"Count on it."

When the ropes were tight again, Chris shoved him back into the closet and closed the door.

* * *

Dwight stepped on the pizza box to flatten it, then shoved it and the wadded napkins into the trash can under the sink. "Well?" he asked.

"Well what?"

"Did you ask him again?"

"Dwight, I don't think that bastard is going to tell us where our money is."

Dwight rinsed the plates. "Maybe if we hurt him some more. Use the lighter on his damned balls, like inside."

"Maybe. But I wouldn't even count on that. If you want the truth, I think maybe Detaglio is a little crazy."

Dwight sighed and joined him at the table. "Well, then?" Chris shrugged.

"Think we should just split? Forget the damned money?"

"Probably." He slammed a fist down onto the table. "It just makes me so fucking mad."

"Me, too. But, Chris, if we hang around here too long, something bad is going to happen."

Chris didn't know why he laughed right then. Not because anything was funny, for sure. But he did laugh. "Sweetheart, in case you haven't noticed, bad things are already happening. The whole fucking world is falling in on us."

Dwight was quiet for a long time, staring at the mottled Formica on the tabletop. "I can't go back inside, Chris," he finally said in a whisper. "I can't."

"I know."

Dwight reached across the table suddenly and grabbed his hand. "I really cannot go back."

"You won't be going back. I swear I won't let that happen, okay? Give it a rest now, willya?" Chris yanked his hand free. "Okay. We'll catch a little sleep, then try once more with him."

"And then?"

"Then we pick up the goods from Talese and split."

"Without the money?"

"If we have to. We might have to persuade Talese to give us the goods if we don't have the bread." Persuade, yeah. He thought about the neat house and the old lady watching soaps on TV. He sighed.

Dwight ran a tired hand through his hair. "And start all over again."

"What else? What fucking else?"

After a moment, Chris got to his feet and walked outside. He sat on the top step. God, what an unbelievable fuck-up.

He suddenly remembered the napkin in his pocket, the one with the address Jimmy Lee had given him. A big score. Right. He stared at the address. Why the hell couldn't this have come along sooner? But now it was too late.

He took out his cigarette lighter and torched the napkin. He dropped it to the ground and watched it burn.

25

It had been a very long day. This was the kind of long, pointless, frustrating day that he hadn't had since leaving the job. Not even two cups of real coffee had helped much. He waved for a refill from the counterman. Maybe a third cup would be the charm, would give him the jolt of energy he needed to keep going.

As he stirred Coffeemate into the cup, a couple of important questions bounced around inside his head: Why the hell should he keep going? Keep going where? And for what reason?

He didn't have a good answer. Not even a bad answer, if the truth were told.

It wasn't much of a surprise to look up as the door opened and see Roger Blank walk into the diner. This place was near the cop shop and Bryan's jeep was parked out front, announcing his presence.

Blank planted himself on the next stool and ordered coffee. The juice of life for a cop. Then he turned to look at Bryan. "So?" he said.

Bryan was contemplating the pie slowly turning in the plastic display case. It looked like cardboard. "Hmm?"

"I was just wondering what the hotshot New York cop had managed to uncover."

"Ex-hotshot," Bryan corrected. "And what makes you think that I've been trying to uncover anything, anyway?"

Blank smiled tightly. "I've known you for a long time, Murph."

Bryan shrugged. "Well, like you told me before, I'm out of my element here. I haven't found out anything. And I haven't found Tray Detaglio, if that's what you're thinking."

"Too bad. I was hoping maybe you'd get lucky."

"Which means, I guess, that you haven't found him, either."

"Not yet."

"But you're still convinced he's your man?"

Blank waved a hand expansively. "Hey, pal, all I need is for somebody to show me different. If you've got some evidence proving that the guy is Snow White, just lay it out. My mind is open."

Bryan decided against the pie. "How about that the broad was involved until recently with Michael Stanzione?"

"I looked at that, of course."

"And?"

"And nothing. It still comes up Detaglio, far as I can see. This is maybe the one crime that Stanzione is clean on, but that's the way it goes. And since you also talked to him, you must know that, too."

Bryan smiled sheepishly.

Blank reached for and lit a Winston. "Actually, I had another reason for coming in here to talk to you. Some news I thought you'd like to know."

"Good or bad?"

Which was a stupid question. When, in the whole, fucked-up history of mankind had a *cop*, for chrissake, ever brought good news?

Blank shrugged. "Well, good or bad sort of depends. If you're a dragging-ass cop with too many cases to clear, it's good, because it sort of simplifies things. If you're a close pal of Tray Detaglio, on the other hand, it's probably not so good."

"Well, what the fuck is it?"

"I got another stiff dumped on me. And a lot of people are upset about this one because the deceased was a parole officer. Guy named Emory Whitson. Mean anything to you?"

"Not a damned thing. And I don't know why you think it should. Tray isn't on parole; he did his time."

"Uh-huh. Well, despite that fact, the P.O. is dead. And Ballistics now says that the gun used to off him was the same one used to kill the Daily broad."

Bryan slowly massaged his right temple. "So, what is it? Now you've got this guy running all over the freaking city killing people? Is that what you think?"

Blank finished his coffee and stood. "Hell, what do I know? I'm just a dumb cop."

The house in Topanga was quiet and dark when Bryan walked in.

He hit some lights and turned on the TV, then sat on the couch and thought back over the last few days. It wasn't until then that he remembered something he should have remembered a whole lot earlier.

Goddamn, he thought, I better get my act together or else drop out of the frigging show.

Taking out his wallet, he searched through its contents quickly until he found the folded paper with some numbers scribbled on it. He studied it. This was the license number of the car that had picked Kathryn up at the Denny's the night he'd found her.

Bryan was willing to bet the mortgage on his house that the man who'd been driving the car that night was involved in all of this somehow. Made sense. After a moment, he reached for the telephone book, looked up a number, and then dialed it quickly.

Bryan Murphy had been a cop for a long time. Consequently, this was not exactly his first occasion of sin. A little falsehood here and there made life easier, and, anyway, fibbing was only venial, not mortal, if he was correctly remembering the Catholicism his mother tried to sneak by the old man's evangelism.

During the phone conversation with a somewhat sullen female records clerk, he didn't exactly claim to be Lieutenant Roger Blank. Not in so many words. Somehow, though, that was the impression the clerk seemed to have. His sin, if there was one, lay in not revealing the truth.

For a change, no computers were down, and so in only moments Bryan had a name, Dwight St. John, and an address in Venice.

Not forgetting to thank the helpful clerk, he hung up carefully. Then he grinned broadly.

Goddamn, he thought, I love this kind of thing.

He got back into his jeep and headed toward the beach.

Why the hell would Detaglio kill a California parole officer named Emory Whitson?

It didn't make any sense, and maybe he was just a stubborn mick, but damnit, Bryan Murphy liked things to make sense. What was it that pointy-eared guy used to say on the TV space show? *It isn't logical.* That's what was missing here: some goddamned logic.

He wasn't familiar with Venice, so it took a while to find the right house. When he did spot the number he was looking for, he didn't stop but cruised right on by. He parked down the block and turned off the engine. Now what?

Well, he could find a phone and call Blank.

But what, really, did he have to offer the cop? Nothing that Roger would take very seriously. So what he had to do was hang in there until he found something *serious*. That old smoking-gun shit.

After another moment, he got out of the jeep and walked back toward the small bungalow. Although the curtains were all closed—strange on such a warm night—there was enough light so that he could see some shadows moving around inside. One of the shadows looked big enough to be the man he remembered from the parking lot.

After just watching the shadows for a time, Bryan worked his way around to the back of the house. There was a Rabbit parked in the drive. He went closer and peered in. It was loaded with duffels and boxes. It looked like somebody was planning on taking a trip.

Suddenly, the back door of the house opened.

Bryan ducked behind the car and crouched there.

"That bastard is crazy," a voice said.

"Yeah, well. We're out of here at dawn, so he won't be a problem very much longer."

"And if he doesn't crack? What do we do then, Chris?"

It was a long moment before there was an answer to the question. "We just manage, I guess," Chris said, sounding worn out. "Like always."

Bryan slid his gun out of its holster and hefted it thoughtfully. Maybe this was the time to make a move. Catch them unawares.

But before he could make up his mind, he heard a sound that was unmistakable. Somebody just beyond the flimsy wooden fence was loading a gun.

He quietly replaced his own weapon.

Not yet.

"He has about one more chance," Chris said.

"Shit" was the only reply.

The door banged shut as they went back inside.

Bryan settled onto the ground and let his breath out in a long sigh. Well, Detaglio was still alive, at least. He assumed, anyway, that the "crazy bastard" they had been talking about was Tray. The description certainly fit.

Now was definitely the time to call in some reinforcements.

But . . .

Bryan told himself that he was being a total ass about this. A quick check of his pulse rate reassured him that everything was beating away as it should. Which still didn't mean that he should try any stupid hero stunts.

But he didn't think that was it. At least, he didn't *think* he thought that was it.

It was simple. The worry was that by calling in a bunch of gung-ho cops and pitting them against the two creeps inside, he might be unleashing something deadly. What good would it be to break the damned case and get Tray killed in the process? All right, the guy was an idiot, but stupidity was hardly a capital crime.

Bryan decided to just stay put for the moment and watch. See what happened. Play it by ear.

Just like the good old days.

26

Chris stopped peering through the window and let the shade fall back into place.

Dwight had fallen asleep in the chair. He dozed restlessly, muttering softly and shifting on the cushions. Probably he'd wake himself up in a panic when the dreams got bad enough.

But at least he could sleep.

Chris tried not to be bitter. He stared at Dwight, hoping that the intensity of his gaze would wake the other man, but no such luck. He stopped his pacing, stood next to the chair. There was a fine sheen of sweat on Dwight's face and Chris reached out an impatient hand to wipe it away.

Dwight stirred a little under the touch, mumbling something that made no sense. But he still didn't wake up. Once Chris had read something about sleep being an escape, especially for people suffering from depression. And this was sure as hell a depressing situation.

Chris still wasn't quite sure how things had descended quite so far into the madness they were now caught up in. All he had wanted to do, from the start, was get enough money to take them away from here, to take them someplace where they could finally be safe. This city seemed like such a dangerous place.

Well, it sure as hell had turned dangerous over the last few days, hadn't it?

Just look at the mess they were in. The deal that had seemed so good had turned to shit in their hands, and Chris didn't see any way to turn it around.

Turning sharply, he left Dwight sleeping in the chair and went into the bedroom. He yanked open the closet door. "Detaglio?"

The bound man peered up at him. "Hunh?" he said thickly, sounding as if he'd just awakened.

Hell, Chris thought, am I the only son of a bitch who isn't sleeping tonight?

He crouched next to Detaglio and, without warning, slapped him across the face. "Wake up all the way. We need to talk."

"I'm awake, I'm awake."

"Good." He took Detaglio's chin firmly between his thumb and forefinger. "Time is running out, sweetheart. I need to know where the fucking money is and I need to know now." He squeezed. The flesh beneath his fingers turned white and Detaglio grimaced. "You understand that I'm a fucking desperate man here? No more fucking games with a Bic. No more pizza." He released his hold and slapped Detaglio again. "You understand that we're going to kill you?"

"I unnerstan'," Detaglio said. A faint trickle of blood had begun from Detaglio's lip. He licked at it slowly. "What if I give it to you? Won't you kill me anyway now?"

"Not necessarily. Not if I'm in a good mood." This slap was harder. "You've been inside, right? You know the goddamned rules, don't you?"

"I know 'em."

"Good." Chris pulled a pocketknife from his jeans and snapped it open. He tested the edge with his thumb. "Man, I just want you to understand something. This is not my kind of thing. Not usually. But I'm like a trapped rat now. So I've got no choice." He drew the knife along Detaglio's chest, cutting through the sweatshirt with no trouble at all and leaving a vivid red line in the skin. "See? I mean business. You ready to talk now?"

The dope had to be hurting: His burned hand was swollen and red. His face was bruised. And now his chest was bleeding. But he didn't say anything. Maybe the pain had made him crazy. He almost seemed to smile.

The knife moved again. This time the line it left was a little deeper and there was more blood.

Detaglio bit his lower lip.

Chris leaned back on his heels and stared at him. "Maybe we can make a deal," he said finally. "Split the fucking bread. That way everybody comes up a winner."

Detaglio looked at him with his one good eye. He spit some blood, grimacing at the pain the action cost. "I don't think I could trust you," he said.

"What choice do you have?"

He shrugged. "Maybe none. But I'm sort of stuck with it now."

Chris felt like weeping in frustration. "What about the broad's share? How the fuck greedy are you, anyway?"

This time Detaglio actually made a sound that must have been a chuckle. "Yeah. Well, Kathryn wins again. I don't know what the hell she did with it. How about that? All that money out there and we can't get to it. She always did have a fucking sense of humor."

"I'm not laughing."

Detaglio blinked at him. He spit more blood onto the floor. "Neither am I, Chris," he said. "Neither am I."

Chris just shook his head.

Bryan moved closer to the window. The shade was just slightly askew and he could see one narrow slice of the room inside. Someone was sitting in a chair, apparently asleep. It wasn't the big guy from the parking lot, so he must be in the other room. It looked like now or never. This was going to be pretty much of a one-shot deal; there wouldn't be a second chance.

He tried the knob and was mildly surprised to discover that it wasn't locked. Everybody got careless once in a while. He just had to be damned sure that this wasn't his time to make a dumb mistake. Very slowly, he pushed the door open and slipped into the house.

The gun was in his hand.

First thing to do was to even up the odds just a little. The sleeping man didn't stir as Bryan approached. When he was right behind the chair, Bryan raised the gun and brought the butt down against the side of the man's head.

He grunted and fell off the chair.

"Dwight?" The voice came from the other room. "You okay?"

Bryan leveled the gun at the doorway and waited.

"Dwight?" The man who had to be Chris appeared. When he saw Bryan, he froze. "What the fuck is going on? Who are—" His gaze feel onto the sprawled figure. "What'd you do to Dwight?"

"Nothing fatal."

"You better hope." The words were soft and yet Bryan sensed the danger coming from the man, who was staring at him.

He was suddenly very glad that he hadn't killed Dwight. "He'll be okay."

Chris glanced across to the couch, where a gun waited.

"Oh, come on," Bryan said. "There wouldn't be a chance in hell."

"Yeah, I know. Who the fuck are you, anyway?"

"Just an interested bystander."

"Which means what?"

"Which means I want Detaglio."

Chris smiled agreeably. "Sure thing. Just as soon as we're done with him."

Bryan returned the smile. "You're done now."

"Not quite. The creep is trying to screw us over."

"Tough. Life is like that sometimes."

Chris was watching Dwight again. He gestured in that direction. "Can I check him?"

Bryan took two steps back, the gun still centered on Chris. "Okay. But just don't get smart."

Surprisingly, Chris smiled again. As he knelt, he gave a hollow laugh. "I don't think there's much danger of that," he said. "Just look at the record." His fingers poked at the skull beneath the curls. "Poor Dwight's gonna have a hell of a headache." He hauled the limp form back up onto the chair.

"Just dump him," Bryan said impatiently.

Chris did, then he straightened and stared at Bryan. "You look like a cop to me. And I'm a fucking expert on cops."

"Not anymore. Once upon a time, yeah, but not anymore."

"So what's your interest, anyway?"

"Mostly just curiosity. And Detaglio is sort of a friend."

Chris shook his head.

Dwight began to stir, moaning a little and reaching toward his head.

Absently, Chris patted his shoulder.

"Where's Tray?" Bryan said.

A gesture toward the bedroom. "He's in there. But he can't exactly walk in here right at the moment."

"You didn't do any permanent damage, I hope?"

"Unfortunately, no. Not yet, anyway."

Dwight finally opened his eyes and struggled to sit up. "What the fuck happened?"

"S'okay. We got some company, is all."

Dwight glared at Bryan. "Bastard."

"Mind your manners," Bryan said. Then he looked at Chris. "Get him out here. Now."

Chris nodded. "We'll play it your way for the moment."

"See, you're getting smarter already."

"Right."

As Chris turned to go back into the bedroom, the first shot crashed through the door. Somebody outside was using a sawed-off shotgun, which meant that he wasn't too particular about what or who he hit.

As another shot exploded through the ravaged doorway, all three men hit the floor. "What the fuck," Chris said, starting to crawl toward the couch, where his gun was.

Bryan flattened himself against the floor, wondering why the hell he was suddenly a target. He crawled to the front window and peered carefully over the sill. What he saw didn't exactly reassure him. He dropped again. "Has to be Stanzione's goons," he said.

"Shit."

Dwight grabbed a pillow and heaved it across the room. "Damnit, we should have been long gone by this time. We should have been in fucking Mexico."

Nobody said anything and then a third blast rocked the room.

"Why don't they just fucking rush us and get it over with?" Chris complained.

"Men like Stanzione don't just kill you," Bryan said. "They like to make a point at the same time. The point is that you don't rip off men like Stanzione. They get mad."

Chris finally got his hands on the damned Magnum. He crawled on his hands and knees to the window and stuck his hand over the sill, firing at random out into the night. He glanced around. "I could use some fucking help here, if nobody minds."

Dwight reached under the couch and pulled out another gun, then joined Chris at the window. Bryan just shook his head and started for the bedroom.

Before he reached the doorway, though, something new crashed through what was left of the door. There was a small *pop* and a flash, and then he saw flames. Bryan moved more quickly and scooted into the bedroom.

A bound, bloodied figure lay in the middle of the room. Bryan knelt beside him. The smell of smoke was getting stronger and he went to work quickly on the ropes. "Can you move?" he asked.

Tray looked up at him. "If the other choice is dying, I can," he said in a hoarse voice.

Bryan smiled fleetingly. "I like your style."

He got the last of the ropes undone and helped Tray to the window. "Wait," he said. He stuck his head up a little and scanned the horizon.

Tray tapped him on the arm. "There," he said, pointing to a crouched figure by the fence.

"Okay. You want to play bait?"

"Oh, sure." Tray started to move gingerly, then paused. "How good are you with a gun?" he asked.

"Nobody's killed me yet," Bryan replied. "Move."

Tray grunted softly as he worked his way over the sill and dropped to the ground outside. As he landed, the figure by the fence stood and lifted a rifle.

Bryan fired twice, holding his breath—it had been a long time since he'd been on the police range.

After one painfully long moment, the man toppled over.

"Got the bastard," Bryan heard Tray whisper.

He shifted the gun to his other hand and hauled himself out of the window. Before they could move away, Chris and Dwight dove out, too.

Chris righted himself quickest and before either Bryan or Tray could react, he drove his powerful fist into Bryan's stomach.

Bryan dropped both the gun and the grip he had on Tray's arm and fell to his knees, retching. He couldn't do anything but watch as Chris and Dwight dragged Tray to the Rabbit and shoved him into the back. By then, he could hear sirens approaching. Cops. Finally.

Chris and Dwight jumped into the car and took off with a roar, disappearing down the alley.

Bryan finally stopped gagging. He didn't get up yet, though. Instead, he just rested his face against the ground and closed his eyes.

So much for the last case of Detective Bryan Murphy.

27

Dwight kept the accelerator pressed to the floor as he propelled the small car through the dark, narrow streets. Chris watched behind them, holding the Magnum and muttering to himself.

Both of them ignored Detaglio, who was being quiet for a change.

"I can hear the fucking sirens," Dwight said. "I can hear them getting closer."

"Drive," Chris said through gritted teeth. "Just keep driving."

"Why the hell did we bring him along?"

Chris used his sleeve to keep the sweat from rolling into his eyes. "Hostage," he replied. "He's a goddamned hostage. In case we need to do a deal."

They sideswiped a parked car and neatly evaded a fire hydrant.

"Deals like that never work, Chris, and you know it. You always said that hostage deals don't work."

"Maybe this time it will. We don't have much fucking choice, do we?" Chris knew damned well that he was kidding himself. As far as he knew, nobody in the history of the freaking world ever got away clean on a hostage deal. It sucked, but he just didn't know what else to do. He braced himself against the dash as the car took a corner on two wheels.

The faster they went, the louder the sirens behind them seemed to get.

"Dwight," Chris said urgently.

"I can't go any faster here, damnit."

The newspaper delivery truck seemed to just suddenly appear out of nowhere. Dwight slammed his foot on the brake. The car fishtailed all over the road as he fought to regain control. "Hold on," he yelled as they headed for the wall.

Chris braced himself again, closing his eyes. The impact jarred his insides but didn't do any real damage. He tried to open the door; it was jammed closed. It took the full weight of his body, pushing and shoving, to get it open. He still had the Magnum clutched in his hand. "Come on. Forget him and let's just get the hell out of here."

Dwight moved and then groaned. "My leg," he whispered. "My fucking leg is broken, Chris."

Chris swore and ran around to the driver's side. He tugged and pulled until that door also opened. "Dwight, come on."

"My leg. Damnit, I can't move."

Chris reached inside and tried to help Dwight get out of the car, but the other man groaned in agony. Chris gave up. He straightened and looked around desperately.

The wailing of the sirens was getting closer.

"Chris?"

He crouched next to the car. "Yeah, buddy?" he said wearily, leaning his forehead against the frame.

"They're gonna get us this time."

"Yes, I guess they are."

"You promised me, Chris. You swore I wouldn't have to go back."

"Yeah. But I was wrong."

Dwight was struggling to move. "Chris, I can't. I can't do more time."

"It'll be all right." He raised his gaze and stared at Dwight, seeing too clearly what was written in the anguished eyes. "Dwight, I can't do that."

"You don't have to do anything. Just gimme the gun."

Chris shook his head.

Dwight grabbed his free hand and held on. "Please. We're buddies, right? If all of it meant anything to you, please gimme the gun. Please don't let this happen to me."

"I can work an angle inside," Chris said.

"Maybe you could. But maybe you couldn't."

Chris looked back suddenly and his eyes met Detaglio's. "Dwight . . ." he said helplessly.

"Please." It was a bare breath the way he said it.

The first squad car must have been only a block or so away, the noise from its siren was so loud. Chris closed his eyes for just a moment. Then he opened them and handed the Magnum to Dwight.

"Thank you, Chris."

"You don't have to do this."

"Yeah, I do. I'm sorry to be such a fucking coward." Dwight put the barrel of the gun into his mouth. Staring at Chris, he winked once.

Chris kept looking.

Dwight pulled the trigger.

"My God," Detaglio said.

Chris leaned against the car, his head bent. "I should take that fucking gun and kill you," he said dully.

Detaglio was pressed against the seat. There were drops of fresh blood on his face. "Are you going to?"

The squad car arrived.

Chris shook his head. "No. It doesn't matter anymore. I can do the fucking time."

He didn't move, even as the two cops approached, guns drawn.

Bryan sidestepped an approaching nurse and pushed his way into the emergency room. Tray was sitting on the edge of the examining table. He had been cleaned up considerably and looked far different from the man who had been hauled out of the wrecked Rabbit. He now sported several gleaming bandages as well as another glorious shiner. One hand was wrapped and gauze covered his chest. From the bright look in his eyes and his cheerful smile, it was clear that a heavy dose of painkillers had been pumped into him.

"Hi," he said.

Bryan nodded.

"You okay, Bry?"

"Me?" Bryan said in surprise.

"Yeah. Chris hit you pretty hard. And your heart . . ."

"I'm fine. No thanks to you. My gut is bruised, but otherwise I seem to have survived."

"Good." Tray was quiet as the doctor poked his ribs. "Ouch."

The doctor nodded as she stepped back. "You'll live, too," she said before leaving the room.

Bryan stepped closer to the table. "What happened in that car?"

Tray was touching the swollen eye carefully. "Dwight shot himself. He couldn't stand getting sent back inside. So he killed himself."

"That's the way Moore tells it."

"Well, it's the truth." Tray looked at him. "Sometimes even cons tell the truth."

"Sure. And speaking of guys getting sent back inside, Blank is on his way in here. He has some questions."

Tray grimaced. "I'm sure." He was looking at the floor now. "Will you stay?"

Bryan shrugged. "I've got no influence with him."

"Well, call it moral support."

"What the hell do you know about anything moral?"

"Hey, you're supposed to be on my side, remember?"

"Says who?"

Tray was quiet for a moment. "What happened to the house?" he asked suddenly.

"Burned to the ground."

Tray nodded, as if the answer pleased him.

The curtain was shoved aside again and Blank came in. He took silent note of Bryan's presence, then turned his attention to Tray. "So, where's the money?"

"Money?" Tray repeated with as much brightness as he seemed able to muster.

"Moore told us the whole story."

"Chris doesn't know the *whole* story. He doesn't know where I hid the money."

"So now you'll tell us."

"Sure. It doesn't matter anymore."

"And why is that?"

"Ever read 'The Purloined Letter'?"

"What?" Blank said.

"I figured the best place to stash the dough was right under their dumb noses. So I doubled back and hid it under their own goddamned porch. I expect it must've burned up with the house. That's a first-class bitch, isn't it?"

"You don't seem all that upset about it."

Tray smiled. "Hey, I'm alive. Maybe my priorities have changed."

Blank nodded. "I guess that could happen. Tell me about Kathryn Daily's death," he said suddenly.

"What about it?"

"You look real good for that killing. Maybe you wanted the whole bundle for yourself."

Tray looked genuinely startled; some of the drug-induced cheer faded from his eyes. "Hey, sir, I didn't kill her. They shot her. One of them. You're not trying to pin that on me, are you?" He glanced urgently at Bryan.

Bryan didn't say anything.

"We're checking every angle," Blank said.

"Well, that angle sucks."

"I should probably haul your ass in, but the jail is overcrowded, anyway, and Murph here has promised to keep you available for me."

"Thanks for that," Tray said, not sounding very grateful.

"Of course," Blank went on, "I don't know what the hell the D.A. might decide to throw at you. This whole thing is a major fuck-up."

"Boy, I agree with that."

Blank looked at them both, then shook his head and left.

"Come on," said Bryan. "We might as well go home."

Tray glanced at him quickly. "I can come back?"

Bryan just walked out without saying anything.

After a moment, Tray followed him.

28

It was nearly noon before Bryan woke up the next morning.

At first, all he did was stare up at the sun-dappled ceiling, a little surprised to realize that he was still alive and, apparently, healthy. And actually feeling pretty damned good despite some soreness where Moore had sucker-punched him.

After savoring the sensation for a time, he got up and went to take a long, hot shower. He found himself whistling as he donned cut-off jeans and a white Polo shirt. Who said he couldn't become a frigging Californian?

When he walked into the kitchen, he found breakfast ready and waiting. Tray waved him into a chair and served up the no-cholesterol scrambled eggs, toast, and juice. Bryan surveyed the meal. "Thanks," he said.

"Well, I figured I owed you. Although it wasn't easy to do one-handed," he added.

"Uh-huh." Bryan took a bite of the toast. "And you figure that cooking me breakfast will even the score?"

"Not hardly. But maybe it's a start."

They ate in silence for a time.

Finally, Bryan wiped his mouth, sat back, and took a sip of the coffee. "You know, Tray, no matter how I might have acted lately, I'm not really a dope. You don't think for a minute that I actually swallowed the garbage you were feeding Blank last night, do you?"

"Which garbage is that?" Detaglio's face was swollen and bruised, but he managed an innocent look, anyway. From the foggy gaze in his eyes, it was obvious he was still popping the feel-good pills.

Bryan just laid a real cop stare on him.

Tray smiled sheepishly. "No, I didn't think you believed it. And I'm leading up to telling you the truth. That's part of what I owe you."

"Thanks for that."

"Hey, you saved my life."

"Maybe."

"For sure." Tray finished his orange juice and licked his upper lip thoughtfully. "There was *some* truth to the story."

"The best liars always include just a little truth. Adds to their plausibility."

"Uh-huh." Tray ate the crust of his toast. "I actually did hide the money under a porch, just like I said. Only thing is, it wasn't that particular porch. It was another house, couple blocks away."

"I see."

Although Bryan made an effort to speak nonjudgmentally, Detagalio seemed to pick up something in his tone because he looked very defensive suddenly. "Well, don't forget what I went through for that money, Bry. Don't I deserve something? I damned well earned it. Why the hell should I have just turned it over to the damned cops? Or maybe you think I should give it back to Stanzione?"

"I don't think anything, Tray."

"Anyway, I wanted you to know the truth."

"So now I know."

"You pissed?"

"No."

"Okay, good." Tray wadded his napkin and tossed it onto the table. "Maybe we could go get it this morning? House with a FOR SALE sign in front. Easy to find."

Bryan nodded slowly. "Okay. We'll go pick it up."

"Thanks. You could probably use some dough around this place, right?"

"I don't want any of it."

"You deserve it."

"Go get dressed. I'll drive you to Venice."

"Sure thing." Tray headed for the bathroom.

Bryan remained at the table for a moment. Then he got up, walked over to the phone, and dialed a familiar number.

They didn't talk much during the trip to Venice.

Bryan slowed the jeep as they went past the burned-out remains of the house. He shook his head, then drove on, following Tray's directions.

"You ran this route? In the dark?"

Tray was slumped in the seat. "Well, when a couple guys are on your ass shooting at you, it sort of provides motivation."

"I can understand."

Tray was quiet briefly. "It's too bad what happened. To Kathryn, I mean. I feel very bad about that."

"This whole mess is too bad," Bryan replied.

"That guy," Tray said softly. "He just put the damned gun into his mouth and pulled the fucking trigger." He mimicked the action with his finger. "Jesus, it was the damndest thing I ever saw." Then he looked up. "That's the place."

Bryan parked the jeep at the curb. They both sat still for a moment. "Well?" Bryan said finally.

"Yeah, I'm going. Just gimme a minute to enjoy this. It's like foreplay." He grinned, then jumped down from the jeep. "They kept asking me where the fucking money was, Bry. But even when they hurt me, I never said a word."

"Why the hell not?"

He shrugged. "I don't really know. It was stupid, yeah. But I just decided it was time I did something. Took a stand. I think I would've died before telling them. So that's why I figure this money is mine. That's only fair."

Bryan didn't say anything.

"Well, I'll get it." He walked quickly to the porch of the empty house and got down on his knees. Bryan couldn't see what he was doing, but after a few moments he pulled out a duffel. "Got it!" he yelled over his shoulder.

Bryan just nodded.

He got to his feet and came back to the jeep. "Okay, here it is, Bry." He unzipped the duffel and they both stared at the stacks of bills inside. Tray ran a hand across the money. He sighed, then looked at Bryan. "All of a sudden, none of it hurts so much, Bry."

Bryan was looking past Tray.

"Morning, Detaglio."

He whipped around and saw Blank approaching. A uniformed cop walked beside him.

"I'll be taking that," Blank said.

Tray looked from him to Bryan. "You called him. You fucking called him, you son of a bitch."

"Yeah, I called him. For your own good, I called him."

"Don't give me that shit. For my own good?" He shook his head. "I can't believe you did this to me."

"The money doesn't belong to you, Tray. That's the end of it."

"Fuck if it doesn't." He closed the duffel savagely and pitched it at the two cops. The uniform bent to pick it up.

"Thank you," Blank said.

"Now you bust me, right?"

"No." Blank stared at him. "Moore backs your story on the woman's death. And busting you for all the rest of the shit you were into wasn't part of the deal. You can thank Murphy for that."

He nodded at Bryan and then the other cop led the way back to the squad car.

"Let's go, Tray," Bryan said carefully.

"Go fuck yourself, Murphy," Tray said. He started to walk.

"Where are you going?"

When there was no answer, Bryan started the jeep and moved slowly after him. "Tray, look, that money was nothing but trouble. You need to break away from all that if you want to stay straight."

Finally, Tray stopped. He turned to look at Bryan. "Leave me alone."

"Detaglio, damnit—"

"One friend doesn't fuck over another friend like this."

Bryan got mad then, too. Was this guy just plain stupid or what? "Fine," he said. "If that's how you see it." He shook his head. "God, you're such a fucking dope. You're so stupid, you don't even know when somebody's giving you a chance."

"Is that what you did? Gave me a chance?" Tray smiled without a trace of humor. "Well, I'll tell you the same thing I told a couple of the creeps in stir who wanted to give me a chance. The chance for easy time. And all I had to do was roll over and enjoy it. Thanks for the thought, but no thanks. To make my point with them, I had to kick them in the balls. That probably won't be necessary with you. Although, believe me, I'd enjoy doing it."

He started walking again.

This time, Bryan let him go.

29

Ann showed up at the house, a copy of the *Times* tucked under her arm. Bryan led the way out to the deck and they sat down to drink iced tea from plastic tumblers.

She unfolded the paper to display the front-page story. "You have been a busy man lately, haven't you?"

He took the paper from her and skimmed the story quickly, then tossed it aside. "Well, it wasn't quite as dramatic as they make it sound. Actually, it all happened pretty fast."

"You're damned lucky it didn't bring a premature end to your retirement."

"Humph" was all he said to that.

"So, where's the other renegade?"

Bryan poured more iced tea for himself. "Detaglio? Well, he decided that the straight and narrow path was too damned confining." She just looked puzzled, so he sighed and explained. "I made him give the money back." He shrugged. "I don't know where the hell he is. Probably holding up a convenience store somewhere."

She sipped the tea. "That's too bad. I was starting to like him."

"Were you?" Bryan was quiet for a moment. "Well, I thought he was gonna work out, but what the hell do I know?"

"So that's it? You're giving up on him?"

"Sure. Why should I waste my time? Besides, he took off."

She nodded and nibbled the edge of the tumbler. "Where would he go, do you think?"

"How the hell do I know?" Why didn't she just drop it? He shrugged. "People generally run for home when things turn bad. So maybe he's headed for Washington. Spokane, I think he said."

Ann stood up abruptly and walked over to stand behind him. She began to rub his neck. Her hands were cold and a little damp from the glass. "Probably having been your bed partner for just one night—an experience I wouldn't mind repeating, in case you were wondering—doesn't really entitle me to have an opinion about your life, but I've got one. If you'd like to hear it."

He was bemused by her interjection and it was a moment before he smiled and said, "Go ahead."

"I think you should try to find him."

"Why the hell should I do that? Do I really need the aggravation?"

She was still massaging his neck. "Yes, as a matter of fact, I think you do. How much more of your life do you intend to devote to painting and playing Mr. Fixit?"

"Well, I can think of a few other things to do with my time now," he said.

She slapped him lightly on the head. "There'll be time for that, too. But you need something to *do*."

"You make Detaglio sound like some kind of damned do-it-yourself project."

"Maybe that's it, a little. But I also think he's a friend, no matter what stupid things he did. And I think we need all the friends we can get."

"Yeah, maybe." Bryan finished his tea. "I probably couldn't find him even if I looked."

"You think he might be heading north. If he's hitching, Highway One is the logical route. What could it hurt to try?"

Bryan thought about it for a moment. Then he jumped up and planted a kiss on her cheek. "You're a smart broad, Hamilton. And you hold that thought about a repeat performance."

She laughed.

Bryan grabbed his keys and headed for the jeep.

* * *

There was only one customer in the truck-stop café when Tray walked in. A skinny black man wearing a worn army camouflage jacket and faded jeans sat at the counter. Tray nodded at him and took a stool at the other end of the place. He studied the menu with an eye to the very limited funds in his wallet and finally ordered the special $1.49 twenty-four-hour breakfast.

"Where you headed?"

He looked at the man. "Spokane."

"Spo-kane?"

"Washington State."

"Yeah, I know that."

"You driving north?" Tray asked him hopefully.

"Nope. Sorry."

"Yeah, well. It's been that kind of a day."

The black man laughed softly. "My name's Charles."

"Tray."

The waitress set down his one fried egg and two strips of bacon. "Anything else?"

He shook his head.

"So, what's in Spo-kane, Tray?"

"I don't know." He did know, really, and after chewing briefly, he said, "Nothing. That's just where I'm from. So I'm going back." He sopped up runny egg yolk with a slice of limp toast. "There isn't a damned thing in Spokane for me and that's the truth."

"Not your mama? Your woman? Some buddies?"

"None of the above."

Charles looked puzzled. "Can I ask you something, my man?"

"Sure."

"Why the hell you going back to Spo-kane?"

He had been asking himself that for the last few hours, ever since he came down off the massive torrent of anger. "I don't know. Mostly because there's no place else to go."

"That's too bad."

Yeah, he agreed silently, it is too bad. But that's life as fucked up by Traylane Detaglio and there's nothing to do about it now.

He finished the meal glumly and said good-bye to Charles,

who didn't seem to be in any hurry at all to get wherever it was he was going.

It wasn't until he reached for his wallet to pay for the meal that he discovered the small leather bag he had taken from Kathryn's neck and retrieved from under the porch with the money. For some reason, he had stuck it into his pocket instead of showing it to Bryan. A good thing, probably.

He opened the drawstring and reached inside. A small key fell into his hand. He studied it for a moment, then began to smile.

Damned Kathryn.

She never did have much of an imagination. Her share of the money went right back to the bus depot. In one of those lockers there was almost $200,000.

And nobody knew about it but him.

Tray walked back out to the shoulder of the road and continued his journey. His thumb went into the air automatically whenever he heard a car approaching from behind. But nobody stopped. He still couldn't get a goddamned lift when he needed one.

As he walked, he kept thinking about the money. Why the hell was he still heading for Spokane, when there was so much waiting for him back in Los Angeles?

At first, he didn't realize that it was the jeep pulling to a stop on the shoulder behind him. He turned finally and saw Bryan.

Neither man spoke as several cars whizzed by.

Bryan turned off the engine. "You all that hot to see Washington State again?" he said.

"Maybe not." Tray stared down the dark highway, then shook his head. "No, I'm not all that hot to go back. Nothing there but some bad memories."

Bryan tapped the steering wheel. "I still have a job open. If you're willing."

Tray smiled a little and shook his head. "Good honest work, right?"

"Well, you could give it a try. Just for a change." Bryan smiled, too, taking the sting out of the words.

"I guess I could. For a change."

"And maybe we ought to make a deal."

He looked at Bryan suspiciously. "What deal?"

"You be a little less a damned con and I'll be a little less a cop."

"That might work."

Bryan reached for the ignition. "So get in. It's late."

Tray climbed into the passenger seat. "Not too late, though, I guess."

"Not yet. Not too late yet."

The jeep made a radical U-turn, in violation of several laws, and headed south.

Tray stuck one hand into his pocket and touched the key. He smiled to himself and settled down in the jeep for the ride home.

30

He was finally alone.

Even the familiar sounds of the cellblock, those noises that seemed to be an almost constant background to his life, were muted and faraway for the moment. Chris stretched out on the top bunk and lit a cigarette. At least he was alone in here. No goddamned cellmate. It smelled just like every other jail he'd ever been in.

Just like he'd told Detaglio, he could do the time.

He started to make a mental list of all the things to ask his Legal Aid lawyer in the morning.

Like, where would they be sending him?

And what, exactly, were the charges, anyway?

And who was taking care of seeing that Dwight got properly buried? Just because he'd been a con didn't mean he couldn't have a little respect when he was dead.

Chris inhaled deeply and shook his head as he exhaled again, sending a plume of smoke into the rank air. It had been a good run while it lasted. Some great times.

Of course, now that he was on his own again, life would be easier.

But he admitted to himself that he would miss Dwight. You got used to a person after so many years. Even a crazy bastard like Dwight. That was the only thing. He thought he might be a little lonesome for a while. Until he got used to it.

He could do the time, though. He could do whatever fucking kind of time they wanted to throw at him. No problem.

He kept smoking and staring at the ceiling.

I can do the fucking time.

MORE MYSTERIOUS PLEASURES

HAROLD ADAMS
The Carl Wilcox mystery series
MURDER	#501	$3.95
PAINT THE TOWN RED	#601	$3.95
THE MISSING MOON	#602	$3.95
THE NAKED LIAR	#420	$3.95
THE FOURTH WIDOW	#502	$3.50
THE BARBED WIRE NOOSE	#603	$3.95
THE MAN WHO MET THE TRAIN	#801	$3.95

TED ALLBEURY
THE SEEDS OF TREASON	#604	$3.95
THE JUDAS FACTOR	#802	$4.50
THE STALKING ANGEL	#803	$3.95

ERIC AMBLER
HERE LIES: AN AUTOBIOGRAPHY	#701	$8.95

ROBERT BARNARD
A TALENT TO DECEIVE: AN APPRECIATION OF AGATHA CHRISTIE	#702	$8.95

EARL DERR BIGGERS
The Charlie Chan mystery series
THE HOUSE WITHOUT A KEY	#421	$3.95
THE CHINESE PARROT	#503	$3.95
BEHIND THAT CURTAIN	#504	$3.95
THE BLACK CAMEL	#505	$3.95
CHARLIE CHAN CARRIES ON	#506	$3.95
KEEPER OF THE KEYS	#605	$3.95

JAMES M. CAIN
THE ENCHANTED ISLE	#415	$3.95
CLOUD NINE	#507	$3.95

ROBERT CAMPBELL
IN LA-LA LAND WE TRUST ... #508 $3.95

RAYMOND CHANDLER
RAYMOND CHANDLER'S UNKNOWN THRILLER:
THE SCREENPLAY OF "PLAYBACK" ... #703 $9.95

GEORGE C. CHESBRO
The Veil Kendry suspense series
VEIL ... #509 $3.95
JUNGLE OF STEEL AND STONE ... #606 $3.95

EDWARD CLINE
FIRST PRIZE ... #804 $4.95

K.C. CONSTANTINE
The Mario Balzic mystery series
JOEY'S CASE ... #805 $4.50

MATTHEW HEALD COOPER
DOG EATS DOG ... #607 $4.95

CARROLL JOHN DALY
THE ADVENTURES OF SATAN HALL ... #704 $8.95
THE ADVENTURES OF RACE WILLIAMS ... #723 $9.95

NORBERT DAVIS
THE ADVENTURES OF MAX LATIN ... #705 $8.95

MARK DAWIDZIAK
THE COLUMBO PHILE: A CASEBOOK ... #726 $14.95

WILLIAM L. DeANDREA
The Cronus espionage series
SNARK ... #510 $3.95
AZRAEL ... #608 $4.50
The Matt Cobb mystery series
KILLED IN THE ACT ... #511 $3.50
KILLED WITH A PASSION ... #512 $3.50
KILLED ON THE ICE ... #513 $3.50
KILLED IN PARADISE ... #806 $3.95

LEN DEIGHTON
ONLY WHEN I LAUGH ... #609 $4.95

AARON ELKINS
The Professor Gideon Oliver mystery series
OLD BONES ... #610 $3.95

JAMES ELLROY
THE BLACK DAHLIA	#611	$4.95
THE BIG NOWHERE	#807	$4.95
SUICIDE HILL	#514	$4.50

PAUL ENGLEMAN
The Mark Renzler mystery series
CATCH A FALLEN ANGEL	#515	$3.50
MURDER-IN-LAW	#612	$3.95

LOREN D. ESTLEMAN
The Peter Macklin suspense series
ROSES ARE DEAD	#516	$3.95
ANY MAN'S DEATH	#517	$3.95

ANNE FINE
THE KILLJOY	#613	$3.95

DICK FRANCIS
THE SPORT OF QUEENS	#410	$4.95

JOHN GARDNER
THE GARDEN OF WEAPONS	#103	$4.50

BRIAN GARFIELD
DEATH WISH	#301	$3.95
DEATH SENTENCE	#302	$3.95
TRIPWIRE	#303	$3.95
FEAR IN A HANDFUL OF DUST	#304	$3.95

THOMAS GODFREY, ED.
MURDER FOR CHRISTMAS	#614	$3.95
MURDER FOR CHRISTMAS II	#615	$3.95

JOE GORES
COME MORNING	#518	$3.95

JOSEPH HANSEN
The Dave Brandstetter mystery series
EARLY GRAVES	#643	$3.95
OBEDIENCE	#809	$4.95

NAT HENTOFF
THE MAN FROM INTERNAL AFFAIRS	#409	$3.95

PATRICIA HIGHSMITH
THE ANIMAL-LOVER'S BOOK OF BEASTLY MURDER	#706	$8.95
LITTLE TALES OF MISOGYNY	#707	$8.95
SLOWLY, SLOWLY IN THE WIND	#708	$8.95
THE BLACK HOUSE	#724	$9.95

DOUG HORNIG
WATERMAN #616 $3.95
The Loren Swift mystery series
THE DARK SIDE #519 $3.95
DEEP DIVE #810 $4.50

JANE HORNING
THE MYSTERY LOVERS' BOOK
  OF QUOTATIONS #709 $12.95

PETER ISRAEL
The Charles Camelot mystery series
I'LL CRY WHEN I KILL YOU #811 $3.95

P.D. JAMES/T.A. CRITCHLEY
THE MAUL AND THE PEAR TREE #520 $3.95

STUART M. KAMINSKY
The Toby Peters mystery series
HE DONE HER WRONG #105 $3.95
HIGH MIDNIGHT #106 $3.95
NEVER CROSS A VAMPIRE #107 $3.95
BULLET FOR A STAR #308 $3.95
THE FALA FACTOR #309 $3.95

JOSEPH KOENIG
FLOATER #521 $3.50

ELMORE LEONARD
THE HUNTED #401 $3.95
MR. MAJESTYK #402 $3.95
THE BIG BOUNCE #403 $3.95

ELSA LEWIN
I, ANNA #522 $3.50

PETER LOVESEY
ROUGH CIDER #617 $3.95
BUTCHERS AND OTHER STORIES OF CRIME #710 $9.95
BERTIE AND THE TINMAN #812 $3.95

JOHN LUTZ
SHADOWTOWN #813 $3.95

ARTHUR LYONS
SATAN WANTS YOU: THE CULT OF
  DEVIL WORSHIP #814 $4.50
The Jacob Asch mystery series
FAST FADE #618 $3.95

AVAILABLE AT YOUR BOOKSTORE OR DIRECT FROM THE PUBLISHER

Mysterious Press Mail Order
129 West 56th Street
New York, NY 10019

Please send me the MYSTERIOUS PRESS titles I have circled below:

103 105 106 107 112 113 209 210 211 212 213 214 301 302
303 304 308 309 315 316 401 402 403 404 405 406 407 408
409 410 411 412 413 414 415 416 417 418 419 420 421 501
502 503 504 505 506 507 508 509 510 511 512 513 514 515
516 517 518 519 520 521 522 523 524 525 526 527 528 529
530 531 532 533 534 535 536 537 538 539 540 541 542 543
544 545 601 602 603 604 605 606 607 608 609 610 611 612
613 614 615 616 617 618 619 620 621 622 623 624 625 626
627 628 629 630 631 632 633 634 635 636 637 638 639 640
641 642 643 644 645 646 701 702 703 704 705 706 707 708
709 710 711 712 713 714 715 716 717 718 719 720 721 722
723 724 725 726 727 728 729 801 802 803 804 805 806 807
808 809 810 811 812 813 814 815 816 817 818 819 820 821
822 823 824 825 826 827 828 829 830 831 832 833 834 835
836 837 838 839 840 841 842 843

I am enclosing $_____ (please add $3.00 postage and handling for the first book, and 50¢ for each additional book). Send check or money order only—no cash or C.O.D.'s please. Allow at least 4 weeks for delivery.

NAME _____

ADDRESS _____

CITY _____ STATE _____ ZIP CODE _____
New York State residents please add appropriate sales tax.